IMAGE *protector*

LILY ALEXANDER

ISBN: 978-1-7345686-1-5 (Ebook)
ISBN: 978-1-7345686-3-9 (Paperback)

Editor: Edits By Sue
Cover Design: Kate Farlow, Y'all. That Graphic.
Interior Design: Stephanie Anderson, Alt 19 Creative

IMAGE SERIES:

Image Adjuster

Image Protector

Image Destroyer (coming in 2021)

HOLLYWOOD CONNECTIONS SERIES:

Winter Bloom

Spring Breeze (coming in 2021)

Summer Storm (coming in 2021)

For my incredible family—you are simply the best.
&
To the wonderful neighborhood ladies, your
support is very much appreciated even if I seem
uncomfortable—I'm still learning how to take a
compliment graciously but I'm working on it. XOXO.

CHAPTER

One

AN INDELICATE SQUEAK of surprise left Nora's throat as she flailed and jumped to her feet. Sand and saltwater went flying out from underneath her as she scrambled, legs tangling a bit in the skirt of her bridesmaid's dress.

A cold, gritty, *wet* nose had pressed into her ear, giving her the startle of a lifetime as she gazed out at the Pacific Ocean. The vast expanse of vibrant orange and gold meeting the azure sky had absorbed her attention completely.

She hadn't even heard the massive dog approach over the steady, heavy heartbeat of the waves and now, he was all lolling tongue and happy panting as he gave her a waist hug with his front legs.

"Rufus! Down!"

A familiar man bounded toward them, panic on his incredibly handsome face. Brown eyes wide, he held out a hand as if to stop his dog from accosting her, but it was already too late.

She recognized him; he was her best friend Devon's brand-new wife's best friend. Stephanie was *her* good friend as well, and he'd come up in conversation more than once. His name was Maxwell if memory served.

They'd been in close proximity many times, but never actually met or spoken without a bunch of distractions, and today, having been Stephanie and Devon's wedding day, had been no different.

"I'm so sorry!" He looked horror-struck at the sandy paw prints his dog had left on Nora's plum-colored bridesmaid dress. "He got away from me for just a second—"

"It's okay," Nora brushed the mostly dry sand off her dress and patted the giant mastiff's head once he dismounted her waist and stood between them just happily panting. She couldn't help but smile at the big goofy face. "He didn't hurt me. Just a little surprised is all."

Maxwell visibly relaxed and ran a hand through his light brown hair. He was still in his wedding attire as well, though missing a few pieces. His suit had been pared down to just dress slacks and white button-down shirt, the cuffs of both rolled up. His feet were bare in the sand, his ankles, a bit of collarbone and tanned forearms exposed.

"Sorry again. I know we've met before—I'd know your lovely smile anywhere, in fact—but I'm Maxwell Caine." He extended a hand to her.

"Nora Chase," she replied, shaking his outstretched hand. Her brain registered that the skin was slightly rough but warm.

"Pleased to meet you again, Nora. We were down the table a bit at the rehearsal dinner and on opposite sides of the altar at the wedding." It wasn't a question, though his grin was teasing.

Nora nodded. "Yes. Friend of both the bride and groom, but the groom in particular."

"Me too. But the opposite. How is it we've never really connected before now?" The question lingered between them, Nora giving a slight shrug. His head inclined to the left, adorably.

At the momentary silence, her eyes trailed off to the rolling ocean for a moment, then back to the reception a bit further down the beach under tents strung with twinkly lights.

Her friends were in there, and their families. They were dancing and toasting and happy. The smile pushed at her mouth, and she finally looked away.

The cool ocean breeze tried to whip some of the blonde hair that had escaped her fancy up-do into circles, and she pushed it away from her face.

Maxwell's gaze hadn't once left her face.

"Nothing quite like bending the wedding rules. I love that I was a groom's maid and you were a bride's man."

His laugh was warm and rolled across her skin very pleasantly. The way his expressive eyes appraised her made her feel things she couldn't adequately process. It was nice. And it was dangerous.

"I was Man of *Honor*, thanks very much, but yes, I agree," he paused, chocolate eyes twinkling as he dipped his head to one side again, a playful smile on his lips. "I had to give Rufus here a stroll so I have an excuse. Why aren't you over there celebrating?"

"I needed a breath of air." She couldn't help but return his grin, Rufus panting in devoted adoration of his master, still planted firmly on the sand between them, though he'd given up standing and had taken a seat.

It seemed that the breath caught in her chest as she looked at Maxwell. His gaze communicated attraction, but in the friendliest of ways.

"At an outdoor beach wedding?" he teased, but then nodded gently. "Honestly, I understand that. Well, I'll leave you to it. Maybe I'll see you later? A glass of champagne, perhaps a dance?"

"Sure."

Nora watched one of the most handsome men she had ever met stride back past the party tents and toward the enormous house up above. She wanted to call him back but realized she didn't have the first clue of what she'd say if she did.

She didn't have these kinds of feelings about men. Hadn't since her last boyfriend, a miserable specimen that she wished she could go back and never meet in the first place. There was no time for dating or relationships between her job and the mess back home that was a feud of sorts between her frustrating, needy mother and independent, lovely sister.

Her fingers twitched, knowing the pile of text messages was still waiting for her. Nora had pointedly left her purse safe with the mother of the groom in the party tent. Her mother would not ruin this day with her insistent attempts at getting in touch with her.

Nora took a deep breath and forced those thoughts away, focusing on the man and his dog instead.

Rufus followed Maxwell at a trot, panting and drooling all over the place. A spot in Nora's chest that had been cold warmed as she watched them wander toward the massive house at the edge of the sand. Her reaction to him worried her a bit, but she couldn't resist the urge to welcome it.

Had it not been for some poor choices earlier in her career she wouldn't feel this way, but that was then and this was now.

Rubbing her hands together to clear some stray grains of black and gold Malibu beach sand, she turned her feet back toward the wedding tent, a genuine smile on her face. Yes, she definitely wanted to see more of Maxwell Caine.

That, too, worried her, but she couldn't quite make herself care.

CHAPTER
Two

Nora's skin was crawling everywhere Ollie Parkinson touched her, even through the layers of her light leather jacket and shirt sleeves. She forced a smile through the discomfort and kept telling herself that it would all be over soon—it was just one scene, probably less than two takes, and then they would be done.

They were on set in sunny Los Angeles; though you'd never know what the weather was like outside while filming an indoor scene within the giant concrete buildings.

Ollie, former model and C-list actor, was plenty easy on the eyes with his fit frame, aqua gaze, and sandy hair. Unfortunately, his smarmy, misogynistic personality left a vast array of things to be desired and more than detracted from his looks. He also had a solid reputation for being a less than stellar human being, and Nora had been lucky enough to avoid working with him until now.

He'd fallen from grace in a major way after getting involved in a fight on-set a few productions back. He punched a fellow actor after a verbal altercation, giving both the actor and Ollie's career a black eye. Not long after that incident, he'd hired her best friend Devon's wife, Stephanie, to pose as his girlfriend for some positive PR and had accosted her in his car.

Needless to say, his reputation was in the trash and there was no telling how much begging his agent had done to get him this, albeit tiny role, on *Destiny Falls*, Nora and Devon's hit prime-time paranormal drama.

She could do this, Nora reassured herself, the words like a mantra in her head. She was a professional actress. She could and would grit her teeth and get through this scene. Soon enough she could take a scalding shower and scrub his excessive cologne and clammy hand sensation from her skin.

Nothing quite like a healthy relationship with your co-workers, right?

The whole situation made her oddly and immensely nostalgic for some of her previous temporary co-stars. James Cromwell came to mind for one. He'd been a gentleman and the very picture of professional grace when he'd appeared as Nora's character Brigid's love interest for all of three episodes. They'd had to be very touchy-feely for their scenes and kissed several times. It had been very clinical, as expected, but not necessarily lacking in chemistry.

Nora would trade away Ollie Parkinson for James Cromwell in a hot second if she could. Sadly, his character had died rather quickly and that character arc was similarly dead.

THE SET THEY were working on was the living room of an elaborate mansion; one she repeatedly wished she could visit for real and take an extended vacation in. It was meant to mimic an old estate home in New Orleans belonging to a family of witches and inhabited by both them and a coven of vampires. The word decadent was the best possible descriptor Nora could think of.

Everything created for the exterior was dripping in greenery and Spanish moss—something familiar to her having grown up in Alabama but totally foreign to the reality of their location in Los Angeles. The props were gilded and antiqued, the fabrics all dark jewel tones and lush textures. The furniture was similarly quite comfortable and extra plush for something that was just set dressing—it put the inexpensive Ikea and second-hand pieces in her apartment to shame.

One day, she'd be well past the growing pains of being a struggling up-and-coming actress bouncing from commercial spots to a solid television show. One day, she'd always have more money coming in than with bills going out and she would buy the plushest, most comfortable sofa she could find. Having contracted several seasons on the show was her healthy first step in that direction and she was grateful.

The set was quite a comfortable space if you could ignore the fact that Ollie was standing so closely. Or that there were no ceilings and only three walls. Instead of a ceiling, you got hot lights and microphones hung on scaffolding or held by crew above you, and about fifty people were watching your every move or milling around while you tried to focus on your part.

Then there were the giant cameras and at least one person yelling at you about how and where to move, how to emote, where to position your body—not great for relaxation if she really thought about it.

Nora fought the frown that had decided it wanted to take up residence on her face. The set was pretty, but no comparison to the real thing after all.

Trying not to feel deflated, she turned her focus on anything and everything positive about where she was, since the person she had to be in closest proximity to quite frankly, was totally repellant.

Nora felt a sigh build in her chest and pushed it back down.

At least she wasn't stuck behind a desk somewhere or waitressing. She'd been total shit at both of those jobs, but they'd paid the bills for quite a long time before she had her big break. Well, fairly big break.

She'd spilled more than her share of coffee on people at the diner, screwed up countless special orders at the vegan cafe, and had been more than terrible at both maintaining spreadsheets and being perpetually perky over the phone at the desk jobs she'd temped at. If having a niche skill was a thing, acting was her first and caring for plants her second. Both could probably make her money, but she was lucky enough to be doing the higher paying one for now.

She ignored her handsome but obnoxious co-star and watched the crew doing their jobs instead; men and women busily bustling around the pretend room. Their hands moved in a steady stream of setting, rearranging, adjusting. Most of them moved around the actors like there was some kind of invisible force field, which always fascinated Nora. They were so focused on the set yet treated the live bodies similar to the furniture. Most crew avoided making eye contact or speaking to the actors unless absolutely necessary.

Inside the imaginary bubble, chatter happened around and with the actors as makeup was reapplied and hair re-sprayed and artfully mussed. To someone from the outside the whole scene right now would look like utter chaos.

But despite some irritating drawbacks, like co-stars that make your skin crawl, Nora *loved* her job. She loved the craft of acting and the way it allowed her to be anything and everything she wasn't in her actual life.

Her acting persona kept her going when her real-self felt like giving up. Bubbly, blonde Nora Chase from Los Angeles could be front and center when necessary instead of introverted, brunette Eleanora Chatzi from Nowhereville

Alabama which was a relief even if it was also a cleverly crafted lie. She adored that she could get paid real money to express herself through being someone else. She loved being part of something like the show she knew she had been lucky to join with her best friend, Devon.

But damn if there weren't also some *major* flaws to this whole thing.

Having to touch, smile at, and otherwise be anywhere near Ollie Parkinson was one of them. A massive, craggy wasteland of a flaw.

It was really too bad because he really might have been quite a pleasure to work with if he weren't a total tool.

He flashed her a smile that was surely meant to be charming but came off instead as slimy and lecherous. Lucky for every girl on set but not so much for him, she already knew way too much about him—and she'd told anyone who'd hold still long enough to hear about it. Nora's friend and Devon's wife, Stephanie, who had been born into the Hollywood world, had made sure to give Nora the run-down of people she'd be best off avoiding should they come up as co-stars, and *why*.

It had been a surprisingly short list, all things considered, but Ollie Parkinson had appeared at the very top. Stephanie's story behind why was as infuriating and terrifying as it was humorous now that hindsight was a factor.

Stephanie had dated Ollie *once*. As an actress who contracted out her services as a fake girlfriend to help boost the image of other actors, Stephanie had taken him on as a client. He had made the grievous error of taking her to an out of the way location with the intent of getting her under him in his car—whether she wanted to or not. Thankfully, Stephanie was not only trained in self-defense but also had a bodyguard on call. Alan, a former MMA fighter and part-time action star (as well as an old family friend to Stephanie) arrived in time to prevent anything from happening aside from some attempted kissing and over-the-clothes touching. Unfortunately, it seemed as though Ollie had forgotten the lesson that Alan had taught him by dangling him over the side of a canyon that day, and that Stephanie had driven home with the only weapon she had at the time—her very pointy stiletto heel.

Nora knew she was probably imagining it, but she could swear there was a round indentation or bruise on his forehead under his makeup. Surely it had been way too long since the event for it to still be there, but Nora liked to imagine she could see it when she was forced to look at his angular and frustratingly handsome face during takes.

From the story Stephanie had relayed to her over manicures and wine at their favorite salon one night, his face and neck had taken the brunt of the damage from Stephanie's shoe when he didn't take no for an answer after their one and only date.

Fake date.

Stephanie's history was even more complicated than Nora's was when it came to relationships, and that was saying something.

The crew scattered once again, and at the director's call, she moved through her lines with Ollie. He wasn't a terrible actor, but he just oozed dirtbag vibes. They did the scene three times, Nora putting her all into every take because she simply needed to be *done.*

"Cut and print, that's the one, thank you!" the director finally called, and Nora gratefully dropped her hands from where they had been perched on Ollie's broad shoulders as everyone began buzzing around to change set dressing for the next scene which would be an exterior shot among the fake live oaks in a lavishly fabricated cemetery.

Ollie, however, didn't let go of her waist as he should have, making her discomfort multiply upon itself.

She didn't say anything, just wriggled enough to give him a very clear indication that she was done standing in that spot and he needed to move his damn hands.

"So soon?" he chuckled. "I was rather enjoying myself."

Nora backed away a few additional steps, making sure not to get in the way of the set runners and prop masters as they adjusted a few things and verified continuity.

"That makes one of us," she said, makeup stepping forward to adjust her hair and touch up her lipstick again.

"Aw, come on. Don't be like that." Ollie tried to be cute or maybe endearing but instead veered into smarmy and gross.

Nora suppressed a shiver—but only just barely, and it had taken significant concentration. Maybe the knowledge of his predatory ways had upped his skeevy level, regardless she had absolutely no interest in him. She sighed and played the card she knew would get him to knock it off.

"I think you know a friend of mine."

His face transformed into a grin that on Devon would have been wolfish and adorable. Ollie, however, couldn't quite break away from the *creep* settings on his expressions.

"Oh? I'm sure any friend of yours could *definitely* be a friend of mine, Beautiful." He gave her a salacious, icky wink. Ugh.

The crawling sensation returned to Nora's skin. She held still as the ladies adjusted her makeup, only pushing a tight smile onto her mouth after the lipstick had been applied and they had scurried off the set again. "Oh, I doubt that. Quite a lot, actually. Not after the story Stephanie told me about you."

Ollie's face blanked and he tensed, as she had predicted. The mention of his previous missteps seemed to remind him that job security was something he certainly didn't have, and toeing the line of being a decent human being was not only desired but necessary.

"Oh. Yes, we've met," he said blandly.

She snorted. She hadn't meant to, but his words just tickled her that way.

"You've more than met. I'm fully aware of your 'date'," she even used finger quotes around the word. "*and* how it ended."

The color quickly and violently returned to Ollie's face and she could see his hands fisting at his sides. A vein pulsed right about the same place she imagined the round bruise on his forehead.

"Right," Nora nodded. "I'm sure you understand why backing off is in your best interest, as is minding your manners. You seem to be running out of last chances to keep working in this town—I'd hate to see you blow it."

She really couldn't give even a single damn about his career, but she also couldn't resist the light taunt.

Ollie's rage was obvious in the vein pulsing away in his forehead, but he nodded tightly. Nora was braced in the event he decided to lash out physically at her, but thankfully he didn't make that terrible choice. It wouldn't have been very smart to do so with all the people around, anyway. She got the impression he was prone to being irrational but wasn't stupid.

After the director called *action* once again, the two performed their scene with as little physical contact as they could manage, and Ollie slunk off at the end of the shoot, presumably to his trailer, without any other commentary. His broad shoulders set in a slight hunch; meaty fists balled up as he went on his way.

Nora let out a breath as she watched him go, shooting Stephanie a text with the shortest possible re-telling of her interaction with Ollie and to let her know he was likely up to his old tricks if he was working anywhere else.

The response from Stephanie was immediate.

S: *Noted. I'll call Maxwell and Alan, let them know to be watching.*

Maxwell.

The mere letters of his name in text on her phone display made friendly butterflies flutter in her stomach. Those butterflies were nearly immediately chased and captured by the net of her anxiety, but still.

Nora had been enjoying any number of day-dreamy thoughts about him since Stephanie and Devon's wedding a couple of weeks before, nearly always followed by a really Debbie Downer inner voice that warned her off of such dangerous thoughts.

She hadn't seen him since that day, but the thought of his beachy blonde hair, dark chocolate eyes, easy smile, and his adorable, enormous Mastiff Rufus were enough to inject a happy smile whenever the idea of him crossed her mind.

It might be the only place she'd get to enjoy him, and she was making the most of it. She'd have to find fulfillment between her daydreams of Maxwell and the random fan texts she had been getting for the past number of months telling her everything from how nice she looked in whatever photo or video they were looking at to the various marriage proposals.

There was no time or space in her life for relationships, and she was doing just fine as a single professional.

Relationships just complicated things. Dating had a history of being hazardous to her blood pressure and bank account.

As she walked back to makeup to wash off the day's touch-ups, her phone buzzed again.

> **S:** *We're back in town tomorrow, btw! I've got a craving for Mr. Woo's. You in? Our place Friday night?*

Nora considered the offer as the makeup ladies helpfully handed her a towel and her preferred makeup remover. She considered her response as she brushed out her hair. With a genuine smile and thanks to the kind women who made her beautiful every day. She headed to wardrobe to quickly change then left the set and headed toward her tiny trailer so she could get her bag. Once it was in hand, she consulted the schedule posted on the trailer door and smiled.

Her call time was early Friday, so she'd be finished by mid-afternoon. Dinner with her friends sounded wonderful.

Devon hadn't been around because he was off on an extended honeymoon and she didn't hang out with anyone else from the show regularly. Or at all, really.

It was complicated.

Probably way more so than it needed to be, truth be told, but Nora had a hard time making friends with co-workers. The nature of the industry left her trusting very few. She'd been burned more than once, and if she didn't love acting so much she probably would be considering a total career change. It had been one of the main things Nora and Stephanie had bonded over when they became friends. Devon was a factor there too, but nobody needed to inflate that man's healthy ego any more than it already was.

Thinking of her friend, Nora couldn't help but smile. Devon knew he was the cat's pajamas, but thankfully his massive head about how great he was didn't get in the way of his ridiculously lovable personality. He'd been her best friend and the closest thing she'd ever had to a brother since they were in college, and he'd do just about anything for those around him; inflated ego or not.

'On stage' Nora and 'Real' Nora were very different people. She thought any number of actors or artists probably felt exactly the same way. Nora believed that it was, at least in part, probably what made them good at their jobs. Compartmentalization in the purest sense—stage persona versus real person. Stephanie had gone so far as to create a whole pseudonym for herself when she stepped away from acting and started painting. Nora thought it was brilliant that she was Stephanie as a person and actress and Alex as a painter. Both were her, but slipping into a certain name like a costume helped define what craft she was honing.

Distracted by her thoughts, panic seized her as she stepped out of her trailer and almost directly into Ollie.

Her grip tightened on her phone. It would be so convenient to have a panic button app like Stephanie had described using for her secret actress dating work. Stephanie had been the *Celebrity Image Adjuster*, and her business acting out fake relationships had saved the reputation of many a bad boy around town before she had fallen for Devon.

Apparently, Maxwell Caine had created it which made it all the more intriguing. She'd be asking about that as soon as possible.

"Hey," Ollie backed up, looking contrite. "I'm sorry. I probably just scared the shit out of you. That was stupid. Sorry. Again."

Nora didn't confirm or deny, but got ready to dash back into her trailer if she needed to.

Ollie held up his hands in a gesture of surrender. At the very least it showed her he didn't have any weapons. He did look genuinely sorry which threw Nora off. He could easily be pretending to atone so she didn't report his ass.

"I'm sorry, really. About this and about earlier. I know I'm an asshole. I don't mean to be. I'm trying to be better. I'm … I'm getting help." He pushed a hand through his short hair and shook his head. His expression was something along the lines of tortured.

Nora's eyebrow lifted. Words were not forthcoming, her tongue stuck to the roof of her mouth as she regarded him carefully. She did finally manage a quiet, "Thanks. And good luck. Asking for help is hard. That's a very honorable thing to do."

Ollie looked at her intensely, seeming genuinely thankful for her understanding.

"Anyway," He nodded and took a few steps backward. "you were right to call me out. That wasn't okay. It was … nice, working with you today."

He nodded again and stuffed his hands in his pockets as he turned and walked away, headed toward the parking lot. Nora stood there in shock for a few long moments.

"Okay," she muttered to herself finally, resolving to ask Stephanie about her panic button app and wondering what the hell had just happened.

CHAPTER *Three*

ONCE SAFELY SECURED in her late model Honda sedan, she texted back her confirmation to Stephanie about dinner and prepared to leave the lot. The smell of old cloth seats and vinyl dash lingered in the afternoon heat. It was a familiar smell, one that made her feel like she could reach out and touch her teenage self if she wanted to.

She had barely begun to inch out of her space when her phone buzzed again, so she stopped and checked it quickly, finding a cluster of happy emoji from her friend. She also found one of those fan texts proclaiming how beautiful she looked, which always made her look over her shoulder to see if anyone was watching her.

The numbers always appeared as unavailable or private, and they seemed mostly innocuous. After getting the messages she usually blocked the numbers, but more always popped up. She hated the idea of changing her number yet again but had promised herself and Devon if things got out of hand, she definitely would do that.

There had been a rather scary situation after she and Devon had gone to the jewelry store together so he could buy an engagement ring for Stephanie. The media had been all over it, spinning it completely wrong, as usual. The store itself had sold footage from their security cameras to the gossip shows showing Devon looking at rings and Nora modeling his selections. They both realized how truly stupid doing that had been after the fact, but when it was happening it seemed so innocent and she just wanted to help her friend out. At the very least, they should have approached the store owner and negotiated for an after-hours appointment or made them sign a document stating they wouldn't sell the footage.

Hindsight was 20/20 and all that.

That outing and the subsequent media spin had caused a huge rift between Stephanie and Devon. Nora still felt a huge pile of guilt over it, even though everything was fine now.

Nora had found herself under attack from fans who pegged Devon and Stephanie as a match. Their 'couple name' was Stephon or Devonie, depending on what team you were on. Nora's part in the whole situation was seen as her trying to split them up and while totally wrong, this was a terrible place to be when rabid fans are involved.

Nora got painted all over message boards and social media as the home-wrecker, a whore, every ugly name in the book by fans of the Devon and Stephanie coupling. She'd had fans physically throw things at her even; everything from drinks to rotten food to human waste while trying to grocery shop, get a coffee, or just going for a walk. It had been rough, but thankfully hadn't lasted long because her friends announced their engagement and the tabloids corrected their story spin, or at the very least moved on and so did the fandoms.

Through the worst of it, she had gotten hundreds and hundreds of messages and had eventually changed her number and taken as many security steps as she could. She had reported any outright threatening texts to the police, and they had researched a few that seemed to be credible. Unfortunately, there hadn't been much they could do. Only when there's an effort for physical harm can the police step in.

Another habitual texter had appeared out of the woodwork around the same time, someone she thought she'd long since gotten rid of. Unfortunately, making *them* go away wasn't quite so simple. And he always managed to get her new number, no matter what. She'd block, report, reject but no matter what she tried it was like he had some kind of inside source providing him with her new number and information.

Nora's skin still broke out in mild hives when she thought about how tense the weeks had been while she'd been getting the messages.

In theory, having super-fans was really flattering. In reality, it could be downright terrifying and took a serious toll on your mental state if you didn't make yourself unplug from media in general on a regular basis. There was no way to avoid feeling bad about yourself when people were telling you how terrible you were, especially when you knew there were plenty of prime examples just behind a flimsy closet door, ready and waiting to fall out and expose you to the world.

Thankfully, things had been fairly quiet except for the positive messages since she changed her number and started avoiding interaction on social media, but she still felt the lingering threat.

A chill snaked down her spine, making her teeth rattle.

She hadn't noticed the car crossing the lot, but Nora looked up to find Ollie Parkinson staring at her from behind the wheel of his beloved Tesla. He was *right* in front of her. Despite her efforts to park as far away from the electric charging stations as possible, the lot had been mostly full when she'd driven in that morning.

He gave a rueful smile and lifted his hand in a friendly wave before driving off.

There had to be something there—some kind of per-sonality or maybe even bi-polar disorder. He ran extremely hot and cold and unless he was faking (which was always possible, he was an actor after all) there had been some genuine remorse for his actions.

Despite his attitude change, Nora waited until he had driven out the gate and onto the road to put her car back into gear.

With a head shake to clear away all the dark thoughts, she swiped her badge at the gate kiosk, waved at the guard on duty, and pulled away from the insulated bubble that was the studio lot and entered the mess that was evening traffic in Los Angeles.

SHE ALWAYS TRIED to use her slow commute to clear her head, but that was easier said than done. Traveling inches at a time toward an apartment she couldn't wait to move out of felt like it was only delaying inevitable disappointment. The saddest part was that it wasn't a terrible location or even a terrible apartment. It was dated, sure, but better than many. And at least had a secure, gated parking lot.

One of the main issues was it consistently smelled of vinegar thanks to old lady Gravitz down the hall who supplemented her meager income by making home-made pickles.

Seriously, tons of pickles.

Cucumbers, asparagus, green beans, carrots, beets—you name it, she'd put it in a jar and make it a pickle. At first, it had been an interesting conversation piece and a pleasant novelty when holidays rolled around to get an assortment of jars as a gift, but now it was a smell that made Nora's stomach pitch and roll and seemed to linger in every article of clothing and even in her nostrils. She had a whole cabinet dedicated to jars of goodies Mrs. Gravitz had traded or gifted her. Re-gifting them was a full-time challenge.

More than an hour and less than 15 long miles later, she finally reached the non-descript yellow stucco building that counted as home. Nora was more than ready for a quick bite to eat and some relaxation before she had to turn around to head to set by 6 am.

Even the palm trees and rolling hills in the background were losing their magic, and that made Nora sad. There was something truly special about southern California and once the luster was off that diamond, she might as well pack up and move back home to Alabama.

She felt her face pinch a little.

No, *not* Alabama. But somewhere.

Trying to ignore the thick layer of vinegar and garlic scent in the hallway, Nora entered her cool apartment on a sigh, grateful for the familiarity of her own space if nothing else.

Crossing the tiny linoleum entryway and padding across the worn and stained beige carpeting of the living room, she took some time to greet and water her green babies first. Nora knew that many would think her totally bizarre for doing so, but she deeply cared for and talked to her plants. She had a collection of all varieties and sizes, many of which needed new pots soon.

Nora wasn't counting anymore, but she knew there had to be close to four dozen, many clustered together near the large dining room windows on the thrift store tables and stands she'd collected, a few others dispersed throughout the apartment's rooms.

Beige walls to match the carpeting greeted her. Neutral on neutral to make things appear clean and more attractive for new renters. It was boring, and everyone knew it. She'd tried to hang some posters and prints but they didn't lend nearly as much personality to the space as she'd hoped. Nora knew that this place was temporary, but having her efforts to decorate and make it her own fall short was frustrating.

She crooned at the plants, telling them how lovely they looked and how big they were getting as she pinched off some dead leaves, watered those that needed a drink, and turned a few to get better sunlight. Caring for her plants made a gentle smile appear and helped her stress levels normalize.

As a child, her grandmother had cared for exotic plants, Orchids mostly, and both Nora and her sister had picked up that gene. Tending to greenery was soothing; therapeutic. Nora hoped to be able to re-acquire the orchids under another's care since her grandmother's passing, but as a renter with no space, it just wasn't possible.

One day.

Once the plants were all taken care of, Nora took the dozen or so steps from the living room into the small but open kitchen. Digging out enough odds and ends from her dated, almond-colored fridge she found enough to put together something that resembled a meal.

The chipped ivory and gold flaked Formica counter-top was limited as far as space, but clean. Nora quickly assembled a hash out of her assorted veggies and leftover Indian food in a well-loved cast-iron skillet, enjoying the smells coming off the pan and the simple act of preparing a meal, haphazard as it was.

Leftover hash was something she would forever equate with growing up on simple means. There were far too many people in the city who had never been poor, and it showed.

Eating while standing over the kitchen sink was not optimal, Nora knew. She could almost hear Devon in her ear, telling her to *go out, meet people, have fun*. Nora's head shook, chasing away her own personal Jiminy Cricket. She didn't have time for a social life, or fun, or dating right now. She had work and a couple of friends she saw once in a while and that was enough.

It had to be.

The consequences of her first (and last) attempt at being a normal girl going out and having fun or being in a relationship still lingered. Her mystery texts were a constant reminder that keeping to herself was a good idea, at least for now. She needed her bright and shiny good-girl image to last in the press while she built up a solid career—especially after the hit that had come from the ring store debacle. Nora had come too far and worked too hard to see it all vanish because of her past bad decisions.

Maxwell's smile popped into her mind unbidden and she could feel her spine straighten. A relationship of any kind was a complication to her life and her focus. Dangerous even.

Getting into the dating world was a surefire way to mess with her stable, clean reputation. Though someone like Maxwell would be a lot more secure than a random stranger she met online or out somewhere.

Regardless, she'd worked too hard to let go of Nora Chase as she currently existed—she was known and loved. As a TV actress, she was still too small-time to be considered *America's Sweetheart*, but she was the next best thing.

There was never any link to her doing drugs or over-indulging in alcohol, she was kind to strangers, children, and animals. As a close friend to Devon and Stephanie; a power-couple who were also comparatively clean-cut and never got into any trouble, her public persona reflected back on them. She had no intention of sullying it, and while it wasn't a lot of effort to stay out of trouble—honestly it was way easier and much preferred to stay home instead of going out partying—even one slip, one photo, one little snippet of footage could bring her image and popularity crashing down. Her past was a house of cards but under someone else's control. One misstep from her and it would all come down.

So why did she feel like throwing caution to the wind where Maxwell was involved? She felt like once she had a better toe-hold in the industry she'd get a bit more wiggle room. Though it's not like he called, or checked with her friends to find out her number or how to reach her. Had he?

Frustrated with herself and where her train of thought seemed to be continuously derailed, she rinsed her plate in the dented steel sink and stalked off to her bedroom to go through her regular evening yoga routine.

She had thus far avoided needing a nutritionist or trainer for her roles for the most part, and hoped to keep it that way. Regular yoga seemed to be working so far and was beneficial to both her body and mental state for so many reasons. Her muscles and anxiety thanked her as she went through the poses on her padded lavender mat.

Once she was finally wound down, Nora tucked herself into her one indulgence as far as furniture—her giant king-sized bed with plush memory foam mattress and 800-thread-count sheets. As her body melted into the bed, sleep claimed her, a tall, gorgeous man on the beach playing a starring role in her dreams.

CHAPTER
Four

DEVON MET HER in the parking lot of his condo complex on Friday evening, all bright smile and wide-open arms.

"Ick, look at you—all honeymoon glowy," she teased, falling into his tight squeezing hug with an amount of relief she hadn't been expecting to feel.

"Super gross, actually. I'm very well fed and all kinds of oversexed too." He was like the annoying, over-sharing big brother she never had.

"Ugh! Nope. No, no, no. I don't need to hear that! I have to look at you and Stephanie while trying to *eat*. Plus, you're touching me right now—I *definitely* don't need to think about you having sex," Nora teased back, wiggling as though trying to escape his enthusiastic hug. "Been a long couple of weeks without you at work. I almost missed you."

He dwarfed her petite frame, and there was no escape from his arms once he decided to dedicate himself to an embrace. She eventually quit fighting and just let it happen, going limp in his grip.

"That's sweet. I missed my fangs."

"Your mean fans? Or your friends?"

"No, my *fangs*. I quite enjoy pretending to be a vampire, just as you like pretending to be a witch," he faked a gasp. "unless you're not *pretending*?"

Nora gave him a sideways look from under her lashes and he chuckled.

"And I missed you. *Of course* you! It was strange not to have to turn up for makeup and wardrobe in the early hours of the morning," Devon took a deep breath. "I feel like I'm Superman now that we're back—there's so much more air here than there was in Colorado!" He gave an extra tight squeeze of his arms to demonstrate, Nora grunting as he compressed her whole ribcage.

"Quit!" she forced out with a giggle. "Could you let go now?"

Nora didn't giggle, either. That was something that only seemed to happen around him and rarely. He brought out her younger side with his playful antics.

When Devon finally loosened his grip, she smiled back at him broadly, his hands holding her at arms-length. To be fair, that was quite a distance considering his height and her lack thereof.

His happiness was evident, nearly overwhelming, and she loved that he was in love. A throb of loneliness spiked through her, but she pushed it away. She had thought she was in love once. Man had she been wrong. Nevertheless, it looked good on her friend and she was beyond happy for him.

Nora's best friend since they had met as college freshmen, Devon was the best kind of man and she was so lucky to have him on her side and in her life. She'd helped him both heal physically and grieve the loss of his scholarship and a professional soccer career after he was injured that first semester at school. Then when he decided to join her in the theater program she'd been thrilled as could be. She couldn't even be mad at him when he'd found success faster and bigger than she did because he was always there cheering her on and offering a hand up where he could. When they had decided to move to Los Angeles, he had tried his hand at modeling first but found that acting was his true love.

She could relate.

So much so that a few bad decisions still followed her around from her earliest days in California. She tried not to think about it, but she could never fully put it out of her mind.

The only thing that pulled at her heart the same way as acting was her plants, and it might be an even comparison between the two, just depended on the day. Both fed her soul, acting as a learned craft and plants because she could see the results of nurturing them along.

Everything was all that much better now that Stephanie was part of the package deal. She got to see Devon both at work and outside of it, and she had a close girlfriend she could relate to in Stephanie.

Girlfriends had never been her strong suit and on top of it all, she missed her younger sister fiercely. Friends, in general, can be really tough in the business. It was difficult whether to know if they are interested in you as a person, not because of what you can offer them or their career. Because of the media spin on how Nora and Devon were involved, she and Stephanie had suffered a rocky start to their friendship but thankfully, things were all worked out now. *They* knew the truth of their situation, and that's what mattered.

"You look good, Kid." He grinned down at her, those sky-blue eyes twinkling.

"Thanks. You look … married," she said, lips tugged up in a grin. "you look incredibly happy, Dev."

His smile was immediate and broad, and that made Nora's heart warm.

"It's the best."

Nora shook her head and turned back to the car to gather her things, ready to be out of the parking lot, no matter how well landscaped and maintained. She wondered if she would ever not feel exposed when out in the open.

"Phae call you back yet?" Devon asked casually. She stiffened at the mention of her sister's name and shook her head. She could hear him sigh behind her. "It's been months, Nor. What's going on that she doesn't want to talk to you?"

"I don't know, but I'm worried. She won't return my calls or texts except to tell me she's okay. That's the entirety of the messages, like clockwork once a week—'I'm okay'. I know she's hiding and mad because of the whole mess with Mom, but I don't get why she's avoiding *me*." She stopped and shook her head again.

Devon knew all about the drama between her mom and sister, but not the deep, dark ugly secret hanging over *her*. She knew she'd have to tell him eventually, but not yet. It was her problem, not his.

His sympathetic gaze truly made her feel like she was his sister, not just his friend. That made her feel like keeping this gigantic secret was a shitty thing to do. Guilt settled heavily in her chest and gut.

"I'll help you figure it out, you know. I wish Phae would call back, but at least she's checking in once a week. Your mom on the other hand … well, we both know she won't stop until she gets what she wants, or at least *feels* like she's won." Devon seemed to know more than she'd told him, which reminded her exactly how easily and how badly keeping secrets from him could blow up in her face.

"I know. I may have to fly home to get it all sorted out, but that will mean a break from the show unless I wait until the season is over. You know how complicated that gets."

Devon nodded and abruptly shifted gears. His eyes tracked some movement outside the gate to the complex. Nora tensed with his movements. It could be someone out walking their dog, just trying to get down the street or it could be a photographer looking for a candid shot to sell to the tabloids. No way to know.

"Come on. Bring that bag that I know has at least one bottle of wine, your crazy neighbor lady's assorted pickled goodies, and probably chocolate cake. Maxwell hasn't shown up with the food yet and Stephanie's getting hangry." He gave her a serious look, eyebrows pinched. "She's *mean* when she's hangry."

"Aren't we all," Nora said, gentle smile back on her face as she gathered her purse and the bag, those nervous butterflies back in her gut, fluttering around and causing adrenaline to pump. She hadn't seen or heard from Maxwell since the wedding, but her interest in the handsome attorney was definitely piqued. Nobody had mentioned he was coming, but she guessed she shouldn't have been surprised—Maxwell was to Stephanie what Devon was to Nora. It only made sense that they see one another when schedules managed to align.

Devon led her toward the building by the shoulders, tugging on her ponytail once or twice like the obnoxious big brother type friend he was. His assessment of what was inside her canvas grocery bag had been dead-on and made her question her predictability. Was she that boring? Did it matter? Or had he just snuck a peek somehow?

Her hormones and nerves, on the other hand, had surged at the mention of Maxwell.

"Maxwell as in Maxwell Caine?" she queried, trying to sound neutral and not knowing if she succeeded or not.

Wearing his trademark smirk, Devon nodded. "Yep. He's Steph's Mr. Woo's dealer and she wanted to see him about as much as I wanted to see you, so we figured why not just have a family dinner? Couldn't we all use some incredibly delicious old Los Angeles Chinese food in our lives?"

Nora felt her head quirk to one side. Family dinner, huh? "She didn't mention that," she accused lightly.

Devon's eyes danced with mirth and his smirk only grew. "Oh no? How strange."

Nora froze just as they reached the dove gray door of the condo.

"Oh my God. Are you guys trying to *set us up*?" Nora asked, feigning indignation she didn't really feel but kind of wished she did. A little. If nothing else, she couldn't seem too eager—Devon would have a ball with that kind of ammunition to tease her with. She had to at least *pretend* to put up a fight and seem somewhat disinterested. She was pretty sure that was in the BFF manual under code of conduct for being set up on dates.

She didn't have time to date. She had a thousand reasons not to, a couple of which were really, really important.

It would never work, not with her schedule and her family drama and the skeleton that kept knocking on her closet door. Not to mention that being hounded by paparazzi was not at all conducive or helpful for a healthy relationship.

Devon opened the door and gestured for her to go in ahead of him, snickering. He no doubt had seen the whole argument she just had with herself cross her face.

"No. We're just putting the two of you—our very best friends—in the same space together. If you think about it, it's kind of important that you like each other. Tolerance, at a bare minimum, is required. You are probably going to be seeing each other a few times a year or more for the rest of our lives."

Well. Put like that, she guessed it was the only logical thing. That didn't stop the anvil in her chest from dropping dramatically into her feet. She didn't like that Devon thought them getting close was an inevitability, even if it was.

Devon's condo was an enthusiastic step up from her apartment. The parking lot was gated and recently paved, the grounds immaculately maintained and the interior of the unit completely updated and luxurious. There was plenty of space for guests, lots of furniture that didn't have a questionable history and enough dishes to go around.

There were reasons she rarely offered to host at her place.

Her friends never seemed bothered by her bottom of the barrel, but still outrageously priced rental—everyone who lived in or around Los Angeles knew the crazy cost of living in Los Angeles—but she couldn't help but be a little self-conscious about it.

Nora was busy taking in all the new canvases on the walls as Devon tugged her along. Stephanie had certainly been busy with her paints. It never ceased to amaze Nora how talented with the brushes Stephanie was.

She painted under the name Alex Felton, and her incredible abstracts were displayed everywhere from the Beverly Wilshire Hotel lobby to celebrity chef helmed restaurants. She was kind of a big deal and deserved every accolade Alex attracted.

They breezed—well, Devon breezed, Nora was tugged—into the kitchen where they found Stephanie putting plates and utensils onto the gorgeous blue and grey granite counter-top.

"Nora!" Stephanie immediately wrapped Nora in a quick hug before relieving her of her bag. "I'm so glad you made it." Her amber eyes were full of the smile on her mouth and Nora warmed, reveling in the feeling of being wanted and included and part of a friendship she wasn't constantly questioning or chasing after.

Or hiding from.

She'd only ever had that before with Devon and a few people throughout high school and college that she didn't speak to anymore. To have it with a female was a novelty she knew Stephanie was also enjoying and adjusting to.

"Me too." As Stephanie reached into the bag, she couldn't help but caveat the contents. "The wine was a gift, so I have no idea if it's any good. The chocolate cake is from La Monarca, so I know without a doubt it's fantastic."

Stephanie made a moaning noise over the cake. "Yes. Oh, man. I have to remember to save room."

Nora laughed. "Pickles of every kind, too. Mrs. Gravitz has been busy and I honestly can't stand most of them anymore because of the smell in my building all the time."

On a chuckle, Devon examined a jar of pickled beet slices, opened them up, and helped himself.

"Good." He nodded, talking over a mouthful of beet.

"You're so gross," Nora gently chided, smiling at her friend. He made her feel young, and in a town that made you feel ancient by the time you hit 25, it was a novel, wonderful feeling.

"Super gross," he agreed, his words muffled. He gave her a broad smile, doing so in a way that ensured he showed as much masticated beet as possible.

"That's disgusting. You're like, what, 12?" Nora laughed.

Stephanie swatted him on the arm without any real effort behind it and shook her head with a smile, turning to open the bottle of wine. "And here I thought I already had you mostly house-trained."

Just as the cork came out, the doorbell rang, and she dropped the corkscrew to the counter-top with a clatter, nearly sprinting to the door.

"Wow," Nora commented, eyebrows up. She felt a bit like a traitor to Stephanie for having that response—she knew damn well that there was nothing between her and Maxwell, and if it were her doorbell he was ringing, Nora would respond in exactly the same way.

Devon nodded, expression solemn. "I used to be a bit worried about that reaction. See, I thought it was for Maxwell. Turns out, it's for the Mr. Woo's, so I don't worry anymore. I know that she'll look at *me* like that if only I show up with a bag of lo-mein, some Kung pow chicken, and extra egg rolls." His serious expression gave way to mirth and Nora laughed heartily, trying to compartmentalize the tingly sensation in her chest that ignited from the sound of Maxwell's voice in the other room.

"Maxwell, you know Nora, right?" Stephanie glided back into the kitchen, both she and Maxwell carrying bags of food.

Nora felt her heart stop for what felt like a full ten seconds as he made eye contact with her. Damn, that was a potent gaze.

"Yes, of course. We met at your wedding, Steph. Among other regrettably brief introductions." He turned the full force of his smile her direction and Nora couldn't help but blush. "Nice to see you again, Nora. You're a bit less sandy than I recall, but that was my fault I suppose. Rufus shouldn't be allowed off his leash when we're on the beach in the vicinity of beautiful women in fancy dresses."

"Yes, very nice to see you again," she managed, blush intensifying as he complimented her. As a distraction, she busied herself by pouring the wine. "Rufus was no bother."

He simply gave her a gentle smile that she could feel clear down in her toes.

As the group dished up and sat down at the dining table, Nora realized that she was focused purely on the pounding of her pulse and wasn't paying any attention to the conversation going on around her. She was embarrassed to realize that Maxwell had asked her a question.

"Sorry?"

"Stephanie said you worked with Ollie Parkinson the other day?"

The mere mention of his name regulated all of Nora's hormones instantly, goosebumps—the unfriendly kind—breaking out on her arms.

"Yes. He's … slimy."

Maxwell nodded gravely, and Stephanie barked a single note of laughter.

"Is he done shooting with you?" Devon asked, unusually serious, an expression of concern on his face.

"Yes, it was just the one day. You may have a couple of scenes with him though, before he's killed off."

Devon considered that for a moment.

"I could always loan Alan to you for a day or two." Stephanie grinned with a playful but also terrifyingly devious expression. She had one eyebrow up, a tip to her mouth that Nora wasn't sure she ever wanted to see again, especially if she were to ever become the target. She looked entirely too amused by the prospect of sending Nora with her gigantic bodyguard for a few days. "As long as you promise to film Ollie's reaction when he sees Alan."

"You're pure evil, aren't you, Lovely?" Maxwell chuckled.

Nora smiled though, genuinely considering it and feeling like a jerk for doing so. He'd apologized, and had truly seemed to be genuine about it. "You think he would? Alan, I mean."

Stephanie pulled her phone out. "I have no doubt it would give him quite a thrill to see Ollie again." She tapped away as she muttered, "He was quite disappointed he didn't get to drop him down the canyon to see if he bounced."

Nora choked a bit on her wine.

Maxwell shook his head. "You indulge that overgrown brute too much, Alex. He doesn't need another toy."

Nora couldn't stop the laugh the bubbled out of her at Maxwell's description of Alan. An action star and honest to goodness bodybuilder, he could only be referred to as a mountain of a man. While perhaps a teddy bear to those he's close to, anyone in their right mind would be wise to stay off his bad side.

"I could swear I saw a circle dent in his forehead under his makeup the other day."

Stephanie gave a similar choke on the sip of wine she'd taken. "Oh my god. It shouldn't be funny, but it is.

It definitely wasn't when it happened." A snort emitted from her mouth. "My Jimmy Choo's *were* a great weapon."

Maxwell just shook his head at her. He and Stephanie, friends since the womb essentially, according to the story Devon had relayed, had an even better shorthand than Nora and Devon did. Their parents were life-long friends, and so they had become close as well.

Nora noticed that Devon was unusually quiet and the grip he had on his fork was pretty intense. Thinking of Stephanie being accosted and having to defend herself with her shoe clearly made him very uncomfortable. And of course it did—she'd worry about him if it didn't.

"I'll keep you posted. Honestly just mentioning your name made him back off." She considered as she moved some food around her plate. "He actually apologized at the end of the day. Said he was trying to be better."

This pleased everyone at the table, but there was still a general sense of distrust for him.

"That's because Steph is a badass."

"A shoe ninja even," Maxwell kidded.

Stephanie tipped her glass. "He said that to me too—that he promised to be better. I'll believe it when he finally checks himself into some anger management classes or therapy or something."

The tension was suitably cut and the meal progressed in a playful manner—Nora eating way too much of the amazing Chinese food and yet still finding room for the decadent chocolate cake; she and Stephanie commiserating with a look across the table in their misery. They did also manage to share a smile because Devon and Maxwell were having a playful discussion and the atmosphere was comfortable and warm.

She would package up that feeling if she could, so it could be opened and meted out in small doses when needed.

Lately, she needed it more and more often, and that thought bothered her. As if on cue, she could hear her phone vibrate from where it rested in her purse across the room.

As she contemplated getting up to check, a thought flitted through her mind. Despite her nervousness around Maxwell and her undeniable attraction to him, even if nothing at all changed between them and they remained in their mutual BFF boxes, only seeing one another at holidays and get-togethers, it would be nice. Warm. Enjoyable.

As a group, they seemed to mesh well and loved to laugh together. That's what friends were all about, right?

Lord knew that she could use more laughter, especially lately. The weight of things outside her control, for the most part, had been weighing heavily. Her normally bubbly personality was beginning to bow under the strain of keeping only to the routine of work—home—work and maintaining her pristine image.

Nora allowed herself a few hours to eat, drink, relax, laugh, and enjoy herself. She ignored her phone completely and tried to imagine what it would be like if her life was like this more often. She wondered if it was actually like this for some people; this happiness. If their lives actually were the happy go lucky social media portrayal of reality.

The feeling of belonging and happiness was light but heady. She wanted to reach out and grab it, but she knew it didn't work that way, and right now that kind of life wasn't hers to take.

Devon noticed the change in her face at one point and quirked a concerned eyebrow. She shook her head and pulled a silly face to put him at ease. He smiled, but he knew her better than that. There would no doubt be an inquiry very soon about what was going on in her brain. At least she had time to suitably prepare a response that might sound somewhat feasible.

It was impossibly sexy, watching the two gentlemen clean up then insist on doing dishes. Rather than load the dishwasher Maxwell washed and Devon dried. Nora met Stephanie's eye across the dining table agreeing they'd move to a smaller setting while the guys finished up.

"I'm with you, sister," Stephanie teased, fanning herself.

Nora chuckled and felt herself blushing. Stephanie just smiled and winked at her, both of them unable to stop glancing back into the kitchen for another look.

At the end of the evening, Maxwell kindly offered to walk Nora to her car.

"That would be great, thanks." She managed to keep the nervous tremble from her voice which she considered a win.

Saying goodbye, Devon couldn't help but slide her a sly wink and she shook her head at him.

"You're the worst."

"You love me anyway. And we need to talk later, about whatever it is that has you so worried."

Nora kissed his cheek in confirmation of his statement but agreed to nothing, hugging Stephanie one more time before stepping out of the condo ahead of Maxwell. His warm bulk behind her made her feel simultaneously safe and nervous—the nerves for a reason she hadn't felt in quite a while and wasn't sure should be inviting.

"This was nice," she said, eager to fill the strange gap of silence.

"It was. Those two are quite the pair." Maxwell's easy grin reappeared and made Nora's insides melt.

"They are. Thanks for walking me out."

The cars loomed just ahead and Maxwell's head bobbed gently. "My pleasure. See you soon maybe?"

Nora nodded, sliding behind the wheel of her Honda. "Sure."

Maxwell gently closed the door once she'd tucked her body safely into the seat. She could see that he waited until she was backing out to get into his vehicle—a little, shiny, red sports car. How he folded himself down small enough to get into the drivers' seat was a mystery.

She expected to feel disappointed that he didn't press further for her phone number, or another date or anything at all really, but that emotion never managed to fully manifest. Something told her to be patient, that she'd see him again—and soon, just like he said. The thoughts warring in her mind then made sure to remind her that she didn't have time or space for a relationship anyway and to quit while she was ahead.

That feeling of lightness carried her all the way home and through her yoga poses, soothing her even into sleep where once again, that blonde hair and smile showed up to grace her dreams, making them sweet and more hormonally agitated than she'd admit.

"THE GOOD NEWS is, we can get you some new representation very quickly. The bad news is, you may not get all the advance money right away because this is technically a delay in negotiations. The studio can hold that money hostage for a while if they choose."

Nora stared at her agent across the large desk in her office. It wasn't the end of the world, certainly, and it was definitely a good news / bad news situation.

The entertainment law firm partnered with the talent agency had up and closed their doors with no warning or forwarding information, leaving the clientele for the whole of the agency without representation right at a time when Nora's contract for the show was pending renewal.

Her agent, Melissa-Mel-normally one of the most on top of it and aggressively aware women she'd ever met, looked embarrassed and even a bit ashamed. Instead of her normal bulldog expression, her vibrant blue eyes, dark hair in a high and tight bun, and red-lipstick covered mouth looked quite tense and bordering on dour.

"Like how long are we talking for a delay?"

"Until filming resumes in the Fall."

Nora's stomach dropped a bit. That wasn't what she'd budgeted for, but she could make it work. She had been socking as much as she could save away, hoping for a newer car or even a different apartment. Maybe nest egg for the future should she not get so lucky for auditions and roles in the future. There was one expense that, if she could cut, would make her whole life easier, but there was no way to do that right now. Not without sabotaging just about everything else.

"Okay. It's okay, Mel. What do I do? Just tell me the next steps. I'll figure it out."

The other woman shook her head gently. "I'm so sorry Nora. Really. We should have had a backup plan for this as a whole. I will be rebating my fees to make some of the sting better, but we screwed the pooch totally and I'm not afraid to admit it. We worked with that firm for so many years we—well, I can only speak for myself, but I assume the others would agree—got comfortable and assumed they weren't going to disappear like bandits in the night. Now we know better." Mel shuffled around a few papers and brought up a business card, handing it to Nora across the desk. "I've been in touch with a different law firm, and they've agreed to take you on as a client if you're interested.

Instead of having our own in-house or a firm on retainer, we are transitioning to client held representation." Mel met her eye and let out a breath. "This firm has some of the best entertainment attorneys in town. Give them a call." Nora took the card, and as her eyes scanned the raised lettering, her heart stuttered a bit as she heard Mel's next words. "If you want new representation as far as an agent goes … I get that too."

"I…" Nora hesitated. "I'll give them a call. I'm not looking to switch agents, Mel. Shit happens." It did. Not usually like this, but Mel had been there when Nora was doing small bit parts and commercials and fought hard to get her better auditions and, in the end, on *Destiny Falls*, one of the most popular prime-time shows the major networks had to offer. She wouldn't feel right abandoning her now. She said as much, and the hint of a smile crossed Mel's face, some tension easing around her eyes.

"I appreciate the vote of confidence, Nora. Truly though, if you are at all uncomfortable, I would understand if you find someone else. I won't hold it against you. Give these guys a call—they've been given a heads up on the situation. I'm betting the firm that pulled this over on us did it all over town."

Mel looked tired, her normally sparkling blue eyes dull and the dark circles peeking through her carefully applied makeup.

Nora nodded, rising from the chair, eyes on the card. Hollywood Law would certainly be getting a call.

IT WORKED OUT that the law office was taking consultations on cases like Nora's immediately. It looked to be a massive group of clients and agents that had been left high and dry by the previous team. Contracts that were supposed to be reviewed and sent back were just left hanging; just sent into what amounted to a giant pending wasteland for 'filing' as they pulled up stakes and dissolved the business right out from underneath their partners.

That old joke about a waste-paper basket being called the circular file was suddenly way less amusing.

Therefore, Nora found herself sitting with at least half a dozen other actors in a lush black and chrome lobby just a few days later, her leg bouncing nervously under her conservative black skirt as she waited her turn to be called back. She had a fleeting worry that she was going to sweat through the white silk blouse before it became her turn—and she hadn't brought a jacket to disguise that if it happened.

She wasn't sure why she was so nervous; she'd done nothing wrong. It was just that ingrained sensation of having been called to the principal's office she supposed. They felt like authority to her—adultier adults than she currently was. No matter her feelings on it, these were people she was essentially interviewing to take her money—she was hiring *them*. She needed someone she trusted looking over her business contracts.

She was the one in charge here. She could even decide that this wasn't the firm for her and hunt down different lawyers if she wanted to.

It just didn't feel that way. Being a grown-up sneaks up on you sometimes.

Her phone buzzed, and she only glanced at it before stowing it again. The messages from her mother were getting more persistent, more frequent, and more frantic. She'd have to rip the band-aid off that situation pretty soon and pick up the phone. Avoiding the drama that had gone down between her sister and mom was clearly not something she could do forever.

The weekly check-in message from her sister had arrived the night before, and while it made her breathe a bit easier every time she heard from her, Nora wished Phae would actually *speak* to her or answer any of the hundred questions she'd asked in her own messages.

In addition to her mother's messages, there was also a very complimentary fan text, which made her smile a little. It proclaimed that she was the most under-rated and beautiful actress of her generation and that she would no doubt be the perfect wife for whoever had sent the message.

Nora could beg to differ on any number of counts, but she accepted the kind intention behind the text. Responding was out of the question of course, but sometimes she wished she could before she hit the block button.

The surely middle-aged but somehow ageless receptionist at Hollywood Law had clearly been doing the job since the beginning of time; she handled the cluster of anxious, stressed out actors with aplomb and grace the likes of which Nora had never seen before.

Hannah, her nameplate read, had offered drinks, kind smiles, and gentle words of encouragement and comfort every time someone approached the desk. She was beautiful in a very soft, pleasant kind of way. She wore her timeless pencil dress with ease Nora couldn't help but envy, and it looked like her French twist up-do and makeup were simply part of her. Hannah led every client to the double doors to the right of her wide cherry desk with a calm, measured pace, and nodded what felt like a very genuine 'You're welcome' when thanks for her help were offered.

Nora could only aspire to such balanced, easy energy. She was a mass of snarled nerves and anxiety much of the time. Hannah's vibe was that of a graceful swan. Nora's was that of a squirrel who'd gotten into some serious caffeine and maybe some sugared donuts somewhere along the way.

Her brow furrowed as she studied the woman, an interesting thought occurring to her. Perhaps Hannah's nature was a by-product of medical marijuana. Nobody would ever know. The thought intrigued and fascinated Nora, making her smile. The image of a hyped-up squirrel at a rave didn't hurt either.

"Nora Chase?"

Nora quickly got to her feet and followed the affable Hannah to the double doors for her meeting with the attorneys.

"Thank you."

"You're welcome." Slight head nod.

Nora noted that Hannah smelled like roses, not pot, and shook away that whole ridiculous train of thought as she walked straight ahead into the conference room she'd been instructed to enter.

An older gentleman sat at one end of the massive wood table, a neat stack of folders in front of him. Her steps faltered a bit as she realized she recognized the distinguished man.

He looked very different in his business style suit, but there was no mistaking that this was the man who had hosted Devon and Stephanie's wedding. This was Mr. Caine.

"Welcome, Ms. Chase." He reached out a hand and shook hers firmly as recognition sparked. "I wasn't expecting an acquaintance such as yourself in my conference room today, but it's definitely a pleasure to see you again." She noticed that his brown eyes were friendly, and the expression on his face was familiar in a way she couldn't quite put her finger on. "Please, have a seat. One of my partners will be joining us momentarily."

"Thank you, Mr. Caine. Your office is just as lovely as your home."

"Thank you very much. I'll be sure to share that compliment with my wife. She's very proud of that house and for good reason." His smile was broad as he spoke of his wife, then his expression grew somewhat serious. "We're glad you're here, but you have our sympathies about the circumstances. It would seem that the Flanders firm did wrong by quite a number of clients." He gave an expression that made her think he was annoyed with the other firm for doing the wrong thing, which earned him any number of points in her book. It would be quite a new experience to end up with a lawyer that had an admirable moral code. "Please call me Samuel, by the way."

"I'll do my best with that, sir."

He laughed, and it was a warm, well-used guffaw. "Very polite, the lot of you today. I can't say I was expecting it, but it's nice to be surprised. Wouldn't you agree?"

Nora couldn't help but smile. This older man was not at all what she'd expected either, so they were on the same page. Their brief introduction at the wedding hadn't been much to go on as far as gauging his personality.

"Yes, absolutely."

There was a rap of knuckles on the open conference room door, and Nora turned, her breath stalling in her chest.

"Ah, there he is. Ms. Chase, I believe you're familiar with my partner, Maxwell."

Maxwell was more than Samuel's law partner. Unless her memory had totally failed her, this pair of lawyers was father and son.

Maxwell's whole face transformed into that well-used, easy smile before he could school it when his eyes landed on her.

Maxwell extended a hand. "It's lovely to see you again, Nora."

"Hello, Maxwell."

Samuel's well-groomed gray eyebrow raised. "Do you two know each other well? Von Feldt-Greene wedding associations aside, that is."

Maxwell took a seat, smoothing his pinstriped tie as he settled into one of the black leather conference table chairs.

"She's a good friend of Devon's so yes, we're familiar. I shouldn't discount that she's Stephanie's friend as well." Maxwell grinned at Samuel.

"Full disclosure if you hadn't already done the math or hadn't recalled—Maxwell is also my son." Samuel let loose his own broad, toothy grin, and it was immediately apparent to Nora where Maxwell had gotten his smile. "The Von Feldts are old family friends, but we've seen the Greene's around the office a time or two as well."

Nora had a sudden sinking feeling. She knew nothing about law, but something about the familiarity felt like it might be a problem. "Will it be any kind of conflict that I know you and Maxwell personally? Or other clients?"

Samuel turned his gentle smile on her, and she felt it like a warm hug from a parent.

"No, Ms. Chase. We'll make sure you're well taken care of and there's no conflict of interest here," he turned his gaze to his son. "because there *is* interest, isn't there Maxwell?" The double-entendre hung there between them. Samuel grinned, a bit of seriousness creeping back in as he continued. "We've got other partners who can handle the particulars of your case if you choose to go forward with the firm so there's no conflict."

Maxwell, clearly used to his father's shenanigans just nodded and looked her way, still grinning. Nora felt the undivided attention in every cell of her body. It was like her pores absorbed it like vitamin D. "Wouldn't *you* like to know about my interests, old man?"

Serious, business Maxwell was maddeningly just as sexy as playful Maxwell. Nora's hormones certainly appreciated his well-cut suit and crisp cologne. They complimented his smile perfectly.

Samuel rumbled a broad chuckle one final time. Before they all settled down and got to business, a third member of the team, Joshua Banks, was invited to sit in as Maxwell, regrettably, stepped out.

Nora's tension level increased slightly without his presence, but Samuel and Mr. Banks—Joshua—seemed more than capable and were immediately giving her and her case their undivided attention. Samuel sat in mostly to supervise, and Joshua handled all the particulars.

Together they reviewed the contract that Mel had been kind enough to send over, stopping at certain points to discuss items of concern with her. The pair of lawyers didn't like some of the language, and they picked up on a few circular bits that made it appear she would be getting additional funds as bonuses but would never see a dime of without some change in terms and language.

It was an interesting duality to watch when the very friendly senior Caine shifted from friendly to full-on attorney mode, and while she'd have been more than happy to spend a bit more time with Maxwell, Joshua was completely competent and left her feeling confident in his abilities to handle her case.

BY THE END of the meeting, she had full confidence that the Caine lawyers would not only take care of this situation to the best of their ability, but also all of her affairs going forward.

As for the other law firm—should the attorneys who disappeared lock, stock, and barrel be located, Nora was certain that between Hollywood Law and the feds they would deeply regret having ever considered taking advantage of their clients and vanishing.

"Nice to see you again," Samuel repeated, shaking her hand as she stood to leave. "Hannah will give you instructions for the next steps on your way out."

"Thank you, Mr. Caine."

He made a noise in his throat. "Samuel, please."

"Samuel. I appreciate your help," as she said the words, and shook Joshua's hand as well, the door of the conference room opened once again, revealing Maxwell.

Nora felt her lips curve upward in response to seeing him. As she passed him in the doorway, she could feel that he had a hand poised near the small of her back, ready to lead her toward reception. It was entirely wonderful, his gesture, although reception was just a few steps back down the hallway and through the double doors. It was possessive, and protective—Nora wondered if men knew how that simple hand placement translated to the female brain.

Especially now, feeling taken advantage of by the situation around her contract, knowing that he and his father had her interests at hand meant a lot.

It probably should have seemed presumptuous on his part; overly intimate even for them not really knowing one another, but it didn't. That alone sent out tiny alarm bells to Nora, but she pointedly ignored them, choosing to appreciate the gesture and the warm caress of his hand through her blouse.

He wasn't just anyone. He was a friend to Devon and the best of friends to Stephanie. It was okay to trust him.

"It's our pleasure," Maxwell intoned, the timbre of his voice sending tingles through her body.

Hannah gave her a pre-printed sheet as she checked her out at the reception desk, Maxwell hovering slightly but looking busy as he scanned the stack of messages Hannah had given him as he approached the desk with Nora.

"You should be all set. One of the partners will be in touch should you need to give further information. They will also contact your agent as they explained."

"Yes, thanks very much."

Hannah gave another one of those completely beatific smiles and Nora turned to leave, Maxwell following her yet again to the main doors.

"Always a pleasure to see you, Nora. Hopefully next time it's not just for business. I'll see you soon?"

Nora could only nod, her lips ticked up into a grin.

Maxwell chuckled, and she felt it in her nipples.

Shit.

She was in deep trouble, Nora realized and was somehow welcoming it with open arms when she should be shutting it down and running the other way.

DEVON WAS BACK on set the Monday after her meeting at Hollywood Law.

Nora was thankful to have her friend back to work with her, and even more so because Ollie was still on the call sheets, though she wouldn't have to work with him.

He hadn't taken any further action or even said anything to Nora, but even after his apology, being in his general vicinity gave her and just about every other female present an uneasy feeling.

"He's very lucky he's still got all his teeth," Devon said to her as they watched him doing a scene between two of theirs. It was one of his last, the very next would be his untimely, gruesome and painful death. Then, thankfully, he'd be gone from the show and their lives. He could go try to be better elsewhere.

Nora grunted her agreement, and Devon turned his smirk on her. "Seriously though. Between Steph and Alan, this guy's lucky to have all his parts."

"Alan seems like a good friend to have," Nora mused, feeling like a total jerk for wishing the man ill. He was creepy, and inappropriate—absolutely—but he really had been on his best behavior. She knew as well as anyone that everyone was dealing with something in their lives.

Devon snorted. "He's great. We'll have to arrange a meeting. You never know when you might need a terrifying, beefy bodyguard."

Nora and Devon waited out Ollie's takes, Nora's shoulders relaxing as soon as he was dismissed and headed off to makeup.

The rest of the day went well, and Nora filled Devon in on the meeting with the attorneys over makeup removal.

"Seriously? That's some incredible bull-shittery. I'm glad Maxwell and Samuel are in your corner," Devon groused, making the makeup ladies work for it as he snapped his head toward Nora.

"Well, Maxwell had to recuse himself because we're … personally acquainted, but I feel comfortable with Mr. Caine and Mr. Banks handling things."

Devon had luckily escaped the mess because his agent already used Samuel to vet contracts.

"I'm pretty sure Maxwell is still in your corner," Devon smirked.

Nora shook her head at her meddling friend. "It will work out," she said on a sigh, realizing at that moment that she really believed that it would. A few days ago, there was no way she would have been so relaxed about the situation. "At least I know I'm employed for two more years." She smiled at Devon and he returned it.

"That is a wonderful feeling, I have to agree."

Damn Maxwell anyway—making her feel safe and cared for. She loved it, and her guarded side kept shouting warnings at the same rate her overbearing mother was leaving voicemails and sending text messages.

On the way to the parking lot, Devon elbowed her. "So, you going to be seeing your new attorney acquaintance outside the office?" He winked playfully at her and despite how used to his ribbing she was, she blushed. "Oh, man. You actually *like* him." Devon looked positively delighted.

"He's nice," Nora said weakly.

"Nice." Devon stopped sharply, just feet from her car.

"What's wrong with nice?" Nora was reminded that she had used that word when Maxwell had escorted her to her car after dinner at Devon's.

"Nothing. There's *nothing* wrong with nice, and I made the mistake of using that descriptor with my gorgeous wife—*once*," he punctuated the statement with a raised finger. "I told her that our phenomenal date was *nice*." His face puckered like he'd sucked on a lemon. "I didn't deserve to recover from that honestly, but things were extra complicated at the time and she was gracious about it. But you … you deserve so much more than *nice*. And anyway, I know better—he's got to be more than nice to basically be Steph's brother from another mother. So, if you like him, go out with him. You deserve *happy*, Nora. Joyful, enthusiastic, overwhelmed with orgasms happy."

"Ew." Nora pulled a face. "I really don't want to talk orgasms with you Dev, no matter how much I love you."

"Tough. I'm getting them—and giving them—and you should be too. Do you want me to suggest that he ask you out? I'll message Steph right now and have her put the idea in his head—"

"No. No, you will not." Nora shoved him, laughing as he pretended—or at least she hoped he was pretending—to text his wife.

"But you like him?" He persisted.

Nora sighed, unlocking the door of her car. "Yes, *Dad*, I like him."

"What's the problem then? We can only arrange so many group dinners, you know." Devon winked at her and held the door while she dropped into the drivers' seat.

"I knew it!" she declared, sweeping her blonde hair behind her shoulders and securing it with a spare ponytail band from her cup-holder after she adjusted the seatbelt.

Devon's quirked mouth gave her all the confirmation she needed.

"Just watching out for you. So, say yes when he asks, okay?"

Nora shook her head and started the engine. "We'll see."

Devon laughed, a full-body chuckle she knew well and delighted in hearing. There had been a time when neither one of them was able to let loose a rich, warm sound like that while laughing and it was a point of pride every time she was able to make it happen or was lucky enough to have him do so in her presence. There had been some tough, dark times after college.

Some of *her* skeletons were still hanging around.

"See you tomorrow," He said, shutting her door and making his way to his car.

As was their routine, he beeped his horn twice to let her know he was ready, and she led the way out of the lot to the ugly snarl of traffic. She went her way and he went his, both of them waving an arm out the window.

Sitting in the parking lot that was rush hour on the 405, Nora's phone beeped. Making an exception since she was at a full standstill, she checked the message, fully expected a message from her mother, or another random fan message. Pleasantly, it was someone else.

M: *Are you free for coffee at all this week?*

There was a brief pause as Nora stared at the message trying to cypher out if the number was familiar.

M: *This is Maxwell.*

Another brief pause.

M: *Caine. I'd like to discuss some things with you
if so. Part business, part personal.*

Nora's face made a wide smile all of its own accord
and her chest warmed, a feeling she had long thought was
reserved for teenagers and those disgustingly in love like
Devon and Stephanie.

Traffic began to move, so she left the phone in the
cup-holder until the next stopping point. It didn't take long.

Deleting and re-typing what felt like a dozen times,
she finally committed to a message.

N: *Not on the call sheets for Thursday that I know
of. There's a place near your office I assume?*

Maxwell's response came through almost immediately,
and Nora was able to scan it before needing to turn her
attention back to the road.

M: *I know the perfect spot. Best pastries in town.
I'll see you Thursday at 10.*

His next message was an address, and Nora shook her
head a bit, strangely pleased by the fact that he'd simply

given a time and place instead of asking. She realized again that coming from anyone else, she'd have thought it presumptuous, but from him, it was just confidence. She wondered what that said about her.

The rest of the trip didn't seem so awful now that Nora not only had Maxwell's phone number but a coffee date to look forward to. She'd told her inner negative voice to hush, and was beginning to wonder if maybe it was possible to have something good and have it last.

CHAPTER
Six

ORA HAD ALWAYS felt her nerves as both a rolling gut and odd tingles that spread from her chest to her extremities. It wasn't a true bout of butterflies if her fingertips and toes weren't alternating between numbish and boiling hot. Oddly, those same sensations were also what she experienced when she drank alcohol, got overly anxious, or had her heart broken.

Put all together like that, she realized it seemed as though she might benefit from seeking some serious medical attention.

She put it on her running mental to-do list.

Nora's mother had instilled in her from a very young age that if you were 5–10 minutes early, you were on time, and that if you were on time, you were late. If you were actually late, you were *really* late. Unforgivably late. *Tacky* would probably have been the word her mom would attach to such a public faux-pas.

This was one of the very small handful of valuable things her mother had bestowed upon her.

Because of that skewed perspective of how time worked, adjusting to life in Los Angeles with the extreme amount of traffic and severe lack of parking had been particularly stressful.

So far, she'd been late (but really, on time) to no fewer than half a dozen auditions and meetings, and just the thought made her anxiety shoot through the roof and her body break out in a cold sweat, the tingles and hot flashes rushing to her fingers and toes.

Thankfully, the coffee house Maxwell had given her an address for was situated very near the large office building where Hollywood Law was housed, and they had an attached parking structure; a rare find in Los Angeles. Nora would happily pay eight dollars an hour to not have to drive around the block hoping she'd find a spot at the curb or in the too-small attached lot.

After parking her little car, she triple-checked that her hair was contained in the sleek ponytail she'd tied it back in before leaving the house and that her make-up wasn't running down her face because of her sudden nervous sweat. The face she wore for the public had to be in place even if she could be mostly herself talking to Maxwell. You never knew when the paparazzi would pop up after all, and image was everything. Her agent Mel was sure to drill a reminder about that into her head every so often.

At 5 minutes until 10, she made her way from the cool concrete underground of the parking structure to the coffee shop. From quite a distance she spotted Maxwell, somehow devastatingly suave and looking like he was doing an ad for Ralph Lauren in his polo and slacks leaning up against the brick wall outside the coffee shop. The only thing not magazine-worthy was that he held a large manila envelope in the same hand that flashed what looked like a Rolex.

It should have come off as some high level of douche-bag couture, but he made it work.

That smooth grin spread over his mouth upon spotting her, and Nora began to sweat again. Her body had it bad for this guy, and her mind was finding it increasingly difficult to feel any kind of negative way about that.

"Right on time." Maxwell received her by immediately putting his free hand to her lower back to guide her inside the bustling shop, and Nora couldn't help the shiver that followed his touch. Other parts of her body were paying attention as well, and while not unwelcome, the sensations were quite distracting. "What can I get you?" he asked.

"Oh, you don't have to," Nora protested with a smile as they stood in line.

"Of course I don't." He grinned. He smelled like the ocean and leather interior, and Nora wanted to lean closer.

His smell was so much more tantalizing than the coffee grounds and baked goods of the coffee shop.

"I'd love a regular Cappuccino then. Thank you."

Maxwell nodded and sent her nerves jangling as they progressed toward the counter, his hand returning to her lower back every single time they moved a couple of steps forward.

"I'm glad you could meet with me," he said, claiming a table on the patio outside after they collected their drinks and an assortment of pastries Maxwell was gazing at quite adoringly.

To be fair, Nora could relate and probably had hearts in her own eyes when she glanced at the cherry danish and chocolate croissant.

Wardrobe was going to have a fit if she couldn't squeeze into those damned leather pants she was supposed to wear for the next episode.

"Me too." Nora could see herself reflected in the warm mocha depths of his eyes.

"First, business?" Maxwell's face did an interesting amount of transformation as he grew serious for a moment, handing her the very official-looking envelope. He explained that it contained a copy of her revised contracts, as well as what effectively was her receipt for costs involved with Hollywood Law taking her case.

Via email, Nora and Mel had both signed off on what amounted to her official statement about the situation with the defunct law firm and request that she not be penalized for the delay in negotiation as she was not at fault.

Nora had to cover up the fact that she had been staring at the length, strength, and shape of his well-manicured fingers as he handed over the envelope with a quick sip of her coffee.

"So. Stephanie mentioned—" Maxwell was cut off by the sudden exclamation of his name from the mouth of a woman Nora didn't recognize. The woman then literally swooped in and embraced him, which was quite awkward because she was in a romper—a super short one—and Maxwell was sitting down. Nora got an unwelcome eyeful of strange woman ass cheek.

"Darling! Here you are. I couldn't reach you! I was beginning to get worried," Strange Woman said, very pointedly ignoring Nora.

"Hello, Olivia. I didn't get any calls or messages from you. Intentionally, in fact." Maxwell looked odd without that trademark smile. He looked downright cold and Nora found that very interesting and a bit frightening.

She decided at that moment that she never wanted to be on the receiving end of that expression.

The woman laughed, and Nora's skin started to tingle and crawl as though the pitch of the sound were interrupting it on a cellular level. Nora could feel the fakery pouring off this woman, and yet…there was something between her and Maxwell. She would have put good money down that they knew what one another looked like naked.

The flare of anger that such a notion incited was unexpected, and she tamped it down before it could take root. She had no business being angry about such things.

"You do have such a hard time keeping up with your phone calls Max, always have."

The use of the nickname crept along Nora's throat like acid.

Without preamble, Olivia grabbed a spare chair from the next table over and plunked herself down with them.

"Olivia how truly unexpected. You're interrupting, actually. This is Nora. She's … a client."

Nora's body went cold. While that label was not untrue, it also felt quite distant. Whoever Olivia was, he didn't want her to know that he'd invited Nora out for both business and … what? He'd said the meeting was both business and personal, but she wasn't sure what exactly that meant. She'd hoped it was so they could get to know one another a bit better. Surely that had been his intention too?

A forced smile on her lips, Nora nodded to Olivia and tried to center her breathing. It was a gorgeous Southern California day and that shouldn't be tainted by wanting to claw the perfectly black liner-winged eyes out of some woman who was taking some pretty intense liberties at a coffee-shop patio table.

No matter how much she wanted to push the woman into the magenta knock-out roses, she wouldn't, Nora decided. At least not in any way that looked like it had been on purpose.

"We're actually in the middle of something, Olivia, if you don't mind?" Maxwell gestured with an arm that he wanted her to leave.

Olivia had the grace to look a bit affronted and then the tiniest bit embarrassed before the rage took over. Her plastic, overly made-up face transformed with anger. Beautiful became hideous in a flash.

"I see. Noreen, is it?"

Nora, a bit stunned but knowing a diva when she saw one, braced for a full-on meltdown. She forced her body to remain relaxed and stared right back at the icy blue eyes made up with an overwhelming and borderline unflattering smoky eye. She'd met plenty of women like Olivia before. They were routinely at auditions. She hated confrontation and was admittedly a bit of a pushover because of it, but she wouldn't cower to this woman. It's what she wanted, no doubt—for Nora to feel inadequate.

"Close. My name is Nora."

"Whatever. Anyway, anything he says? Don't believe it. You're never going to be the only one in his life and his job is always going to come first. That revolving door to his bedroom won't stop because he told you that you're special."

Oof. That claim hit right in the feels, but Nora knew better than to trust this woman, no matter how scorned she seemed. Alarm bells were ringing—Olivia was trying too hard. She had clearly come to make an impression, and it was working—just not the one Olivia probably intended.

"Noted."

Nora's lack of reaction and simple response seemed to only infuriate the drama queen further.

Maxwell cleared his throat and Olivia got up in full huff, her ridiculous waist-length, pin-straight black extensions flying out behind her as she spun to face him. The romper needed to be rescued from her nether-regions as well—it looked like things were bordering on painfully uncomfortable there.

"Fine. We'll talk later, *darling*. You know you can't live without me, just like I'm miserable without you," she said, and planted one hell of a smacker right on his stunned mouth. There was an obscene red lipstick smear on his face when she pulled away, and he knew it was there—he immediately reached for a napkin and began to wipe.

Nora didn't have any reaction for a moment, and it looked like Maxwell was struggling to breathe through a red mist of rage. She stared at him, realizing that he was a quite angry—his jaw was clenching repeatedly, making those muscles twitch and raising some concern for the health of his molars. His expressive eyes were less open, but gave a clear indication he was thoroughly pissed.

There was no doubt in Nora's mind that he was, though. His body language very clearly communicated that he was totally uncomfortable and royally ticked off.

Just when she thought it couldn't get any stranger, at least half a dozen bodies pressed forward, most of which taking pictures.

What. The. Hell.

Nora picked out a handful of actual telephoto lens point and shoot units among the gaggle of cell phones as Olivia flounced off toward her car, which was conveniently—and illegally—parked in the handicapped space just at the front of the coffee shop. There were some shouted questions directed at herself and Maxwell and plenty of photos taken as well.

Nora just knew she'd see herself on TMZ later.

After some short and to the point responses from Nora about how she knew Maxwell, and some expertly given, very lawyer-like non-answers from Maxwell, the paparazzi finally grew bored and moved away, leaving them in peace. There was one man who hung back as though hoping he'd get the scoop by waiting around, but before long he too gave up and moved on. Nora couldn't seem to shake the feeling that he was watching her a little too closely and that she'd seen him around before.

She brushed off the more than somewhat icky thought off as foolish. Of course, she recognized him. Most of them were regular photogs, many actual employees of tabloids. It was only natural that she'd find some of them familiar when they continually popped up.

The activity had died down quite a bit, but they were still the center of attention for the people on the patio and dozens of eyes were turned their way from behind the glass windows of the shop.

Of all parts of her job, Nora hated those moments the most. It nearly always felt like a violation. She hated feeling like they were out for a pound of flesh and she owed it to them somehow when she was doing something mundane like getting her hair cut or shopping for groceries. It was part of the territory though, and she tried to be grateful they were interested in her. Loss of interest might mean the loss of a job. No job meant no money, and right now, money was necessary.

"I'm so sorry," Maxwell said, a frown on his face, lines between his eyes from the pinch of his forehead. It seemed his rage had depleted, leaving only regret and apology.

Nora had learned it was silly to pout about the drawbacks of being famous.

"That's alright. I don't get nearly enough drama on set at work." Nora shrugged and picked up her mug, taking a hearty sip of the cappuccino, hoping he didn't notice the tremor in her fingers as the adrenaline surge wore off. She didn't want him to feel bad—none of that drama had been anyone but Olivia's fault.

Maxwell regarded her carefully for a moment and then laughed, the sound warm and booming and a balm to the nerves that stood up and paid attention the moment it started to roll out of him.

"Well. You're something else, Nora Chase. My apologies. She's … a lot."

"Seems that way. Is she—"

"*Not* my girlfriend," The words came out vehemently. "not for a long time. Not since she decided to cheat on me with a mutual friend in such a dramatic fashion that there was no way for me *not* to find out by walking in on them. Well, ex-friend, I suppose." He looked thoughtful for a moment and then his handsome features relaxed again. "I honestly have at least as many questions about what the hell just happened as you do."

Nora watched him carefully, and couldn't detect any bit of falseness.

A cool breeze whipped through the umbrella that was blocking out the bright morning sun. She sat there for a few moments, the sound of traffic on the street noisy behind them, the smell of the coffee being brewed wafting out every time someone opened the cafe door.

"I don't know about that—I have quite a few," she said finally, cracking a smile and reaching for the chocolate croissant.

Her grin seemed to make Maxwell's tension drain away and he nodded. "I'm sure. Can we start over?"

The glint in his eye and the interesting dance his forearm muscles did as he lifted his coffee cup soothed her even further.

"Sure."

The paparazzi having moved on to greener pastures, the pair attempted to restart the discussion as they finished their drinks and ate the amazing pastries. The high praise had been no exaggeration on his part; they truly were the best she'd had in the city. Unfortunately, their conversation just couldn't seem to get off the ground or past some light small talk and clever banter about their mutual friends. The death blow was when the conversation came back around to business with Maxwell saying that he was confident that the firm could help her both with her current and future legal needs. It was awkward and felt uncomfortable for everyone which was a sad way to end their coffee date.

"Thank you," Nora said, genuinely happy she'd come to meet him, regardless of the dive-bombing conversation at the end. Despite the strange interruption in the middle, it had been an enjoyable cup of coffee. "for the coffee. And the show, I guess."

She basked in the warm smile he gave her. He did seem truly appreciative of the way she'd handled the situation, and she was pretty impressed by how she'd reacted as well, honestly. It could have been a whole lot worse, but perhaps not much stranger as far as coffee dates go.

Reality was, she needed every penny, and having good attorneys fighting on her side was both necessary and more than welcome. A glance at her phone confirmed that her mother had left two more messages since they sat down.

"Shall we maybe try again some time?" Not usually so forward, her words were a surprise even to Nora herself.

That toothy, lackadaisical grin warmed her soul, and everything inside of her that had been telling her, no, she didn't, she couldn't, was overwhelmed by the explosion of happiness his friendly smile and words brought.

"Absolutely. I'd love to take you to dinner sometime."

They went their separate ways after Maxwell saw her safely back to the parking garage, even getting her ticket validated so she didn't have to pay.

Who said chivalry was dead?

AFTER RIDING THE friendly high from the end of the coffee date most of the morning, the afternoon crash hit her extra hard.

Not only was her face plastered all over TMZ, someone had filmed and submitted the entire interaction with Olivia to the tabloid shows and YouTube.

Nora and Maxwell were hot gossip, and none of the speculation was even close to true. Unfortunately, that didn't mean people wouldn't believe whatever spin was getting put on it.

Her gut twisted and rolled as she watched the whole thing unfold on the TV in her apartment.

Someone had leaked that Nora had been seen at Hollywood Law in the wake of the now widely known contract scandal as well, and the current gossip was saying that something dirty was up with her and Maxwell—that they were more than friends, more than client and attorney (which honestly, was true, though not like they were trying to imply) and she was flipping her hair and batting her eyes at him to get more than her share of the funds that had been taken from the clients. How that would even work was well beyond Nora's pay-grade to figure out and beyond ridiculous. It didn't seem to matter that her image and actions were as far from that as you could get. That was an Olivia type move, not a Nora type move. After five minutes of arguing about it, someone suggested as much and Nora took a breath. At least they were seeing some reason and her image wasn't going to be dragged through the muck over speculation.

Nora felt the beginnings of a headache between her eyes. Sometimes, this fishbowl was just ridiculous. Most of the time really, if she was being honest with herself.

There was a little dirt on Olivia, too. Nora learned that she was reportedly Maxwell's on-again, off-again lover, and it was up in the air whether or not they were currently on or off. By all appearances, they were *way* off, but the show managed to put that seed of doubt into Nora's mind.

She hated that she felt that way too, and tossed the remote with more force than necessary after the show ran the clip for the third time. Nora had seen firsthand what the media had done to Devon and Stephanie and didn't want to fall victim to the same fabricated out of whole-cloth, clever editing nonsense.

As she busied herself with caring for her plants, her phone buzzed.

> **D:** *I see the bottom-feeders found you out in the world today. Please don't worry your pretty head about it. It's all lies.*

Nora released a breath she didn't realize she was holding and felt her shoulders fall away from her ears a bit, forehead smoothing out. Well, only for a moment, because the Gravitz pickle factory was going strong down at the other end of the hall and every breath felt like it was burning off her nostril hairs on the way into her body.

Her fingers hovered for a moment as she considered a response.

> **N:** *Not bothered. It was a really weird few minutes, don't get me wrong, but we're all good.*

Devon sent back a kissy-wink emoji and Nora couldn't help the smile that came. He was as goofy as they came, and he was right.

Taking a deep breath—then regretting it because it hurt all the way down, thanks to Mrs. Gravitz's vinegar—Nora tapped out a new message, finger hovering over the send icon.

> **N:** *Were you serious about dinner?*

There was a very short pause before the response popped up.

> **M:** *Absolutely. Are you free Friday evening?*

Nora quickly popped out of the text and checked her calendar.

N: *Yes, but not until after 7 most likely.*
M: *That's perfect. Can I pick you up at 9?*

Nora grimaced, her inner old-lady homebody cringing at the suggestion of such a late dinner. She didn't want to put him off though.

N: *Would it be easier if I met you somewhere?*

The three dots danced for a moment.

M: *I hate to admit it, but maybe. I was considering pulling out the big guns to woo you. Do I need to woo you, Nora?*

Nora's cheeks flushed with heat. From a text. It was ridiculous. She could picture that panty-melting grin that no doubt lit up his face. Her reaction answered his question though—nope. No wooing needed, not even a little apparently, much to her frustration and a tiny bit of amusement. What was it about this man that made her react this way?

N: *I'd rather enjoy a comfortable meal with good conversation. Wooing is sometimes a side-effect of*

*that though. Big-guns wooing in this town leads
to blindness by flashbulb and death by gossip.*
M: *Too true. Can we meet at Cleo then? Around
8 instead?*

Nora pulled up the restaurant he mentioned on her phone and mapped it. It looked reasonable for travel time and honestly really delicious.

N: *That sounds great. I'll see you Friday?*
M: *I can't wait.*

Anticipation didn't quite cover the feeling Nora had about dinner. It took a glass of wine, an hour of plant-puttering, and a double dose of yoga to settle her down after that short text conversation.

And still, she dreamed of that easy smile and beachy blonde hair.

CHAPTER
Seven

T HE ANXIOUS TINGLES were in full effect as Nora navigated toward *Cleo*, a very hip and popular Mediterranean restaurant in West Hollywood. Being nervous was expected, but also inconvenient when your toes and fingers were giving you hot and cold flashes.

Traffic was actually cooperating pretty well for a Friday evening in Los Angeles, and she hoped to be a few minutes early again. A smile tugged at her lips as she remembered Devon's expression when she not only dashed off-set at the end of the day but very breezily mentioned why.

His face had gone very blank and then lit up like a theater marquee on opening night.

He'd barely been able to get out a quick—"Don't do anything I wouldn't do!" before she slammed her car door in his face, gesturing for him to hurry up and get into his car so they could leave. She'd count herself lucky if he didn't blow up her phone with texts the whole date.

Nora parked, pleased to find that there were a bunch of open spaces in the smallish lot and that it was too early for mandatory valet service. Her mapping service had neglected to mention that she was right in the middle of all things Hollywood tourist attraction, and what felt like just steps from the Capitol Records building. There was plenty of tourist foot traffic and were no doubt photogs lurking nearby.

Maxwell seemed aware enough of that kind of thing to steer clear, especially after their coffee date debacle. Nora felt a little confused but wanted to trust that he hadn't set them up to be ambushed. She would happily stay off TMZ for at least a week.

She sat for a moment, just taking deep breaths and willing her blood pressure to drop just a bit. She was excited. She was nervous. It was all a bit much but also very welcome in a really perplexing way.

She kept proclaiming both loudly and to herself that she didn't have time for a relationship, but the universe didn't seem to care one little bit about that. Or maybe it just didn't agree with what she was counting as limited time. Either way, annoying, but also a thrilling prospect.

After checking her hair and makeup in the visor mirror, she put on her confident face complete with a charming grin and made her way toward the entrance. Out of habit, her eyes immediately started scanning the asphalt and brick for any sign of lurking paparazzi. Thankfully, there didn't appear to be any, and she breathed a little easier. The sunshine all day had left the pavement oozing a nice warmth and it rose up to her feet as she moved. The evening was a bit cooler than she'd expected, and the breeze—despite the smoggy overtone—was welcome.

Once again, Maxwell was lounging sexily against the red brick exterior wall, a vision in khaki slacks, and a sky-blue button-up dress shirt.

He pulled away from the wall, leaning in to kiss her cheek lightly as she approached.

"The map was clear that the restaurant was on Vine, but I guess I wasn't picturing the location well in my head," she said, looking down at the pink terrazzo stars trimmed in brass decorating the sidewalk.

"Good surprise, I hope?" Maxwell's face looked a bit pinched with concern. It was endearing that he seemed nervous.

"I think so," she admitted. "I've actually never really done the touristy thing."

"We should definitely change that soon. I'm glad I could accidentally get you a head start."

His broad smile lit up his face and she couldn't stop herself from basically floating as he guided her through the double doors with a large, warm hand at the small of her back.

After they were seated in the blue and gold dining room at a bar-height table, Nora found herself blushing under the intense scrutiny of Maxwell's dark chocolate gaze. He had taken the liberty of ordering what seemed like one of everything off of their happy hour menu so they could sample small bites through the meal, complete with glasses of wine that paired with well their food.

Most any other time, she would have been a bit put off by her date ordering for her or assuming what she wanted, but he didn't do it in a way that felt controlling or domineering. It was as though he was proudly showcasing a bounty he'd procured just for her.

Nora sighed internally. This was so bad. He was changing her very brain chemistry and making her a silly, love-struck girl.

"I'm glad this worked out," Maxwell said, sipping at his glass of wine.

"Me too." Nora smiled, a chuckle teasing at the edges of her words. "Our mutual friends will start planning our wedding if we tell them too much, you realize."

Maxwell laughed loudly, the sound stroking her nerve endings in a very pleasant way.

"Stephanie less so, I think. Devon did seem rather giddy about the prospect of us coupling up though." His lips tilted in a friendly way and she nodded.

"Absolutely. I think I could say with relative certainty that they—well, he at least—would continue to arrange 'family dinners' and similar, thinly veiled double dates as often as possible if we didn't try it out ourselves."

Maxwell took one of her hands into his on the tabletop, the pad of his thumb rubbing over her knuckles gently as he carefully examined a ring on her middle finger. It had been her Yiayia Lou's. A simple but significant size amethyst in an emerald cut, it was her most treasured piece of jewelry. It took up nearly one whole knuckle of her finger.

"Well, I do love beating Stephanie at her own game. Not that I'm certain she's playing one that is, this may all be Devon's scheming." He met her eye. "He is a schemer too, though a playful one."

She couldn't help but nod at his assessment.

He continued, "I imagine it's no different with you and Devon, the competition part. I'd have been very pleased to take you out regardless, but that does add a little bit of positive incentive, does it not?"

Nora nodded, regretting that their hands had to part as the first round of food was delivered by a sweet, pretty waitress who seemed to have recognized her while asking if they needed anything else before the next batch of appetizers were served.

The waitress lingered just a fraction of a second too long and Nora smiled at her, trying to acknowledge that she appreciated that the girl was a fan while also not making a big deal of things. This also meant maintaining the delicate balance between real Nora, who was about to enjoy dinner with Maxwell, and on-screen Nora who was much more boisterous and bubblier and naturally eternally grateful for her fans, even if they did make regular social interactions the tiniest bit awkward.

Maxwell had picked up on the waitress' hesitation, that same grin on his lips as he looked over the selection of plates.

"Seems you have an admirer. Besides me, of course."

Nora nodded, selecting a few items for herself. "Yes. Hopefully, I don't throw her too far off her game. I've had servers get so nervous they were spilling things a couple of times."

Maxwell nodded, chewing thoughtfully. "Been there. Not over me, naturally, but I spend enough time with Steph that it's happened." He pointed at her ring. "That's quite lovely. Is it a real stone?"

Nora nodded. "Yes. My Yiayia's—my grandmother's."

"You don't see many amethysts set like that anymore. It suits you." The small, gentle grin went straight into Nora's heart. "Family heirlooms are often the best pieces."

There was simply no way she could agree more. Her Yiayia had been the best kind of person, and she treasured every memory. The ring helped her keep them close. She had been the one to teach Nora gardening as well. Her mother had black thumbs, but Yiayia Louise could grow anything. Orchids had been her favorite plant, and she'd had hundreds at the end of her life. Hopefully, the expert they'd hired to care for them after she had passed was doing a good job.

If Maxwell noticed her slip into other thoughts, he didn't give any indication.

"This is all fantastic," she said, enthusiastically tasting her way through the collection of dishes on the table. Nobody had carried on the tradition of Greek cooking after Yiayia had passed on either, and many of the dishes were variations of things she grew up eating with her. Nora's mother was a miserable cook all the way around, and neither Nora or Phae had acquired more than passing skills themselves.

Nora shared that little tidbit and Maxwell grinned again.

"Well, a happy accident, but that's immensely satisfying. I'm glad I could give you back some good memories. Food is fantastic for that."

By the time the third round of plates were brought, Nora wasn't sure she could eat any more, but she definitely gave it her best shot.

She and Maxwell had quite easily gone through the obligatory first date conversation topics throughout the meal. Strangely, Nora felt very comfortable with him, and while knowing some additional things about him helped round out his past, not much of it seemed relevant.

He was handsome, he was kind. His smile could melt panties at 50 yards. He was obviously good people and quite successful. The ease with which she decided she could get close to him made her a bit nervous, but at the same time was very soothing. It was a sensation not unlike thinking 'there you are' when you find something you've been missing. Or some*one* you didn't realize you were missing to begin with.

The dining room had filled up as the hours passed, and it was quite a bit louder than when they first started. The sun had set outside the large windows, and foot traffic had increased on the sidewalk.

"I can't eat another bite," Nora proclaimed as she folded her napkin on her plate. "thank you, this was lovely."

Maxwell signaled the waitress—who to her immense credit, had not had another stumble since she first recognized Nora—and relayed his credit card when she returned with the leather envelope for the bill.

"I'm glad you enjoyed it. I haven't had such a relaxing meal out in ages."

Nora glowed with that compliment.

Maxwell signed off on the bill and Nora reached out for the pen. The duplicate receipt was still tucked inside the folder, so Nora used the blank back to write a quick note.

Thanks for the lovely service. Dinner was fantastic! —Nora

Maxwell seemed momentarily embarrassed that she was looking at the bill—and what he'd left as far as gratuity most likely, though there was no cause for concern there at all—but when he realized what she was doing he relaxed and that perpetual grin slid back onto his generous mouth.

His hand warm on her back once again, he guided her out of the restaurant as though they'd done this a thousand times before. Their stride matched and everything felt easy.

It was a heady feeling, and Nora leaned into it instead of questioning it like she probably should have.

They could see the waitress' face light up through the window as she spotted the note, just as they exited the restaurant. She looked up and met Nora's eye through the expanse of glass. The broad smile was truly lovely, and something Nora never tired of seeing on a fan. She raised a hand in a quick wave and the waitress nodded, holding the leather folio close to her chest.

Moments like that were worth every second of dealing with people like Ollie Parkinson and the more aggressive paparazzi.

As if conjured by her thinking the word, photographers materialized in front of them.

There were only a couple of guys, but the violent flashes of light in her face and aggressively shouted questions effectively destroyed the happy little bubble that Nora had been in with Maxwell. Feeling her stiffen, Maxwell wrapped his arm around her shoulders and hustled them both to the parking area where valets were now manning a podium.

"That's unusual. I wonder if someone called them," Maxwell grumbled softly; Nora's cheek pressed against his chest. He got her to her car before loosening his grip. Thanks to the on-site security, the photogs couldn't follow them past the valet stand into the parking lot proper.

"Hazard of the job." She forced a smile.

Maxwell's hand rose and cupped her jaw. "I know, but I thought hiding in plain sight might work." That easy smile was a bit strained. "Sorry to have ended a nice dinner on that note."

"It's alright." Nora had to forcefully resist the urge to turn her face into his hand. Hormones bounced wildly around her body, willing her to get as much physical contact as possible with him. "I truly did enjoy tonight." The smile that came to her lips was much more natural.

His was too. "Me too."

Without warning or permission, he dipped down and placed a soft kiss on her mouth, waiting for her reaction before deepening it just a bit and then slowly moving away. She could feel the regret in his movements as he straightened up. There was also an overtone of restraint. He wanted to continue, she felt it—he was just being a good guy.

Nora's thoughts were completely scattered by the simple press of his lush mouth to hers, and she knew she probably looked shocked as he gazed at her afterward, a playful, satisfied smirk on his mouth. It should have come off as arrogant, but it translated instead as pleased.

"Goodnight Nora. Next time, I'll pick you up so we don't have to say goodnight in a parking lot with photographers trying to get a shot of us kissing."

"Sounds like a wonderful plan," Nora heard herself say, realizing that was basically admitting that there would be another date. And that it might go further than kissing at the car or the door.

Who was she kidding, there would be as many as possible if her body had any say in the matter. Maxwell seemed to just fit, no matter how much she protested about not having time or space for dating. Her body missed affection and sex, and he felt like someone she could trust.

He made her promise to text when she got home safely, and that concern for her safety just that made him just that much more attractive.

She got flutters noticing that he waited to fold himself into his little red sports car until she was fully out of her parking space. They lifted their hands in a mutual wave, and she pasted on a smile for the photogs who were lingering at the exit.

Once again, she had the feeling that she recognized at least one of the men half-hidden behind giant cameras with enormous lenses and obnoxious flashbulbs.

Thankfully traffic moved well even though it was heavy, and she was able to pull out onto Vine and get down the road before she was totally blinded by the bright flashes and resulting black spots in her vision.

As she made her way home through the twinkle of the city lights to her small and kind of sad apartment, her mind replayed every time Maxwell had brushed her with his fingertips, how he had protectively pulled her into his arms and away from the paparazzi, how he smelled like leather and spice and how the sound of his laugh made her want to take her clothes off.

Dealing with the mass of tangled up emotions that revelation brought was going to be a whole thing, she could feel it.

As she dragged herself up the worn concrete stairs to her apartment, something occurred to her. The errant thought made her frown as she dug around in her bag for her door key. She took a moment to notice that the hallway was thankfully relatively vinegar-free for a change as her eyebrows pulled together and her mouth turned down.

Nora hoped that Jessica the waitress wasn't the reason the paparazzi had showed up. She didn't want to think badly of the sweet little brunette, especially after having seen the amount of tip Maxwell had left her.

Once safely locked inside her quiet, out of the way apartment, she went about her plant care and yoga routine, already thinking about the next time she could see him.

She felt a bit ridiculous, and like she was too old to be acting this young, but her give-a-damn about it was little to non-existent.

Her fingers tapped out the requested text, and he responded almost immediately, confirming that he too was home and reiterating that he'd had a great time. She responded in kind, then wished him a good night, not wanting to do that silly 'you hang up first' thing over text, no matter that she felt exactly like that kind of goofy teenager with raging hormones at the moment.

She pointedly ignored the three messages Devon had left, all teasing and asking how it was going. One threatened Maxwell's manhood if he wasn't behaving himself. There was also one from Stephanie apologizing for her husband and letting Nora know that she'd taken away his phone.

A laugh rose out of Nora's throat. She took a moment to revel in the warm feels she was having. Devon was a goofball, but he was *her* goofball, and the closest thing to a brother she would ever get. Stephanie was a fantastic friend. Maxwell was … a promising new adventure.

Just as she was getting ready to get into bed, her phone chimed again. She told herself not to check, but she couldn't resist. Butterflies swarmed as she unlocked her screen, because what if it was Maxwell again? What if he was sending something racy? A girl could hope.

All happy thoughts crashed to the floor as she read over the text.

Blood fled from her face and pooled in her gut, her wonderful dinner curdling and rolling in the surge of acid the words released. Cold crept in, vaporizing the warmth she'd been enjoying.

> **Private:** *You looked gorgeous tonight. You shouldn't have been out with him, though. What would he think of you if he knew the truth? What about your career? My price just went up. You're running out of time.*

CHAPTER

COMPARING CALLING TO her mother to ripping off a band-aid was a huge exaggeration about how painful taking off those magical plastic strips of healing was. At least if you were taking it off, it had fixed something underneath.

Nora felt like hitting that call button was something more akin to pulling out her fingernails with pliers.

Their relationship hadn't always been contentious. It was about the time Nora realized her thoughts and feelings were valid and normal and she deserved to express that, things really fell apart between them.

But once it had started down that path, it became a lot like a boulder rolling downhill. There was no slowing it, no stopping it, and anything or anyone that got in the way was bulldozed right over.

There was nearly always a complete mess left all along its path and it was almost guaranteed that there would be a disastrous crash anywhere it finally came to rest for a while. Her mother seemed to delight in giving that boulder a good push to get it rolling again every once in a while too, no matter how destructive the last explosion had been when it finally hit the bottom of the hill. Drama was what her soul fed on.

Nora had long since given up her own Sisyphus tendencies. The rock stayed at the bottom of the mountain; it was simply not worth her time or energy to try and fix anything between them or roll that enormous ball of stress back up the hill. She'd been rolled over herself one too many times, and Phae had tried too.

Standing in front of her collection of plants for some centering and strength, looking out her window at the small but tidy little grass courtyard of her apartment complex, Nora forced herself to press the call button. Her eyes roamed over the majestic coconut palms that would forever say 'Hollywood' to her and into the bright blue sky above. It was another gorgeous day, and Nora had decided she was not allowed to leave her apartment until she took care of this task.

After weeks of messages that revealed nothing but her mother's increasing impatience, Nora thought perhaps just calling would resolve everything so they could both move on, going back to their sporadic check-in messages instead.

The phone rang in her ear as she looked over the massive bougainvillea climbing the pillars between unit doors, all the way from the ground floor up to the third level balcony. The magenta blooms were bright and beautiful, all of them turned as much toward the sun as they could be. As always, looking at a happy, thriving plant improved Nora's mood.

She loved that particular plant but was not a fan of the thorns. There was a metaphor in there somewhere about beauty and pain, or something along those lines Nora knew, but she was so distracted she couldn't quite pin it down. Besides, there was always the sister plant, Mandevilla, with all the same beauty and no risk of blood or injury. Maybe it was a metaphor about choosing easier paths? She shook her head, unable to make her brain have those kinds of deep thoughts at the moment. Perhaps they were just pretty flowers.

"*Weeks* of trying to get in touch with you and you finally call back at precisely the wrong time." Her mother didn't even bother with a greeting, just launched directly into a long-suffering sigh and accusation.

"Hi, Mom," Nora said, putting on her bubbliest tone of voice, knowing full well it was just going to piss her mother off.

"*Hello*, Eleanora. Hold on."

Nora waited, beginning to pace a little and poking at her plants while there was a scuffling noise on the other end of the line, like plastic being crinkled.

"If it's a bad time, you can just call me back, Mom."

There was a snort. Her mother sounded a bit muted and far away like she'd set the phone down on the counter. "So you can avoid me some more? Please, darling. I'm smarter than that." The sarcastic endearment scraped at Nora's nerves as it was no doubt meant to.

A few more moments of background noise, some muffled words like her mom had covered the mouthpiece with her hand and was giving instructions to someone.

Nora could picture her mom in the small wood-paneled home where she'd grown up. A cottage right out of the late 1960s, it had needed improvements it would likely never get since the day it was built. Nora would have put money down that her mother's brown hair was likely up in curlers and perhaps even soaked with a fresh round of five-dollar box dye to perpetuate the active denial of any gray strands creeping in. There would be a long, slender cigarette burning away in the glass ashtray on the coffee table and while tidy, the place would reek of old smoke and aged carpeting.

"There. I was right in the middle of applying Golden Chestnut Glow to my hair."

Nora stifled a laugh. That would only enrage her mother and have them beginning their conversation with screaming. They had plenty of time to work up to that; no need to rush into it.

"How are you, Mom?"

"Don't even try it, little miss. You know exactly how I am and how I'm going to continue to be if you don't talk some sense into your sister."

Nora took a deep breath. So they were going to dive right in after all.

"She won't even talk to me, Mom. I'm not sure why you think I have any kind of power over this situation. Besides, I don't think what she's doing is wrong."

"Try harder! You're the only one she listens to. It's just not right! She can't stay in that house. Surely there are other options. She's just doing it because I don't want her to. I don't understand why she'd want to hurt me like this. I'm not sure what I ever did to raise two completely rebellious, ungrateful daughters. It breaks my heart." An exaggerated sniffle came over the line and Nora's eyes rolled back into her head.

There it was; her mother's favorite emotion and provocation all in one tidy package. Guilt. Best applied in a thick layer over one's offspring at regular intervals.

Nora took another deep breath and watched a green and blue hummingbird flit around between the bougainvillea blossoms, sipping, and moving on to the next.

"You know that's unfair, Mom. We aren't ungrateful or rebellious. We simply moved on with our lives in a way that you didn't agree with. That doesn't make it the wrong thing. It's her senior year of college. She was miserable last year in the apartment with all those catty girls—this is a good choice for her. Phae is happy where she's at."

Nora was fairly certain that wasn't untrue, but the lack of direct communication with her sister lately had her second-guessing how sure she was.

Sadness forgotten, her mom huffed on the other end. She was like a toddler. "You just have an answer for it all, don't you? You're living the high life out there in Hollywood while we waste away in this dying little town and your baby sister is living like a common whore up in Auburn. She's just following her big sister's example, you know."

Jaw and fist clenching at the same time, Nora raised her eyes to the ceiling, seeing if the will to keep from screaming was somehow written up there in the tacky swirled plaster texture.

It wasn't.

"How much do you want, Mom?"

Her mother at least had the grace to sound affronted by the words, but there was no denial.

"That's not the reason I was calling, Eleanora. We were talking about your sister."

Sure it wasn't. Nora felt herself vibrating with frustration. Her mother was the only person on the planet who could push her buttons in exactly the right combination to make her feel this way.

"Mom, you'd know if you ever decided to use the open invitation to come visit me," Nora gritted her teeth over those words—the last thing she wanted in the world was for her mom and Charlie to visit her in California, but she had to at least pretend to offer. "But I live in a tiny, dated apartment that always smells like vinegar because of the old lady down the hall is constantly making large batches of pickles. I drive the same car I had in college—and it was old *then*. If anything major goes wrong with it, I might be taking the bus back and forth to work—"

"Oh please. Exaggeration doesn't suit you dear, actress or not. We both know your beloved *friend* Devon wouldn't let that happen. He's making quite a bit more than you I take it? And he married that lovely heiress or something like that? That must have been quite a blow dear—I know you've been in love with him since college."

The digs were well placed and burned as they dug into her flesh.

Nora knew her mother was only trying to get a rise out of her, but she couldn't resist responding.

"You know Devon and I have never been that way, Mom. Literally *never*. Stephanie, his amazing wife, is actually a good friend of mine." She forced a deep breath, tempering her tone. "The car is just one example. Any nice clothes I have were probably sponsored by the studio or loaned to me from the designer. My groceries are the opposite of extravagant and I take advantage of craft services at work as much as possible to keep that spending down. I'm not living a lavish lifestyle out here, just so we're clear on that. Yes, Devon does make more than me and substantially so. My part is not as central to the *Destiny Falls* plot as his is—as I'm sure you're watching, I'm sure you already know that." Mentally she cheered her own successful jab. "And I'm not even going to validate what you said about Phaedra, because that's nothing but rude and totally wrong." She didn't address the jab that accused her of being a bad example. That part was maybe partly true.

There was a short, sarcastic chuckle in her ear. This was an argument they'd rehashed so many times it should have disintegrated into dust. Her mother simply couldn't believe that an actress on a popular show wasn't living in a penthouse and being driven around in a limo all the time and eating nothing but caviar and drinking champagne. She had it in her mind that Nora was holding out on her, and nothing, not even photos would change her mind. Nora had even considered bank statements, but screw that.

"You forget how entertainment TV works, my dear. I see you on that TMZ show all the time out and about. You can't tell me that those fancy restaurants don't cost a fortune to eat at." Her mother paused, waiting for Nora to say something, but Nora couldn't—she was far too busy biting a hole right through her tongue. "That man you went to dinner with the other day seems like a real catch. Handsome too. Is he an actor also?"

Nora continued on as though her mother had never mentioned Maxwell. She'd be damned if she'd give away his name. Athena was baiting her anyway—if TMZ had shown pictures they almost certainly had said Maxwell's name and profession. He wasn't a true unknown because of his connection to Stephanie and his own notoriety because of the law firm.

Engaging with her mother's bait was *never* a good idea. Their conversational style could be called pothole—they avoided and dodged a ridiculous amount of things to keep from falling in and getting damaged.

"I'm also in the middle of some legal issues because the lawyers who used to work for my agent's firm did a shitty thing and screwed a ton of actors over as far as their contracts were concerned. I'm not living high on the hog, Mom, no matter what you think. But I know that's at least part of the reason you called. Let's just go ahead and get that out of the way."

Athena wouldn't be deterred from her insistent match-making course without one final hit.

"What about that lovely man you dated before? David."

Nora's blood ran cold. "What *about* him?"

There was a tsk before she continued. "Why not see if he's still interested, dear? Wasn't he a successful director or something? I thought the two of you were an excellent match. He still messages me now and then to check-in, you know. Like he never quite gave up on the two of you. You should give him a call."

Nora felt the stunned words she wanted to say but couldn't get out backing up in her throat; a fresh coating of bile making them burn.

"Do you talk to him, Mom?"

Athena sighed. "Not really. He's just being sweet and making sure we're doing okay. Which is more than I could say for my own daughters."

The dig landed square in Nora's chest. She could barely breathe.

"*Mom*. Please stop talking to him. He and I are *never* going to happen. You know why." There were SO MANY reasons.

Her mother gave a pitiful sigh. "Fine." There was a stagnant pause. Finally, Athena said, "I need at least five grand to get us by until Charlie's disability comes through in a few weeks."

Nora's eyebrows went straight up into her hair and she turned away from the window, walking quickly to her worn love-seat and plopping herself down. Suddenly her ex was the least of her worries.

"I just sent you *ten thousand dollars* a couple of months ago, Mom." Silence. "Help me understand. You own the house out-right, you have for years—there's no mortgage unless you've refinanced and didn't tell me. You have barely five hundred dollars a month in utilities. I know about what your car payments and insurance run. Why do you need that much money?" Nora fought hard to keep her tone neutral, but her mother was not known for her subtlety or her maturity. She *was*, however, known for her needling and insults.

"If you don't want to send it, just say so," she snapped.

"I didn't say that Mom. I'd just like to know where it's going."

She had a pretty good idea where her money was ending up. There were several casinos nearby at the resorts in Mobile, and she knew better than to think that Charlie, Phae's father—Nora's step-father—was completely reformed from his gambling addiction. Especially now that he had gotten injured and couldn't go back to work.

Hell would freeze over before he or her mother would admit to it though.

"We'll figure something out. We always do." Her mother pouted. "If your sister had stayed here to help me at the department store instead of going off to college, it wouldn't even be an issue."

Nora gripped the phone tightly. "That's not even partly true either Mom, and you know it. Her living at home and working retail doesn't change *your* situation. It's *good* for Phae to get out of there. College is a *good* thing." She decided to try a different tactic, knowing full well there wouldn't be any difference in her mother's response but needing confirmation that she was right to feel the way she did about her mother's neediness and apathy. Nora and Phaedra shouldn't be the parents in this situation, but more often than not, they were. "Aren't you proud of us? We're accomplishing big things, doing more with our lives than you were able to." The acid was clear in her stinging words. Nora was tired of this old song and dance. Just because Athena Chatzi-Stewart was stuck in the same old place doing the same old thing with no ambition for anything different didn't mean her daughters should be stuck too.

"Look at you, Miss High and Mighty. I'm not sure why I even bothered to reach out. You clearly don't care about us and it only hurts my feelings when we talk."

Yes, *clearly*. Dropping ten grand here and five there into what amounted to a giant hole was definitely a sign of not caring. Nora said nothing, just letting her mother's words hang until she could find something to say that wasn't completely inflammatory.

Growing up, Nora hadn't had a label for people like her mother. She did now, thanks mostly to character research and Phae's Psych 101 class.

Nora's mother was a textbook narcissist.

Nothing was ever her fault. Ever. Control was her drug of choice. She had once been the homecoming queen, the girl the whole town smiled at. The beautiful girl that boys chased and girls wanted to be friends with. She had always been a little bit of a conceited bully, mostly because she could. Nobody expected any more from her and nobody expected any less. Nobody corrected her terrible attitude, though surely Yiayia Lou tried. Now, she was losing her good looks to age and had never done a thing with her life other than skate by on her appearance and was suffering for it. She'd never even moved past her high school job at the local department store. The only difference was that now her name-tag said 'Manager', but she was still working the sales floor and trying to bat her eyelashes to make the sale for her pitiful commission.

Nora sighed, suddenly swamped by pity and guilt she knew she shouldn't have. She felt tired. Deep tired, down into her bones. "I'll see what I can do about sending some money, Mom, but I can't guarantee it will be five thousand dollars. I don't just have that lying around."

No response, just a sniffle.

"I'll talk to you soon, okay? I'll keep trying to get in touch with Phaedra."

She didn't say goodbye even, just hung up the phone. It was a land-line too, so Nora got that satisfying 'click' when her mother hung up on her.

As expected, she felt terrible following the call, but at least it was over. She promised herself she would take a few days to think about writing a check instead of just sending what her mother had asked for out of the guilt that had settled heavily over her like a blanket and what was surely a really distorted sense of duty since she was the oldest child and doing well for herself.

Unable to sit around the house any longer, she gathered her things and headed for her favorite local garden center.

Wandering the aisles, picking up plants that had seen some hard times and just needed some TLC to revive them was fantastic therapy. She ended up choosing three new babies and a handful of clearance pots so she could transfer a few of the ones she already had into new homes. A bag of soil, some cute plant charm decorations, and an hour later, she headed back to her apartment, significantly lighter.

NORA SPENT AT least another hour playing in the dirt and nurturing her new babies, terrible mood leveling off from her talk with her mom. The comforting meal of a cheeseburger, fries, and chocolate shake she'd gotten from In-n-Out didn't hurt either.

Once she'd cleaned up her mess and washed up, she found herself hovering by the windows again, hands on her phone. Deciding that there was no harm in trying, she dialed her sister.

To her disappointment but not surprise, it rang through to voice-mail, so she decided to change things up and leave a message instead of just hanging up and texting.

"Hey. I miss you. I just want to hear your voice, Phae, more than what's on your greeting for the voice-mail box, okay? I talked to Mom today. Spoiler alert—she wants more money. Can you just call me? I need to know you're okay. I know you say that you are in your texts but I'd like to hear it. I love you. I miss you."

Phaedra had arrived a year after her mother married Charlie, which had been just shy of two years after Nora's father had divorced her, surprise, for dating Charlie. Her dad lived in Georgia with his new wife who didn't have much use for children, even grown-up ones. Nora hadn't seen him since she graduated college but did get a card in the mail every birthday and Christmas. Phone calls were sparse and awkward.

That was the one relationship Nora wished she could get a do-over on.

At first, Nora hadn't liked the idea of a little sister, but she had quickly changed her tune. She'd been five when Phae came along, so she had been able to help with a lot of things (much to her mother's relief no doubt) and she grew to feel quite responsible for her little sister. It had been very hard when Nora went off to college because Phae was just about to start high school. There were many nights spent on the phone, talking through all the teenaged angst and high-school hormonal things that had come up, not to mention advice on how to navigate their mother when she got into a snit. Charlie was a decent guy but thought their mom hung the moon. He wasn't good about getting between her and Phae, even when he didn't agree with what she was saying or doing.

Nora had also openly shared what she was going through in college, trying to plant the seed for her sister that there was a way out, it would get better and that there was a grand adventure waiting for her on the other side of graduation if she could just hang on.

Yiayia Louise had impressed her love of gardening on more than just Nora, and Phaedra had earned a Horticultural Sciences scholarship to Auburn University. Nora was immensely proud of her sister—that was an incredible accomplishment. She had no doubt that Yiayia

Lou would have been over the moon if she were still alive to have seen that happen. Phaedra had told her that her ultimate dream was to open a nursery that specialized in exotic items like Yiayia Lou's orchids.

Nora agreed and was never too many thoughts away from trying to figure out a way for that to happen. Naturally, their mother thought it was a total waste of time.

The big blowout had come when Phaedra's living situation changed this year. With no more dorm requirement, a year worth of terrible roommates behind her, and extremely limited money, Phaedra had agreed to move into a house close to campus with four men and only one other woman for her senior year.

Shit. Hit. The. Fan.

Athena had called Phaedra every name in the book and insisted she come home immediately. Phaedra refused. Nora got pulled into the middle because, for some reason, she was supposed to be the voice of reason. Things got downright brutal when she sided with her sister and claimed she didn't see a problem—the rent was affordable and living there allowed her to work fewer hours while balancing a heavy course-load.

Phaedra was an adult, the choice was hers and if she liked the house and the roommates, as far as Nora was concerned, there was zero issue.

Nora's mother pulled out the bad example card, as though nobody in the history of the world before her had ever made a mistake in a relationship. Even knowing why she and David had split, her mother was still speaking to him and had the vague hope of them coming back together. No. Way. Granted, Nora's mistake had been pretty epic, but it felt like a bigger one that she'd told her mother about it.

Her mom and sister still weren't speaking to one another and Nora was happily sending her sister a monthly check to cover rent and some groceries and maybe a little extra that their mother had no idea about to make sure she could finish her schooling without totally burning out.

Nora tossed her phone onto the cushion next to her. Her body couldn't decide if it wanted to be tense or relax. The call with her mom had wound her up tight and digging in the dirt settled her. She could feel her shoulders back up by her ears stressing about getting in touch with her sister. Forcing herself to breathe and stretch helped a little bit.

Just as Nora was settling in with a giant bowl of popcorn and the remote, her phone buzzed. Her breath left her in a rush when she saw her sister's name on the screen, and more than just a couple of words indicating she was alive.

> **P:** *Sorry you had to talk to her. Why in the world does she need more money?*
> **N:** *Supposedly to get them by until your dad's disability catches up. When I asked her to elaborate she did what she always does.*
> **P:** *Don't fall for it. I am pretty positive Dad's gambling again.*

Nora sighed. At least she wasn't totally off base.

N: *I'd love to hear your voice, P. Can I call you instead of texting?*

There was a delay while the three dots bounced up and down.

P: *Can't today. But soon, I promise.*
N: *I'll hold you to that. Are you really okay? Do you need anything?*
P: *I need you to tell me who you were out to dinner with the other night. He's gorgeous!* 😍
N: *Sorry, can't explain that by text. Voice only.* 😌
P: *You're the worst.*
N: *You love me.*
P: *I do. I miss you, too. I'll call you soon, I promise.*
N: *Love you, Phae.*
P: *Love you too big sister.*

Nora felt her shoulders relax and released a breath she didn't realize she'd been holding. Her sister was not answering any of the questions she didn't want to answer, but she seemed okay. If she could only get a short text conversation out of her, she'd take it.

It was not lost on Nora that she'd give anything to talk to her sister in person, for a decent amount of time and would prefer to never really do that with her mother.

Deciding she'd had entirely enough peopling for the day, she flipped on a new movie on Netflix, dug into her popcorn, and zoned out for the rest of the evening.

CHAPTER
Nine

"SO, YEAH. YOU and Maxwell." Devon's eyebrow lifted as he showed her the screen of his phone. He playfully hummed the 'sitting in a tree k-i-s-s-i-n-g' melody.

They had just been allowed to vacate their chairs in the make-up trailer and were on their way across the back-lot to wardrobe.

The picture was of them leaving *Cleo* after their date, both of them smiling. Maxwell had his hand on her lower back and she appeared to be leaning into his touch. They looked comfortable and familiar. Happy even.

They definitely didn't look like they were on a first date, either, which was strangely satisfying and also just a little bit strange.

Remembering how his warm hand felt on her body made her lips curve upward. It was just seconds later they had encountered the paparazzi near the parking lot. That particular shot appeared to have been taken from across the street.

"Dinner," she said simply.

Devon grunted in frustration and followed her into wardrobe.

"*Obviously*. How'd it go?"

Nora shook her head. Devon was enjoying this entirely too much.

"Why are you so anxious to get the two of us together? I don't understand why it matters so much to you."

Devon clucked his tongue at her, eyebrows drawn together as he *tsk*ed. He gathered the clothing meant for him and she did the same. They efficiently changed in small curtained cubicles next to one another.

"You've dated, but you haven't had a real, *serious* boyfriend since that weirdo in college. What was his name? John? Jack? James?"

Nora knew he was being ridiculous on purpose. He was also wrong. It was one of the few secrets she'd ever kept from him.

"Jacob. You know that."

"Ah yes, Jacob the art history major." Devon pulled a face and gave an exaggerated half-gag.

"He was nice."

Devon's arm flew out, pointing directly at her as she adjusted her blouse and wiggled around in the leather pants she had been assigned. She could swear that the wardrobe ladies were only making her wear them because they hated seeing her enjoy food. Though they really did make her ass look good. She shrugged at herself in the mirror as she looked over one shoulder at her backside.

"*Exactly*. Nice." He looked like he'd sucked on a lemon. "We've already had this conversation."

With that, he turned on his heel and strode quickly out of wardrobe, Nora hustling to follow him to set.

"At least he wasn't a huge jerk. Or have constant onion breath. Or another girlfriend." Those things may have been just a few of the things she'd encountered on dates since graduating and moving to Los Angeles.

None of those were the big bad ugly either. Devon knew about the man she'd seen for an extremely short amount of time named David, but he didn't know what he'd done. What he was still doing. Devon had him classified in the three dates or less category which to him didn't count. In reality, they'd dated seriously for a few months.

Keeping a secret like that from Devon had been no small feat, and she was beginning to feel like the clock was ticking for how long she could keep it up.

"True, but still not worthy of you, my dear." That smirk appeared and Devon slung his arm over her shoulders. "Tell Uncle Dev all about it."

Nora sighed, knowing she was going to be trapped with him for a while as they finished shooting a different scene. There was no getting around her best friend or his nosiness.

"We met for dinner. It was amazing Greek food and reminded me of Yiayia Lou. Paps were waiting when we left. That was less than awesome, but he used his body to block them for me." She inclined her head, knowing this tidbit would please him.

Devon's eyebrows rose up, and he smiled. "Good man."

Nora's head nodded shortly. "Yes. He's very *nice*," she teased.

He growled. "Don't make me text my wife. I will."

A laugh rose out of her chest. "You text her all day long, anyway. And I think you just love calling her that. Simply saying the word *wife* brings you joy. It's weird. You know that it's a little weird, right? Based on your 'three dates and done' history?"

Devon beamed. He didn't apologize or deflect or anything. Just smiled. In return, so did Nora. She loved seeing him so happy.

"Besides, if I needed her advice, I'd go directly to *her*." He scowled at her, which made her smile. She tossed him a bone. "It was a lovely dinner. Ten out of ten, would do it again."

In truth, everything had been wonderful except the threatening text at the end of the night, which Nora purposely avoided mentioning to anyone. There had been about a dozen random messages since then as well, but nothing that felt threatening or off-color. Mostly they were some version of telling her she looked great and that she and Maxwell (though they didn't reference him by name) were a beautiful couple. She avoided logging into her social media accounts if she could avoid it, but since the photos were being passed around, she had a fair number of tweets with the same commentary, plus a few asking how the restaurant had been.

She had responded enthusiastically to the ones asking about the food.

"When are you going out again then?"

Her head shook as she chuckled. "You're impossible. I don't know. We didn't talk over the weekend." Before Devon could get started on a rant, she filled him in on who she *had* spoken to. His face crumpled up, ire pouring off of him as he spoke.

"I hope you know better than to fall for any of your mother's drama. I'm more than happy to provide ample reminders of Athena's terrible demonstrations of 'love' if you find yourself feeling bad for her. Charlie must be gambling again."

Nora felt her chest warm. Devon really was just the best possible friend.

"That's my thought too. And Phae confirmed."

Devon jerked his head her way at that. "You talked to Phae?"

She shook her head. "Not really. She did text me some complete sentences though, instead of just a few words."

His brow furrowed. "That's progress I guess, but still not great. Do you think she's okay? Like really okay?"

"I think so. I'm not totally sure. I'm hoping I can go visit relatively soon. Summer isn't that far away and we'll have a break from shooting then."

Devon nodded. "I haven't been home in a while. Maybe I'll go with you."

"Your home isn't anywhere near mine. Or Auburn, for that matter." She smiled at him.

His return smile was gentle, but his eyes serious. The combination sent his words straight to her heart. "That's not true. My home is always your home. You know that, right? If you need something, you ask, no hesitation. Especially if I haven't managed to offer first." That icy gaze penetrated right into her soul.

At that moment the surge of gratitude for this man, this friend, nearly made her knees buckle and tears welled in her eyes. Maxine in makeup would not be happy if she needed a total reapplication, so she blinked rapidly to chase the waterworks away.

He was great at identifying when she needed something and conveniently offering it before she could over-analyze how to ask for help.

"You're not just a *you* anymore Dev. What about your wife?"

He shrugged. "She's never been to Alabama. I imagine she'd jump at the chance to see where I grew up. Lord knows Mom, Dad, and those three jerks that call themselves my brothers wouldn't mind. You know I always enjoy checking in on the foundation in person." That smirk was back. Nora knew she was in trouble now—that look meant that he'd decided they were all going, and so she'd better just be prepared for him to email her itinerary and ticket soon.

The director called them then, so their conversation was brought to a halt. It never really got back off the ground, for which Nora was grateful. Dropping into character and playing an immortal witch surrounded by shifters and vampires for a while was a much needed and very welcome distraction from the spaghetti bowl of tangled thoughts her brain was.

She emoted her lines of dialogue and pretended the decadent southern estate home was both her family home and real. Devon smirked and flashed his fangs while she mixed up spells and potions and threw out curses she knew would get some CGI help in post-production.

It was fun, and exhausting in the best way.

They said their goodbyes in the parking lot well after dark that night, which meant that traffic wasn't nearly as bad as usual but Nora was twice as tired. She picked up some take-out on her way and allowed her couch to cradle her day away as she consumed what was probably far too much Thai seafood curry and jasmine rice.

Her phone had died halfway through the shoot, and when she finally got it plugged in and turned back on she saw there was a text from Maxwell.

M: *Had a great time the other night. You busy Saturday?*

The smile that it brought to her face was immediate, the rush of adrenaline making her sweat. Never had she ever had such an intense and instantaneous attraction and reaction to a man. It was thrilling and also a bit worrisome.

What if they crashed and burned? Where would that leave their friendships with Devon and Stephanie? It would be awkward forever and they'd always have to navigate avoiding one another or forcing cordial conversations if they pursued a relationship and it didn't work out. Never-mind the other issue hanging over her head. If she couldn't keep paying, her secrets would be out and Maxwell may not want to be involved with her, anyway.

Realizing her beaming smile had turned into an intense frown, Nora shook her head and responded to his message.

N: *Free all day. You have something in mind?*
M: *I have some business in Malibu. Care to join me at the beach?*

It would be chilly, but it would always be beautiful. Topanga was her preference when she went on solo trips. Malibu was right next door though, and always stunning. How could it not be? She adored driving the long way through the canyon and just meandering around the curves and turns. There was never anyone there, either, which she could never understand.

N: *Any chance Rufus will be coming along?*

Really? She asked about his *dog*? Embarrassment rose into her face as a hot blush and caused her fingers and toes to grow warm, then cold.

M: *Actually yes. I have some business at dad's place—where Stephanie and Devon's wedding was held. Thought we could make a day of it.*

Nora delayed messaging for a moment, trying not to look overeager. Inside, she was about to burst out of her skin. She wanted to say something clever about returning to the scene of their first meet-cute, but resisted, not wanting to look like a total idiot.

N: *Sounds like fun.*

She felt ridiculous giving a bland answer like that, but she could barely coherently string words together. It was obnoxious how rapidly he made her heart beat and thoughts scramble.

M: *Alright if I pick you up around 10?*

Her face fell. She didn't want Maxwell to see her apartment. After an anxious moment, she realized she was being ridiculous. If he had a negative thought about her because of her shitty apartment, that was 100% on him, and it would thoroughly and quickly remove him from her dating pool and as much of her life as she could manage.

N: *Sounds perfect.*

Before she could stop herself, she texted him her address.

M: *Looking forward to it. More than you know.*

Oh, she doubted that, but it made her smile. The anticipation was heady and she found herself wandering her apartment, all tiredness having evaporated.

To keep her hands busy, she tended to her plants, which would probably tell her to knock it off if they could; she was over-loving them and they would start dropping some yellow leaves in protest soon. Yoga wasn't calming either, though her muscles appreciated the stretching. Eventually, she just went into her room and put together a few things for Saturday.

It was more than likely venturing into the land of over-prepared, but if they were going to be on the beach she'd at least need a swimsuit and a towel and a change of clothes. If he wanted to go somewhere to dinner, she'd probably need something nice to wear in the evening. Shoes too. Sunscreen was important, plus moisturizer and lip balm.

Before long, she had a full-on overnight bag packed and was fairly horrified with herself.

"Jesus, Nora. Get your shit together."

Frustrated but still excited about her weekend plans, she stowed the bag on a chair near the front door and made herself get ready for bed.

NORA'S CALL TIMES were extra early to really late all week, but she didn't mind. The show was doing what she felt was some fantastic episodes, and she was so pleased to be a part of what was going on that she couldn't even stress about how tired she was.

Stephanie, who didn't often take acting parts anymore had even agreed to cameo at Devon's persistence—both with her and with the director—so, there was an extra layer of positive energy on set for the rest of the week as Devon got to see his beloved wife at work and Nora got to see what she had begun to think of as her best girlfriend.

Failing to mention her impending day-trip to Malibu to either of them was completely intentional but at the same time virtually impossible. She was excited and for one of the first times in a very long while, she truly wanted to talk about things with a girlfriend but didn't want to spoil anything by doing just that. She vowed to do so after the date happened and if things seemed to be headed in a positive direction overall with Maxwell. The waters were muddy because of the close friendship pool, but it was also really nice—albeit strange—to be able to tap Stephanie for some insider information if she had questions or concerns.

For all the positive, there had to be a negative—for balance, she supposed—and that was coming in the form of messages from her mother. The first was unusually sweet in tone, asking if Nora had decided to send a check. That nice one was followed up by a fairly neutral one asking if she'd decided how much she might be able to send. The third asked quite directly when she planned on putting the check in the mail. The fourth was business as usual; a threat, an insult and a demand for the full five thousand, sent immediately, and if Nora 'couldn't be bothered to write a check' the suggestion of just sending it via phone app.

Devon happened to see the last one over her shoulder. "Don't you dare."

Her head snapped up, heat rushing to her cheeks. It was as though he'd caught her doing something naughty.

The instant guilt reaction and the desire to hide messages from her mother were all the indications that she needed that he was right though.

"I still hadn't decided what I was going to do," she muttered. "but I was definitely leaning toward saying no."

Devon was in full vamp makeup and fangs, shaking his head at her. He looked murderous—which was normal for his character but slightly terrifying for himself.

"Don't send her a dime, Nora. You know she's just playing you. I mean it."

Nora's heart warred with itself. "I don't want to, Dev. I swear. But I would feel guilty if I didn't send anything at all. What if they really *are* struggling?"

He crossed his arms and pinned her with an icy stare.

"No. Just no. HARD no. Don't fall for that. Remember all the nasty things she said to you just a few days ago. The things she says in her messages and *every time* you speak. Remember why you don't go home to visit. Remember why Phaedra wants nothing to do with her right now. You just sent her a huge check, what, like a couple of months ago? Charlie's gambling isn't your problem. That's *your* money. *You* earned it."

Nora knew he was right. If she sent her mother anything other than the requested five grand, it would be cause for more bad blood and another fight. There would be crocodile tears and accusations that Nora didn't love her, that Nora had never accepted Charlie as a parent and that she was a terrible daughter and sister. The list would go on and on and she would feel all the accusations like tiny arrows aimed at her heart. They would all make a cut and she would eventually fold and have to talk herself out of feeling exactly the way her mom wanted her to feel.

Nothing new. And totally healthy.

Devon raised one eyebrow at her, questioning whether or not his opinion and reminders were sinking in. They were. She gave a short nod, feeling something in her chest twist and then lighten. Permission to not go along with her mother's plans was a heavy weight relieved, but the guilt lingered.

"I know you won't, but I'd like to strongly suggest and formally lobby my vote that you block her. Or change your number again. I know she's your mom, but that way you could contact her on your terms and not be constantly harassed."

Nora nodded again because she had thought about doing both of those things. More than once. The number changing for more reasons than just her mother, but she wasn't about to open *that* can of worms when Devon was feeling feisty.

And changing her number would just assure all of her secrets went public.

"I send Phae money every month." Where the confession came from or why it mattered, she didn't know—it just came out of her mouth.

That seemed to be happening to her more and more lately.

Devon's lips tilted up. Doing so revealed a fang.

It was strangely funny that it was so normal to her that it barely registered that it should be unusual. It did increase his danger quotient, and he was already handsome.

She could see why ovaries all over the country exploded when he made that expression. Thankfully hers were quite immune.

"I know. I mean, of course, you do."

Her happiness bubble popped with surprise at his statement.

"You know?"

He gave a short nod, and they took their places as the director called out.

"Of course. There's nothing you wouldn't do for Phae. If I'd been in a better position sooner, I'd have done the same thing for my brothers. Unlucky for them, they were all born a bit too soon after me and neither my soccer or modeling careers took off or paid as well as acting does. Plus, there are three of them. Those assholes have to fend for themselves, mostly, but Phae has the chance to actually enjoy her college experience without working herself to death because of you. She's lucky. And she loves you for it. And so do I."

Nora smiled at her friend before schooling her expression into character. Of course, he knew. Of course, he'd have done the same. They had enjoyed their college experience immensely, but if she could prevent Phae from having to figure out how to survive on less than 6 hours of sleep a night, cheap pasta, canned meat, and frozen veggies she'd do it in a hot second.

Every single time.

WHEN SHE FINALLY made it home that night, it was nearly 11 pm. She was dragging her tired carcass up the steps but found a bit of a bounce return when she saw the lavish bouquet sitting in front of her door.

A smile spread over her lips as she picked up the bundle. It was a decadent mix of gerbera daisies in bright pinks and oranges, alstroemeria in the same color family but more muted in tone and a handful of rust and orange tiger lilies. An unusual and unique choice, but beautiful all the same.

Nora thought roses were pretty but highly over-rated. The fact that there were none in this bouquet gave her a heady thrill for some reason—like a secret she'd been keeping had been accidentally figured out.

The card had only three words on it, no signature.

See you soon.

Nora couldn't stop the silly grin as she entered her apartment and dug out a vase for the blooms. She thought about texting Maxwell her thanks but decided she'd just tell him in person when he came to pick her up since it was already so late. Too tired to think about much except falling into bed, she did just that once her flowers were settled in their new home and she'd done some gentle stretching. Thankfully there had been food catered on set for the late shoot or she'd be dying of starvation.

Honestly, she was grateful for the exhaustion—it kept her from not being able to sleep out of excitement for the following day—she was much like a kid before Christmas, and couldn't wait to see what tomorrow would bring.

CHAPTER
Ten

ORA HAD A feeling that Maxwell didn't know how to be anything other than prompt, and strongly suspected that his definition of 'on time' pretty closely matched hers. For no real reason really, aside from the fact that he had been earlier than she had to both of their dates so far.

This suspicion was summarily confirmed when he knocked on her door at precisely 9:55 Saturday morning. She wouldn't have been surprised if he had stood in the hallway for a bit, just waiting for the minutes to tick over. Not that she'd done that same thing innumerable times herself or anything. The notion that they were in alignment on such a silly thing gave her a rush of endorphins that brought a glow to her cheeks and a warmth to her skin.

Nora opened the worn white door to reveal the charming man who was quickly getting under her skin in the best way possible, his easy smile and familiar impeccable grooming in place. It was an interesting experience every time she realized how large he actually was. He filled up her doorway in a manner that was more comforting than it was imposing. He was a pretty boy to be sure—probably dropping just as much money on his grooming habits and certainly more on his clothing than Nora could ever hope to; but it felt like a self-care thing, not an out to impress thing. Perhaps it was both.

Maxwell stood in her doorway awaiting her invitation to enter. He was wearing another polo, this one flamingo pink, and he definitely had no right to look half as good in it as he did. The bright shade made the blonde in his careless, beach-ready hair more obvious, and darkened the tan that turned his skin golden. Instead of slacks, he wore khaki shorts and he had a pair of dock-siders on his feet. Nora took a moment to wonder how much time it took him to get his hair to look that effortless.

She couldn't stop the grin from forming in response to his toothy smile. It was a heady feeling to be on the receiving end of a Maxwell Caine smile that reached his eyes and then some. There was no escaping the pull of this bastion of joy—it was all-consuming and made you feel as though you were the only person in the world he found worthy of his attention. It was dangerous.

Nora's panties were not appreciative of this effect, but her fluttering heart was.

She had dressed in a simple knee-length lavender and pink ombre sundress, thinking it was the most multi-functional and appropriate choice for a day spent on or near the beach. Amusement flowed through her as she realized that by sheer accident, they had color-coordinated their outfits.

"Good morning." Maxwell's deep tenor rolled pleasantly against her skin.

"Hi," she said, unable to form intelligent or coherent words, apparently. Because she couldn't be trusted with language, she gestured for him to come in and set about gathering her purse and overnight bag.

He was examining her large cluster of plants with interest.

"That's quite the green thumb you've got."

"It's a fulfilling hobby. I find it quite relaxing," she confirmed. He turned his warm gaze back to her, focusing on the bag. Nora was forming the outline of an explanation in her brain, but he beat her to the punch.

"You're on top of things. I was going to suggest you go pack a few things, but it looks like you're way ahead of me." Those full lips tilted up, and he reached a hand out to take it. His melted chocolate gaze conveyed his pleasure that she had felt comfortable enough to put together a bag of things to take with them.

"And I was worried I was over-prepared and perhaps presuming too much," Nora didn't plan to say that, but the words tumbled out, anyway. Despite some embarrassing verbal vomit, she liked how she was around this man. It was an unusual confident flirty feeling; much more on-screen Nora than the normal, everyday version.

"Never." Maxwell beamed. "I didn't want to freak you out by texting that you might want to bring spare clothes. Felt a little … dirty." He raised his eyebrows a bit and Nora laughed. "Ready to go?" His gaze slid to the bouquet on her breakfast bar. She couldn't discern what his expression was when he spotted it, but him noticing that she had them displayed made her smile.

"Yes."

Nora locked up and Maxwell led her down to his sporty red roadster. After stashing her bag in the trunk, he opened her door and she slid in, welcoming the embrace of the supple leather seat and the smell that came with it.

There were two coffee cups in the center holders, and Nora smiled because they were both fresh—they had that telltale little plastic steam stopper in the spout. There was also a bakery box that could only contain pastries on the dash.

Maxwell slid into the drivers' seat and saw her grinning.

"I couldn't let you go hungry or under-caffeinated. That's a serious offense."

"Much appreciated."

"Between my mother and Stephanie, I know much better than to come unprepared. Snacks are mandatory, no matter how long the drive."

He started the engine, and she opened the pastry box. Nora selected a chocolate croissant, and Maxwell a cheese danish. The labels on the coffee were their names, and Nora noted with pleasure that he'd remembered her drink from the other day.

"All set?"

"Yes, thank you."

Nora settled in with her breakfast and coffee as Maxwell navigated them toward the 101.

There was no forced conversation for which Nora was grateful. Her nerves were on a default setting of strung tight, but she was incredibly at ease with Maxwell. She thought that should make her more vigilant and perhaps wary, but instead, it just made her happy.

"I was thinking I'd go through the canyon. Is that okay? Are you in a hurry to get to the beach?"

Nora's face was going to be sore if she kept up all this smiling.

"No, that's fine. When I go I always take 27, anyway. I like that drive through the canyon and fantasizing about the people who live in those houses perched on the sides of the hill, wondering what the floor-plans must look like. It ends right at Topanga Beach too, and that's where I usually go. I hardly ever go into Malibu proper. I *have* been to the lagoon once or twice—I'm not a total heathen."

Maxwell laughed warmly. "I've got some friends who live in some of those interesting hillside houses. Perhaps one day you'll find out a layout or two."

A thrill lit up Nora's veins, but no words sprang to her tongue. She wanted to say something clever, but only half of a cappuccino wasn't quite enough to provide that ability.

"Does your father not live at the Malibu property then?"

Maxwell shook his head, mountains, and cityscape mixed together as they traveled down the freeway.

"Not full time. My parents are actually headed back to the city this morning—we'll cross paths on the road probably. The commute is too much for every day. They keep a small house in the city as well, though if my mother gets her way, they'll retire to the beach full time fairly soon."

She nodded, then realized they were missing a member of their party.

"And Rufus?"

Maxwell beamed. "That giant furry lug *does* basically live at the beach-house full time, the moocher. It's just worked out that either I or my parents were there consistently the last couple of months so he's stayed instead of traveling back and forth with me. I miss him when he's not around, the slobber-box, but it's easier not to have to cram him into this little car every few days and he's got free reign of the big house and yard. He wouldn't have that at my condo."

Nora smiled. Maxwell clearly adored his dog. If that wasn't a positive indicator of a genuinely good human, she didn't know what was.

The little car zipped around the curves of the canyon and around the bits of traffic through town alike, smoothly navigating the twists in the road and making the trip feel like a fun adventure. Her cappuccino hadn't been gone for very long when they turned off of 27 onto Highway 1, the bright azure water always a breathtaking sight. The expanse of it, the white caps of the rolling waves, the way the sun sparkled off of the blue depths always made her sigh. As much as she liked the drive through the canyon, the moment when the road dumped out directly in view of the water was her favorite. It never ceased to take her breath away.

Having grown up on the Gulf coast, the temperature of the water was the only thing she would like to change about the Pacific. She was used to bathwater, and the Pacific was more like cold shower. She did, however, appreciate that there was no concern about amoeba in the colder water—it just took some getting used to once you decided to go in, especially in the months that weren't the punishing heat of Summer.

They drove through what she thought of as 'town' for Malibu proper, and traffic depleted some by the time he pulled the car into the large driveway of the beach estate. For the wedding, many of them had parked at a large lot a short distance away and been shuttled in, but she recognized the house immediately.

Nora's imagination ran for a moment as Maxwell gathered her bag from the trunk—he'd dashed around the car to open her door, like a true gentleman—and unlocked first an iron gate and then a massive wooden front door.

Her thoughts ran wild. What would it be like to live somewhere like this all the time? Would you become immune to the sensation of wonder being this close to the waves provided? What would it be like to be rocked to sleep every night by that fantastic sound? How different would a regular hair and makeup routine be with humidity in the air? What kind of plants could you grow?

That thought stuck because Southern California was certainly an excellent choice for Orchids. She needed to tell Phae that.

"You coming, Gorgeous?" Maxwell had on a lopsided smile, one hand out for her, the other holding the door as she daydreamed in the courtyard that boasted both dwarf Lemon and Avocado trees, plus some fantastic hibiscus and enormous jade bushes.

"Yes. Sorry." A blush warmed her cheeks as she made her feet move past the threshold and onto the white marble flooring of the entryway.

The house was no less lovely now than it had been for Devon and Stephanie's wedding. There had been quite a few more twinkle lights and decorations then, but everything had its place and there was nothing that didn't look staged by a professional designer. It also somehow felt incredibly well lived in. The dichotomy made Nora's forehead furrow a bit.

Maxwell led her through the open living and kitchen, placing her bag on one of the kitchen chairs.

Without delay, Maxwell kept right on moving, throwing the sliding glass door off the small eat-in kitchen area wide open and whistling.

Nora heard Rufus before she saw him—a heavy thud of paws on the wooden decking and a loving whine as he all but knocked Maxwell off his feet with his massive furry body.

"Hey, buddy! I missed you!" Maxwell braced for the onslaught of dog kisses like a pro, just scrunching up his face and taking it, his hands ruffling the dog's ears and fur and a laugh rolling out of him. "Okay. Down, boy."

Rufus did as requested, prancing around in a circle with a half-growl, half-whine. Maxwell leaned down and did some more petting until Rufus calmed a bit. Nora heard herself laughing, and that turned both the man and his dog's attention her way. Rufus bounced like he was about to pounce on her as well, but Maxwell headed him off. "Sit." Rufus reluctantly obeyed but was rewarded with a head pat for his efforts.

"May I?" she asked.

Maxwell nodded, looking pleased. "Of course."

Nora started forward and held her fingers out knuckle first for Rufus to inspect. His tail thumped against the deck and he sniffed, then licked enthusiastically. She accepted his permission and rubbed his short silky fur, paying special attention to his soft, floppy ears. This had the giant hound lowering his whole body to the side, exposing his belly.

"Well. Seems you've made a friend." Maxwell didn't sound surprised, but he did seem happy about the idea. "Doesn't suit to be jealous of a dog, does it?"

Nora obliged and rubbed Rufus' belly, laughing at Maxwell's commentary. Abruptly, Rufus decided that he'd had his fill and left them on the deck. He, it seemed, had an urgent need to sunbathe, and did so just off the side of the deck in the sand.

"I've never had a dog, but always loved them," she confessed.

Maxwell looked scandalized. "Never had a dog? How is that possible?"

Nora shrugged. "My mother isn't a fan of any kind of animal. Phae and I begged and pleaded for a dog or cat or even a fish but my mother wouldn't budge."

"I can't imagine never having a pet. They make so many things about life better." He watched his dog lounging for a short moment and then turned his attention to the waves before looking at her. "Phae is your sister?"

Nora nodded. "Yes. Half-sister technically, but we never really counted that. She's at Auburn."

"Good school. What's she studying?"

"Horticultural Science."

Maxwell's eyebrows went up and his lush mouth pulled into an interesting shape of surprise.

"I have to say, that's not a major I would have guessed, even if given a hundred guesses. You don't hear that often." He smiled. "I take it you share her love of plants? Based on your collection I mean."

Nora returned his grin and followed him as he started back into the house.

"Yes. Our Yiayia taught us what she knew about growing things. Her green thumbs skipped a generation—my mother kills any plant she even looks at—but thankfully Phae and I inherited the green things gene."

Maxwell collected two bottles of water from the massive industrial-grade fridge and offered her one.

"I've got a couple of things to do here in the house. You're welcome to stay here if you like, there's a TV in the living room. Or you could go on ahead to the beach." He gestured vaguely.

"Can I help you with anything?"

"Not really, but you could keep me company."

Nora felt the smile stretch her mouth and the tension between them crackled with electricity.

"Okay."

Maxwell nodded once, closing the sliding door behind them and leading her upstairs.

IT SHOULD HAVE felt like he was trying to do nothing other than to get her in bed—and to be fair, maybe he was—but Maxwell was too kind and too playful for it to come across as a proposition. Nora felt the first flares of anticipation as he led her up the stairs, but no jolts of warning from her intuition.

She chose to ignore the fact that her body wasn't sending out danger signs and take it for what it was. She deserved some happiness. The cost might be high to pay later, but she *needed* this.

Upstairs were three large suites for bedrooms, and Maxwell walked into the one at the front right of the house. There was a deck with access from both bedrooms on that side of the house, complete with comfortable furniture plus a fireplace and a miniature outdoor kitchen.

The other half lived well, she noted. Quite well.

She wasn't even tired and Nora felt like she could crawl up on the massive bed and take the best nap of her life in its fluffy, pillow-bedecked embrace. Everything in the room was shades of grays and yellows and blues—true beach neutrals to be sure—but she could feel a slightly masculine edge to the decor.

"This house is something else." Nora sighed, turning herself around to take in the space.

Maxwell chuckled.

"My mother is very proud of this place. I'll be sure to tell her you like it."

Nora felt a moment of crippling anxiety and shame. She knew it wasn't relevant, but the truth was that she'd grown up in an old cottage with dark wood paneling, terrible linoleum, and walls that were basically two-ply wallpaper. Just being in a multi-million-dollar home on the beach was a novel experience and not something she'd ever been brave enough to dream of doing. But here she was.

And Maxwell was going to tell his mother about her opinion. As if it mattered.

Shaking herself mentally, she tried to exist only here, only now. She deserved to be here. This was her actual life. She was successful and had famous friends. This was *real*.

As Nora battled internally, Maxwell settled behind a glass-topped desk, waking up a very expensive desktop computer and gathering some documents from a file cabinet with efficiency.

"You're not *working*, are you?" Nora teased.

Maxwell smiled at her around one side of the massive display screen.

"Not like you think. I'm not a lawyer today. I do however have a few other projects that need some attention and I mostly tend to them when I'm visiting here."

Nora took a seat on the plush white chaise lounge that was stationed near the desk and under a floor to ceiling window. She thought it would be the perfect place to read a book with the deck door open for a breeze, or to relax and watch the waves roll under the moonlight.

There was an expression on Maxwell's face that sent blood-flow to parts of her body that had been long ignored. His pupils looked at bit blown out and it seemed as though he was gripping the edge of the desk a little tightly. Her imagination was good enough to recognize his lust, and her own rose up in response.

The chaise would definitely be wonderfully multi-functional for amorous activities. Before she could stop her mind from going there, she was picturing herself draped forward over the back of the chaise, Maxwell on his knees atop the cushion behind her as he—

Maxwell cleared his throat and her train of thought derailed in a spectacular explosion of pent-up hormones and exhaled breath.

"What, ah, what else do you do? Besides the lawyer, thing, I mean," she managed to say. The blood rushing to the surface all over her body was hot, and she desperately resisted the urge to press her hands into her cheeks to cool them down. "that day job seems quite time-consuming."

He shifted noticeably in the desk chair, widening his legs, and she tried to keep her eyes on his. She was mostly successful.

"It is. I dabble in security apps."

"Apps? Like for phones?" She was familiar with what he'd made for Stephanie but wanted to hear him talk about it.

"Yes." The warm smile that lit up his face as he tapped on the keyboard and moved the mouse was almost shy.

Nora thought that it was an interesting expression for this confident, exuberant man to be wearing.

He explained the app he had designed for Stephanie, to keep her safe in the event of an Ollie Parkinson situation during the time she was dating other celebs but not for real. She had been hiring out her acting services, nothing more. It was how she and Devon had met. Nora found herself quite awed by what he described. That was serious tech and serious talent.

"That's fantastic, Maxwell. Could it be altered for everyday situations? Like instead of contacting the agency a regular phone number or emergency contact?"

His grin widened and he plugged in a couple of thumb drives, no doubt copying files.

"That's exactly the plan. It's been hard to get all the permissions in place, but we're nearly there. I think monetizing the service could be incredibly profitable—and beneficial."

He launched into his ideas for how to market it to university campuses for the students, to any school really, or to companies whose employees traveled or worked in dangerous conditions or areas.

Nora beamed at him. She was proud of him. This was a fantastic idea, and he was going to make it real.

"That's amazing, Maxwell. Truly."

Thumb drives stored safely in a zipper pouch, he shut down the computer and stored both the pouch and a number of folders full of paperwork into a briefcase.

"Thank you. I'm quite proud of it."

He took her hand and helped her to her feet.

"One project down. Would you like to sit on the beach for a bit? I can make some calls from out there and that way we'll have the afternoon free."

Nora felt her skin heat with his close proximity. The chaise was still at her back, she could feel it hitting just behind her knees. With him close enough to kiss she was very likely to do something wholly out of character for herself if she didn't move away a bit.

"The beach sounds great. I'll get changed."

Maxwell nodded, one eyebrow quirked up when her voice caught.

He knew she was having dirty thoughts, Nora realized. Perhaps even trying to make her do so, but at the very least hoping she was.

"I'll meet you downstairs." His voice was low and quiet, and Nora very nearly shuddered at the way it felt vibrating through her skull and a lot more southern, more interesting places.

She moved toward the bedroom door, feeling as though her body was resisting her efforts the whole way and that she was crawling through molasses, his eyes trailing her hotly the whole way.

CHAPTER *Eleven*

NORA WAS PRETTY sure that while Maxwell's motives had been mostly pure asking her to accompany him to Malibu, they were both now caught in a tempest of hormonally charged innuendo.

She was sitting on a beach towel atop the soft white sand in her plum bikini, trying not to be too obvious as she alternated between watching Maxwell and the waves.

He was a vision in navy swim trunks, his toned upper body shining in the late morning sun as he paced back and forth across the sand. He was far enough away that she couldn't hear what he was saying, but once in a while, the wind would bring the sound of his laugh to her ears.

Where a man who practiced law in an office for a living got off having a body like that, she'd never know. It was ridiculous. She decided that he must spend the hours he should be sleeping working out.

Nora felt her lips lift a bit and purposefully moved her gaze back to the teal waves. The taste of salt coated her lips, mixed with the sunscreen Maxwell had very helpfully assisted her in applying. She shivered, remembering how warm his hands had been on her skin. The July day was more than warm but the breeze off the ocean was brisk when it turned her way. They'd been out nearly an hour, and Nora was pretty sure her skin was about finished playing nice with the sun.

It was odd, the sensation rioting in her body. She'd never felt this drawn to or needy for another human being in her life. Her body didn't do this touch-craving, instantly aroused *thing* that Maxwell seemed to provoke. It was strange and new and oddly welcome. She was realizing quite rapidly how little she'd been enjoying her life.

The lies she told herself about how she was and had been doing what she *needed* seemed very thin and pale as she examined them over the bright light of the midday sun at the beach.

She felt Maxwell coming closer more than she heard it, and he plunked himself down on the giant towel next to her with a sigh. There was a peaceful smile on his lips as he watched the water.

"All done?" she asked.

"Yes. Thankfully. Sorry for having to use some of your time like that."

She shook her head.

"No apology needed. Me and the sun and sand were enjoying ourselves just fine. Good news then?"

He nodded, unabashedly running his gaze up the length of her stretched-out body. She could feel his eyes like they were leaving a warm trail in their wake like they were somehow physically caressing her.

She adjusted how she was holding her upper body up with her arms to disguise the shiver of pleasure that gave her. Maybe there had been some kind of love potion in her cappuccino. Perhaps she could blame the magic of the chocolate croissant.

"Yes. I am likely to have some committed investors come next week, so I can proceed with the app development."

"That's great." Nora smiled at him.

He covered her hand with his, twined his fingers through hers and lifted, pausing a moment to look into her eyes before he kissed her palm.

They said nothing, just allowed the moment to exist around them. They turned their attention back to the ocean, watching as waves crashed, and gulls dived in an organized kind of chaos into the waves for snacks. Rufus half-heartedly chased the birds, splashing in the shallow surf and then shaking off before starting again. A woman and her greyhound jogged down the beach toward them, raising a hand to Maxwell as he nodded that it was okay for them to continue through what was their private slice of beach. The moment was quiet, but the kind of quiet that is heavy with meaning.

Maxwell was on the verge of doing something truly fantastic, and he had invited *her* here to share that moment with him. They were sitting in the spot where they'd first met, and though they'd only been on a couple of actual dates—not counting the dinner that had been set up and sponsored by their scheming mutual friends—and yet she was the most comfortable in her skin and most relaxed with the person near her that she could remember being in … maybe ever. There was no reason to slip into her 'working' Nora skin—she was wholly herself and it was a refreshing change and an incredible weight off.

She worried that she should feel suspicious or afraid of that feeling, but pushed that away in favor of just leaning into it. Maxwell was everything she hadn't known she was looking for. The universe had presented her with a gift and she had enough Southern manners to accept graciously and say thank you. Maybe she'd even send a card. And a couple of jars of pickles.

She felt him move and turned her face toward him. The smile on her lips died of nervous anticipation as he brought his hand to cup her jaw. Her own free hand held it in place as he leaned in and captured her mouth in a kiss that evaporated all the air from her lungs. She decided that it didn't matter either; she'd happily go without breath for this man, this kiss, this moment. He moved his lips over hers with a hunger she was shocked to find she could match. His hand disengaged from hers and wrapped itself around the back of her neck, pulling her closer until she was in his lap, straddling him quite inelegantly but also very effectively.

There was no avoiding what was between them, quite literally. His length pressed into her bikini bottom as he made love to her mouth, using every tool he had available to him—tongue, teeth, lips; it was the most in-depth kiss Nora had ever had. She was fairly certain she wouldn't be able to say no to anything he might ask her to do under the influence of his embrace and the potent drug that was *that kiss.*

And she'd thought his smile was bad.

She'd had no idea what kind of weapons he had at his disposal.

Just about the time she felt his fingers tug lightly at the string of her top, Rufus barked and she could hear a significant splashing noise, followed by a rough gallop that seemed to come closer and closer.

Maxwell pulled away, the look on his face urgent as he shifted their weight and rolled on top of her.

"No! Rufus, stop!"

It was too late though, the very large, very wet dog was charging their way, kicking up sand and throwing what amounted to pea-sized mud balls at them in his enthusiasm.

Fortunately, Maxwell was very effective as a full body shield, for which Nora was grateful.

She desperately tried to ignore how wonderful it felt to be under the weight of his body and his gaze, but she couldn't escape the way he was looking at her like he'd happily devour her whole right then and there.

All of his parts were lined up with hers, and the pressure was enough to make her need to stifle a moan.

Rufus, seeing an opening to break the tension again, shoved his nose under Maxwell's arm and she was treated to a face-full of muddy wet nose right on the cheek and in her ear.

The giggle that came out of her mouth following the shriek she let out felt so carefree she wanted to luxuriate in the sound of it. She didn't giggle. That just didn't happen and yet here she was. It felt incredibly freeing.

Maxwell was laughing, still hovering above her, her head caged by his arms. The tension returned for a moment as he gazed down at her, a smirk that could rival Devon's on his lush mouth.

"Nothing like a good dose of reality after very nearly committing indecent exposure on the beach." He dipped down and planted a quick kiss on her mouth before helping her up, employing a spare beach towel to helping get the sand out of her ear.

"*Private* beach though. Nobody would have seen except maybe the jogger and her dog. Maybe the little drone I saw flying around over there when we first came out. Is going topless not allowed here?"

Maxwell growled. "Jesus." He sucked in a deep breath, his chest rising and falling. She watched his face transform from amused to tortured then back again. "You're not helping."

Nora shrugged, embracing her inner vixen, loving that she had this effect on him.

"Wasn't trying to."

He shook his head, a laugh booming out of him. Rufus returned to his master's side, soaking wet and very pleased with himself.

"Come on. Let's get everyone cleaned up. There's an outside shower on the side of the deck."

Nora bent to gather up her towel. Maxwell stood with his legs spread wide, and she could relate to the ache he must be having between his thighs. She could feel her pulse pounding just about everywhere herself. She tossed him a playful wink and walked ahead of him back toward the house, the resistance of the powdery sand allowing a lot more sway in her hips.

"Quit looking at my ass," she teased.

"Not a chance, Gorgeous." He winked at her before she turned back around, following the exuberant Rufus who kept turning around to be sure the humans were coming along. "Thankfully, the shower is ice cold," she heard him grumble, her smile ear to ear and her body lighter than it had been in years.

AFTER A QUICK rinse outside, Maxwell offered her the shower in the guest room—the room on the other side of the upstairs deck—while he cleaned up in the room with the tempting chaise lounge.

She took her bag up and reveled in the luxury that was the suite, enjoying her spa-like experience for what should have been just a simple, quick shower.

The guest suite had been decorated from the same beach-neutral palate but was decidedly more feminine with tones of peach instead of blue over the gray and yellow. Another massive, fluffy bed took up a portion of the room, and instead of a chaise lounge, there was an overstuffed chair, likely from the same set. She stood by her assessment that it was good furniture to read or take in the stars over the ocean from, regardless of her dirty thoughts about the chaise.

River stones massaged her feet as the rain-shower head delivered a deluge of water to her hair and body. There was cause for deep sighs as she scrubbed off the layer of salt from her skin with spa-quality soap and five-star hotel shampoos.

A girl could definitely get used to this kind of luxury.

Nora dressed in her back-up outfit, which was a similar style dress but in muted shades of emerald and plum. There was no shortage of appliances with which to style her hair, but she didn't think Maxwell was interested in fully-coiffed Nora, and she certainly wasn't interested in putting on that mask right now. She towel-dried her hair and braided it away from her face while it was wet. It would have a nice wave to it when she took it out later on. Makeup similarly was not a priority, and she settled for some tinted BB cream with sunscreen and her favorite lip balm.

Appraising herself in the mirror—and realizing that in this moment she looked more like herself than Maxwell had seen yet—she smiled. There was no back-biting mother voice in her ear insisting that she put her face on, no inner monologue about covering flaws. There was a strange sense of calm that if Maxwell was who she thought he was, this version of her was exactly what he was looking for.

She collected her cast-off clothing and tucked them into the duffel, leaving it by the doorway of the guest room before going downstairs to see if he was ready.

Her stomach gave a growl just as she entered the living room where he was scrolling his phone, body totally relaxed. He had one arm up over the back of the couch, one ankle on the other knee. She envisioned herself tucked right under that arm, up against his body as they watched something on TV or had one of those wonderfully pointless, endless conversations.

That dangerous smile appeared on his mouth, in response to both her appearance and the grumble of her stomach.

"You look stunning, as usual," he said, getting to his feet, planting a kiss in the soft place behind her ear. She couldn't suppress a shiver. "good enough to eat, honestly, but let's worry about stomachs first, shall we?"

Nora smiled at him, trying to ignore the flutters in her chest and stomach. "What did you have in mind?"

"There's a little fish shack not far. You feel like a bit of a walk?"

She nodded at him and he grinned, checking his pockets before leading her out the front door and down the street.

It was only a few blocks to their destination, and before they got very far at all she could see the legitimate wooden shack they were headed toward. There was a line out the door and a cluster of picnic tables mostly full of patrons.

"You don't have any aversions to things that are deep-fried, do you?" He smirked as they joined the queue.

"Definitely not." She shook her head.

He beamed.

She couldn't stop the words that fell out of her mouth, no matter how much she wished she could take them back once they arrived. This was quickly becoming a major concern for her. She had no filter around this man.

"I'd bet Olivia doesn't eat anything but kale, black coffee, and the souls of her enemies."

After a full five seconds, during which Nora stewed in abject mortification, Maxwell barked a laugh and threw his head back.

"Nailed it," he said, appraising her stunned face with something akin to glee. "There are few things sexier than a woman who likes to eat. Maybe one who not only likes to eat but also doesn't bother with full war paint application for a day at the beach." He winked, and she let go of the embarrassment, latching onto a wholly different emotion as he twined his fingers through hers on the table and brushed her knuckles with the pad of his thumb.

A feeling bloomed in her chest. It was warm and wild and she knew it was going to hurt her something fierce at some point, but she couldn't bring herself to care all that much about it.

Between them, they ordered an assortment of seafood to share, plus the requisite fries, hush puppies, and even a dessert. Naturally, there was some coleslaw in there too, but that was mostly just for show—not unlike the huge leaves of parsley under the lemon wedges.

Maxwell chose a table that was tucked out of the way of the bulk of the restaurant traffic, and Nora deeply appreciated the gesture.

"Thank you for that," she said softly, choosing a giant prawn to start with. It was more like a tiny lobster than a large shrimp.

"What, exactly?" he queried playfully.

"There's probably not paparazzi here, but several people were looking at me a little closely. I appreciate that you picked something out of the way of all the staring." She realized how that sounded. *Poor little TV star, everyone is looking at you.* And what if they weren't? What if they were just looking at a pretty couple? Then she seemed totally conceited. No winning, either way.

"Did I?" Maxwell glanced over his shoulder and then did a scan of the nearby beach. "I guess I must have. It's kind of a habit I suppose. Going out with Alex—Steph—all these years I've probably gained some habits I didn't realize I had." He bit into a French fry and grinned at her. "Olivia made sure we were seated front and center, right where everyone could be sure they saw her. Just in case you're still comparing."

She could feel the blush creep up her neck.

"There's no comparison, by the way," he added. "I'd rather be here with you eating my weight in trans fats with some sand in my teeth and between my toes than anywhere with her. *Anywhere.*" He emphasized his last word, gaze pinning her.

Nora swallowed and he tracked the movement, the tension between them ratcheting back up in a palpable way. She hadn't agreed to join him today to hop in his bed—that hadn't really even been on her radar if she was being honest—but she was very clearly getting the notion that that's exactly what would be happening if her body had a vote on things.

That wasn't at all how she operated. She didn't think that's how he worked either and based on a few comments Stephanie had made it wasn't. He wasn't pressuring her to do anything but relax.

Whatever this was brewing between them was intense and real, and Nora didn't want to miss it just because she was feeling totally out of her depth.

Maxwell filled the silence between them with details about the house and the area as they ate. It was clear he'd done lots of research on it, and his parents had owned the house for many years. It was only recently that they'd finished the extensive remodeling and opened it to events for friends and family like the wedding.

She had been hungrier than she realized, and made some significant headway through her platter of food in very little time, noticing that he managed to put away quite a bit of fish as he talked as well. Something about the sea air maybe.

"Would you ever want to live here full time?" she asked.

He thought. "I love the house. I love the beach. I'm not sure this is the exact spot for me though." He smiled. "Steph is renovating the apartment across from hers. She teases me all the time about buying it from her so I can decorate it how I want before she chooses all the final touches."

"That's in Santa Barbara, right?"

He nodded, dusting his hands free of crumbs before wiping the grease on a napkin.

"Yes. Everything's different at the beach. Doesn't really seem to matter which one." He looked wistful almost and sighed. "I'm constantly telling her no, but inside I'm actually considering it."

Nora smiled broadly. She had spent many a Summer day watching re-runs of 80's shows with Phae and Yiayia Lou. "That feels like the makings of a hit sitcom."

Maxwell threw his head back in that rolling, warm laugh of his again. "It kind of does." He leveled her with his playful gaze. "Tell me something about you, Nora."

"What do you want to know?"

"I know it's what's on your SAG card and how you signed our paperwork, but are you Nora Chase?"

The question stunned her for a moment. Legally, yes, she was. But no, she wasn't. Not really. His question sent a quick spike of fear through her veins, but she quickly caught the sensation and made herself relax. She could trust him, and it didn't really matter, anyway. She only had the one major skeleton in her closet aside from her mother and *she* was not hidden at all. It was a good distraction if anyone were looking too hard.

She shook her head.

His head cocked to one side. "No? Well. That explains it then."

"Explains what?"

"Stephanie is Steph, but she's really Alex." Maxwell briefly explained the history there—that when she'd been an angry teen she'd declared she would be called Alex and her parents had played along for a moment, but for Maxwell, it had stuck. She was Alex to him, and always would be.

Nora nodded. She knew the pseudonym that Stephanie painted under, but hadn't known that the history of the name went that far back.

"Who are *you*, really?" Maxwell asked. It was a deep, philosophical question disguised under his tilted, amused lips.

Nora leaned in conspiratorially.

"Do you really think you can handle that information? Can you keep my secret?"

His eyes darkened and focused on her mouth.

"You bet, Gorgeous."

She was enjoying this game, perhaps too much. Hear heart pounded against her ribs, playfulness disguising her underlying fear.

"I might need some wine and a good beach sunset first, Handsome." She winked.

He laughed, gathering their trash and leftovers into a container.

"I'm sure I can accommodate your needs."

Nora had absolutely no doubt of that, and she was very much looking forward to him proving it, in fact. With a smile, she took his offered hand and they walked the short distance back to the house, linked hands swinging, stride loping, attraction building.

Once again, Nora found herself welcoming the dangerous temptation that was Maxwell Caine with open arms, even if it meant her certain destruction.

CHAPTER
Twelve

AXWELL HAD ACCEPTED her challenge with an enthusiasm she probably should have expected. Sunset was nowhere near close—it was barely past 1 pm—but he opened a bottle of wine and they continued their relaxed conversation under the shade of an awning on the second-floor patio, taking full advantage of the plush outdoor furniture made of wicker and stacked deep with cushions and the view of the rolling Pacific.

Rufus seemed to have worn himself out for the day and joined them, napping so deeply he was snoring on one of the love seats.

"And here I thought I was going to have you in suspense for a while." Nora smiled at Maxwell.

"There's no getting around the fact that I'm a lawyer, Gorgeous. I have my ways of getting information."

She nodded, enjoying the warm buzz the wine was supplying to her bloodstream. That tease didn't hurt either.

"Ask your questions then, Counselor."

He tilted his head a bit, looking deep into her eyes with his own. Nora noticed that his melted chocolate irises were flecked with spots of black and tan.

He seemed to like hearing that title outside the courtroom.

"Who are you, Nora Chase?"

The smile lifted her lips as she looked out to the water.

"My mother calls me Eleanora. Eleanora Demetria Chatzi."

Nora turned her eyes back to her date, and he smiled back victoriously.

"That's exceptionally Greek."

The sharp laugh burst from her mouth.

"Yes. Yes, it is."

"What's your sister's name?"

"Phaedra Helena."

Maxwell grinned.

"Your mother was setting you up for greatness with those names."

"She was setting us up for something, alright." Elementary school jeers echoed in the recesses of her memory.

He tilted his head a bit. "Do I sense some tension there?"

"Isn't there always tension between mothers and daughters?"

Maxwell laughed.

"While probably true, I feel I need to congratulate you on a truly well-formulated non-answer. My inner attorney is beaming with pride."

Nora shook her head and sipped at her wine. She saw Maxwell's face turn unusually serious.

"It's serious then. Anything I can do to help?"

Her heart leaped at the offer. It was sweet, totally unnecessary, and completely genuine.

"No, but thank you. Hollywood Law taking me on as a client was the best possible help for that situation."

He grunted, setting his glass on the table and scooting closer to her on the cushions. He took her free hand and began to do a very precise massage on her fingers, pushing tension she didn't realize she was holding in those delicate joints out with his strong fingers.

"It's money related then?" He deduced, moving on to the top of her hand before rotating her wrist and beginning to work on the pressure points in her palm.

"What makes you say that?" Her whole body was turning to mush between the massage, the wine, and his very dedicated attention.

"It usually is." His expression darkened, and it was so strangely endearing that she very nearly threw herself into his arms.

"Yes. She thinks I have something I don't. She and my sister had a fight which only complicates things because I agree with my sister and my mother would prefer I talk some sense into her. Sense that is only actually sensical to my mother. We believe my step-father is gambling since he can't work. It's all a mess."

Maxwell gently kissed her now wholly relaxed palm and reached out for her other hand.

"I'm sorry."

He poured his apology into the massage, relaxing the second hand just as effectively as the first. The silence stretched between them, the crashing of the ocean a steady heartbeat in the background. Without any actual thought, when Maxwell pulled on her arm, she allowed him to tug her against him on the broad couch. Her back pressed against his chest and their arms both wrapped around her, entangled. His legs sat alongside hers, his body effectively containing hers. He just held her there.

Emotions welled up almost aggressively as she realized that she felt *safe* there. Taken care of.

Given time, she thought she could feel loved.

That in and of itself was panic-inducing. He seemed to sense her tension and he spoke slowly, and very softly.

"Did you ever go by anything other than Nora?" Maxwell asked, nuzzling her hair away from her neck, lips tantalizingly soft against the curvature where her neck and shoulder met.

Her tongue darted out to wet her suddenly dry lips, the flavor of salt and her lip balm marrying with the wine she'd been drinking.

"Not really. Eleanora is an awkward mouthful. I briefly considered Demi. Demetria is a lot to say too, and that one seemed a little pretentious. Though it perhaps explains my affinity for plants." She could feel his smile against her skin. "I was Nora Chatzi all through college and Nora Chase was available when I registered for my SAG card so I went with it."

Her whole body flamed up with desire as he moved that sinful mouth up and down her neck, managing to get a bit of collarbone as he nipped along her skin. He inhaled a deep breath in the shallow space behind her ear, arms unwinding from around her chest so his hands could explore the planes of her stomach, her hips, her upper thighs.

"Mmm. You feel like an Elle. Nora doesn't really suit you. This you. The one without the make-up and mask and put-on smile for the cameras. Day at the beach you. I feel like this is maybe the actual person you are. I like her. A lot. Can I call you Elle?"

She couldn't even form complete thoughts but she knew that she shouldn't enjoy this special endearment as much as her body was telling her she did. She should acknowledge that he'd seen the woman behind the curtain and that alone could be dangerous to her public persona. She shouldn't want to take her dress off right there on the patio and surrender her whole self to this man. She was too far gone to figure out *why* she shouldn't though, and that was the key to resisting the mysterious pull he had on her.

"Maxwell," She breathed the word as his thumbs teased the underside of her breasts. "We shouldn't."

He grunted, shifting to the other side of her neck as his hands moved upward and cupped her breasts completely, thumbs teasing her nipples into hard pebbles.

"Why not, Gorgeous?"

As she began to drown in sensations she had long thought she was immune to having except by her own hand or battery-operated device, Nora for the life of her couldn't think of a reason.

"I don't know."

He chuckled and shifted, turning her enough that he had access to her face. That sinful, full, warm mouth of his descended on hers, bringing every sensation directly to the surface of her skin like a bruise as he softly touched and explored and tweaked her body into full wakefulness and total arousal.

"May I have you, Elle? Do you want me to have you? Do you want to have me too?" he asked quietly, fingers poised under her dress straps, teasing along the edges.

She took the pause his questions provided and tried to swim up through the haze of arousal, searching for the evidence she needed to shut this down. Nothing presented itself. Her mouth moved before she'd given it permission.

"Please, Maxwell." She wasn't even sure what she was asking for, but she knew he'd give it to her.

He made a noise deep in his throat and captured her lips again, positioning their bodies on the couch so he could push her dress up past her waist and then her chest, her back arching as he drew it up over her head and off her body. He made similarly short work of her bra and panties, teasing her through them with his mouth and fingers before pulling them away from her heated flesh and discarding them in a pile on the patio floor.

Nora heard herself making noises she might have been embarrassed by in other situations. Maxwell seemed to thrive on them though, adjusting the pressure of his caress on the bundle of nerves at the apex of her thighs, his gentle exploration of her lower lips, the pressure of his mouth on her breast, the depth of his kiss on her mouth when she made them.

He worked her body like it was his job, leaving a trail of hot kisses down her stomach when he finally had his fill at her breasts and went lower. He teased her open with his tongue and she felt nerve endings spring to life at the warm, moist touch. Impatient, he pulled her legs over his shoulders and started to feast, making love to her body with all the same enthusiasm and skill he had her mouth. Maxwell licked, sucked, and even gave small nips to her, driving her to the brink of absolute madness what felt like all too quickly. She called out his name as her body locked up, her thighs clamping unforgivingly against his head, his fingers continuing to work inside her spasming body to draw out her orgasm.

As she came down, she opened her eyes, feeling a sudden shock and rush of shame realizing that they were still outside, albeit on the second floor and mostly covered from prying eyes.

There was a light buzzing sound around them as she tried to remember how to breathe properly and blood rushed in her ears.

Maxwell gazed down at her, mouth shiny with her arousal. That easy smile looked downright feral.

"Elle," he all but growled the name, and she nodded, not fully knowing what he was asking or telling her—it didn't matter really, she agreed. He had her full consent.

He scooped her up and swept her into his room, setting her carefully on the bed but catching her glance at the chaise.

"Next time," he promised, clearly on the same wavelength.

Maxwell quickly divested himself of his clothing. Nora looked him over approvingly and reached out a hand, running her palm up and down his generous shaft. He groaned and pulled away, muttering the same phrase again. "Next time." It sounded like a promise, but he wasn't making it to her.

He retrieved a condom from the bedside table and sheathed himself, crawling up onto the mattress, caging her head with his strong arms again as he angled his hips toward her raised ones.

"Elle? You with me?"

Nora felt her head nod enthusiastically, and she reached down, slicking her wetness around a bit with her fingers before he pressed forward. Her slippery fingertips lingered at her clit, circling gently. She felt her breath hitch as the pressure inside her increased. Maxwell lowered his hips slowly as he filled her, her breath leaving her in a rush when he was fully seated.

She noticed that he was sucking air like he'd been sprinting, which she took as a compliment. Also, she could totally relate.

"Maxwell?"

"Yes, Gorgeous?"

"Move."

He chuckled and complied, thrusting in and out at a slow pace, the drag of him against her inside walls delicious and maddening and intense.

She tried to adjust his speed by moving her hips, wrapping her legs around his waist, but he was having none of it.

"Next time," he repeated.

Nora heard herself grunt in frustration, and he smothered that with a kiss, making love to her mouth as he worked himself in and out of her body. He snuck a hand between them and all but slapped hers aside. He skillfully pressed the pad of his thumb into her clit, rubbing it in slow circles that matched his methodical thrusts.

Sensation burst to a new level of intensity as he played her body. She moaned into his mouth, tightening her legs around his waist so hard her thighs ached. His thumb began to circle faster and his thrusts matched it, and Nora felt herself tightening inside from what felt like her toes to the roots of her hair.

She coiled and folded in upon herself and he plunged in and out of her until she simply didn't exist anymore, her climax sweeping through her body like wildfire and leaving nothing but overwhelmed nerve-endings in its wake.

Maxwell pushed into her a handful more times before finding his own climax, gently collapsing on top of her afterward, both of them struggling for breath, a pressed mass of sweat-slick skin, and heavy breathing.

"Thank you, Gorgeous."

Nora managed to mumble something she was sure didn't make any sense. Maxwell didn't seem to mind.

He stroked her hair for a moment and then rolled away, disappearing to clean up and returning with a warm wet cloth which he reverently used on her.

"I told myself I wouldn't ask if it didn't seem like you wanted to," he started, pulling her up toward the pillows and covering them both to the waist with the blankets. He was just holding her against him again, both of them reclined against the mountain of fluff piled in front of the tufted headboard. "But I feel like we've long passed that landmark here. Would you consider staying over tonight?"

Nora found herself smiling.

"What makes you think I want to stay? Perhaps I've gotten what I came for and I'm done with you now."

Maxwell chuckled and sucked at the flesh of her shoulder. She liked the easy way they were with one another. She liked this beachy bubble and wanted to stay in it as long as she could.

"Nothing in particular," He teased as he ran his fingertips along her arm. "but I suspect you're not like that any more than I am. In fact, I'd wager you're wondering how we ended up here after so few proper dates, just like I am. For the record, I was planning to offer you the guest room. But as things have…escalated…"

Nora could feel her eyebrow lift and he gave a short grunt in acknowledgment of her confirmation.

"I've wanted to see more of you ever since Rufus tackled you during the wedding reception," Maxwell sighed, her skin prickling gooseflesh where his touch trailed. "Lucky for me, Devon was quite quick to latch onto the idea of a group dinner."

Nora felt the smile broaden on her lips. Feeling vindicated in her assumptions about those arrangements, her body relaxed even further.

"I'd love to stay," she replied, falling into his warm embrace, reveling in the happy sensations, appreciating the afterglow.

There was quiet for a bit as they just existed, and Nora could see the sun beginning to drop in the sky from the shadows against the wall. Maxwell's fingertips roamed her skin, and she touched back. He breathed her in and she bent her head back to ensure that he sipped from her lips as well.

When her stomach finally rumbled out, he chuckled and moved to get out of the bed.

"Stay," she said quietly.

"Just going to get reinforcements."

Nora used his bathroom while he was gone, appreciating the dewy, flushed appearance of her skin in the mirror over his sink.

She had just climbed back into the crisp white sheets when he came back, regrettably dressed in a plain white t-shirt and some shorts.

He didn't say anything, just inclined his head toward the patio. His hands were full of what looked like a full cheese board and another bottle of wine.

Her dress was still on the floor of the patio, so she strode out in her birthday suit to retrieve it.

"Playing with fire there, but I'm not complaining," Maxwell smirked at her after she'd pulled it over her head.

The sun was rapidly dropping, and he set the offering on the table in front of the couch they'd defiled, offering Rufus his own treat as a bribe to leave theirs alone. There was a glass-rock firepit in the center of the patio, and he lit that as well, the evening breeze off the water downright frigid.

She plunked herself down next to him and joined in selecting some of the finger foods. Fresh glasses of wine were poured, and they were quiet as they made their way through cheese, cold cuts, crackers, even olives, and apples.

"Where'd you come up with this on such short notice?"

Maxwell made a thoughtful noise in his throat. "Mom is prepared for just about anything. All I had to do was put things on a plate."

Nora smiled. "She seems nice."

That word again. Devon would be traumatized.

Maxwell smiled at her, and it was radiant. "They're both fantastic. Terrifically and disgustingly in love, all these years later too. Always have been. I'm very lucky that way."

Nora nodded. She jostled him gently with her elbow a moment later.

"You did manage to get me my sunset and wine after all."

"I told you I'd deliver." He feigned shock. "You wound me. You had doubts?"

She shook her head.

"No. Not for a minute."

This pleased him, she could see, and he turned a full-volume smile her way before planting a resolute kiss on her lips.

"What happens now?" she asked, to her own mortification. It seemed she was only in control of her brain or mouth part of the time.

"Well, that depends," Maxwell responded saucily, waggling his eyebrows, not at all bothered by the question and choosing to treat it like a challenge.

"That's not what I mean." She laughed, taking a drink of her wine.

"Well, that's a bit disappointing, but we can come back to it. What do you want to happen now, Elle? Is it alright that I call you that? I rather think it suits you perfectly."

Nora stared into his handsome face, itching to trace it with her fingertips. She settled for pressing her palm to his cheek. He held it there with his own hand, moving it a bit so he could kiss her palm, then her knuckles.

"I like it." She smiled. "I like *you*, Maxwell. More than I should. It scares me."

That playful, sinfully handsome grin grew beatific.

"I like you too, Elle. More than I probably should, but I'm not scared at all. I don't think you should be either, because I'm of the mind that if it feels right, it probably is. What are you scared of?"

Nora's gut began to shift uncomfortably.

"My life is complicated." It sounded lame even as she said it.

"So is mine. We'll figure it out."

He watched her closely for a moment, his gaze so intense she could feel it in her spine. Her thoughts could not provide a single, reasonable argument to put forth. Not one. And she had a feeling that even if they had, the lawyer in him would find a very logical response.

Finally, she nodded. "Okay."

He raised an eyebrow. "Okay? That's it? No more debate or resistance?"

"No. You're trained to out-argue me any day of the week. So, okay. Let's like each other."

Maxwell chuckled.

"Music to my ears, Gorgeous, and you're right, though I imagine that at some point down the line I'll have to concede an argument or two. We'll cross that bridge when we get there."

They sat there for hours, eventually depleting the wine and the cheese board and dragging out a couple of fleece blankets from one of the ottomans that served as storage. Even Rufus gave up on them and went inside to find his bed.

The stars came out and twinkled above them, the pair chatting a bit but mostly just absorbing one another's presence in the quiet.

Nora was mostly unconscious, cuddled up against Maxwell under the blankets. His voice rumbled under her chest.

"Elle."

"Mmm?"

"Let's go to bed."

She grunted something in agreement and stumbled inside, grabbing her bag and brushing her teeth in his sink before stripping down and taking out her now very messy braid. Climbing between the crisp white sheets made her sigh. The weight of the blankets was a very welcome embrace.

Maxwell left to close up the house. Through the door, she could see him putting out the flames of the fire pit and gathering up their dishes before he disappeared downstairs to check the locks. He went through his own routine in the bathroom before finally joining her in the bed, pulling her close.

They fell asleep spooned together like they'd done it a hundred times before.

Nora didn't miss her solitary yoga routine even one little bit.

Chapter Thirteen

NORA KNEW THE weekend in Malibu had to end at some point—after all her day trip had turned into an overnight—but she tried to hold onto the magic as long as she could.

At some point in the night, she was awoken by his tender touches and he sank into her body from behind in the dark, making love to her slowly and gently as the scant silver moonlight shone in through the windows and the crashing of the waves set the pace for his languorous thrusts.

Just as the sun was coming up, she felt a kiss on her shoulder, and then his weight leave the bed. The shower ran for a few minutes and Maxwell reappeared clean, dressed, and grinning.

"I'm going to go hunt down some coffee. Use whatever you need."

Nora's grunt in return made him laugh. He sat down beside her on the bed, sweetly brushing some strands of hair away from her face.

"What time is it?"

He consulted the large Rolex on his wrist. "Just past six."

"It's *Sunday*," she complained, squeezing her eyes shut.

His deep chuckle rolled over her skin and she felt his lips press to her forehead.

"Not an early bird, I see. I'll be back in a few—just going to forage for some coffee and breakfast."

Nora made a noise that he took as agreement and the dip in the bed straightened out. His scent left the room with him.

Try as she might, she couldn't go back to sleep again. She pulled her body out of the warm bed and trudged to the guest room next door, taking a very hot, very long, and very luxurious shower to wake herself up. She was just finished pulling on her very last change of clothing—a simple tank and shorts—when Maxwell appeared in the doorway, a cup in his hand.

"Damn, just a bit too slow," he teased.

She gratefully took the paper cup he offered and followed him downstairs, bag in tow.

"Are there plans for today?"

Maxwell's face fell.

"Unfortunately, I have to get back to the city before lunch."

Nora's gut twisted. "Oh."

He turned, a horrified look on his face. He was suddenly gathering her into his arms. "That definitely felt like a brush off. It's not. This was not a hit and run, Elle. I swear. I got a call from an investor—they had a last-minute opening this afternoon and I'd really like to get their money."

She relaxed into his embrace, willing herself to believe the truth of his words. He'd been honest with her so far, there was no reason to think he'd start lying.

She chose to believe him.

On the small table in the kitchen, there was an assortment of muffins and some baked egg cups that were very popular with the low-carb crowd.

Nora could feel Maxwell's eyes follow her hand as she chose, and she realized she was being tested.

"Oh no," he sighed, a miserable expression on his face as he took in her choices.

She'd picked an egg cup with vegetables and sausage with a side of massive blueberry muffin.

"What's wrong?"

"You chose the egg thing with *sausage* in it. And the muffin with fruit instead of chocolate chips." He sat down in one of the chairs, taking two of the egg cups with bacon for himself. "We may be doomed before we truly begin after all."

Nora felt the laugh beginning to rise, but it was more a nervous one, not one borne of humor. Surely he wasn't serious?

"I can't live on buttery pastries filled with chocolate alone." She smiled carefully at him, taking her seat and sipping at her coffee. "Was this some kind of weird psychological compatibility test? Did I fail?"

The smile returned to Maxwell's lips.

"I did also feed you fried fish and cheese," he joked. She watched the play of his muscles as he leaned forward onto his forearms atop the table. "That depends. Tell me why you picked what you did."

Nora looked at him thoughtfully. Even ridiculously early he was playful and gorgeous.

"Well, for starters, I prefer bacon but if I'm going to eat it, it has to be crispy. Soggy, undercooked, gristly bacon fat makes me gag. There's no way to get it or keep it crispy when you cook it in the oven inside scrambled eggs, I don't care who you are." His grin turned positively radiant as she made a face, feeling the squishy texture of undercooked bacon in her mouth just by speaking of it. "And this blueberry muffin has what looks like brown sugar and butter streusel on it. You never refuse streusel. Never." She took a huge bite of her muffin to punctuate her argument.

Maxwell laughed, that sound quickly becoming one of her favorite things in the world. She was also developing an interesting Pavlovian tingling response to it in her private parts.

"Well. Turns out you passed with flying colors, Elle. We're going to get along just fine after all. The Caine household is and has always been team crispy bacon." He cocked his head a bit and looked at her with eyes squinted. "Where do you fall when it comes to Twizzlers versus Red Vines?"

SHE HAD TURNED on her phone for the first time since Saturday morning while in the car on the way back to Los Angeles. There were a total of 17 text messages and she instantly regretted ever looking. Regret, both because she didn't want to deal with her real-life just yet, and because looking at her phone while in the canyon was apparently a sure-fire recipe for her to get a bit carsick.

Nine messages were from her mother. *Nine.* After a brief hesitation, she wrote back a simple sentence stating she would send the five thousand, but that it would be the very last time she did so. No reasons or excuses, just that she couldn't anymore. Sending the message left Nora feeling simultaneously guilty, free and terrified. Before she could change her mind, she logged into her banking app, requested the transfer to her mother's email address and logged right back out. Devon would certainly be giving her a lecture when he found out—and it was a when, not an if with that guy—but she'd deal with it. She was done with her mother's extortion and guilt tactics. If it took one last lump sum to get there, so be it.

Four were from unknown numbers, all innocuous enough and complimentary but it seemed like she was getting progressively more of them. She was strongly beginning to consider a new number. Maybe Maxwell knew of some tech to help keep her private number truly private. His app sounded like a better and better idea all the time.

Two more messages were Devon being Devon and asking inane and invasive personal questions he knew she wouldn't answer about her date, and one was Stephanie, apologizing and advising that Devon had lost his phone privileges. Again.

Those left her smiling, and her face fell hard when she opened the last one.

That last message had sent pure ice rushing through her veins and her body started alternating between cold and hot instantly.

> **Private**: *You're playing with fire. You know you shouldn't be with him—how's he going to feel when I send this film to the press? I've even got a few new pictures that might surprise you. Clearly, I'm not charging quite enough for you to make reasonable decisions where your reputation is concerned. America's Sweetheart getting railed in every possible position on camera is sure to be very click-worthy.*

Maxwell heard her gasp and turned his attention to her. "Everything alright?"

Nora looked at his worried expression and felt something inside her soften. She was not one to turn instantly to a man for comfort or protection, but she was feeling that kind of draw to Maxwell. It was foreign and every bit as annoying as it was interesting.

This man had effectively gotten completely under her skin in the span of days. His genuine concern made her feel cared for and she wasn't quite sure what to do with that.

"No." She released a heavy breath. Admittance was the first step, right? No reason to sugar coat things or tell a lie, even if it was her knee-jerk reaction to say 'everything's fine'. Everything was not *fine*. "I have a bit of a … stalker-ish problem with a guy I dated when I first moved to Los Angeles. He resurfaced once the show got popular, and then last year, around the time Devon and I went ring shopping so he could propose to Stephanie, things got way uglier." Maxwell nodded, inviting her to continue. Everything in her defense mechanisms told her to clam up, and she fought to get the words out, even if they weren't the whole picture. "He was also an aspiring director. I think he's angry that I made it bigger than he did. He texts me now and then. Ugly things. There are … pictures. Of us."

"Oh. Is he threatening you with them? That's a dick move, but also illegal."

Nora considered that all a massive understatement, but appreciated his lack of horror at the revelation.

"It's been mostly quiet since I got a new number and the media figured out that I wasn't actually with Devon." She met his eyes as he looked away from the road to give her his attention. "I just got another message and, yes, he's threatening me again. It's nothing new, but he's escalating."

She included information about how many random texts she was getting and how they were mostly complimentary but some knew things that they shouldn't unless she was being followed. It felt right to also tell him that she felt like the same handful of photogs were always following her around and she was beginning to think one of them was somehow in league with her ex.

Maxwell's face contorted into something like rage, and it was so opposite from his normal, easy-going expression that Nora had to resist shrinking down in the leather seat. Angry Maxwell was formidable and terrifying.

And also beautiful, if she was being honest.

"Have you reported him? What do we need to do?" he asked, and just the fact that he *asked* instead of taking immediate control warmed her insides. He was white-knuckling the steering wheel to be sure, but he wasn't bulldozing over her trying to take care of the problem by himself.

Also, he'd said *we*.

"I have to find the card for the police officer that was helping me before. I'll give him a call after you drop me off."

Maxwell nodded tightly and the rest of the drive passed by in a tense blur. Nora wished repeatedly as they came ever closer to the city that she had waited until she'd gotten home to turn her phone on.

She wanted the peaceful, comfortable quiet back.

She wanted to go back to the playful bubble they'd built in Malibu.

MAXWELL CAREFULLY GUIDED her into her apartment once they got back, blocking her body with as much of his as he could, looking around suspiciously to see if they had any attention or followers. She didn't see anyone unusual, but that didn't mean anything. At this point, she was suspicious of anyone and everyone, including Mrs. Gravitz down the hall.

He waited while she dug around in her desk drawer for the card, and casually listened in while she called.

Detective Rutherford praised her for calling in so quickly and suggested a basic list of increasing her personal security on top of telling her not to delete any of the messages. He also advised that he could meet her at the station later that afternoon to start the ball rolling on re-opening the investigation and she readily agreed she'd be there.

Maxwell sighed, consulting his watch. "I'm so sorry to leave you right now. I really don't want to. But...I need to make this meeting."

Nora smiled at him. "I understand. It's okay, there's no immediate danger. It's mostly extortion, honestly. He's not violent. I'll go see the detective and get a game plan from there."

Maxwell's gaze landed on the bouquet again. He reached out for the card. It should have felt like he was invading her privacy, but since they were from him it was just kind of sweet.

"I'm not usually the jealous type, and it's really none of my business. But who will you be seeing soon, Elle?"

Nora's body went cold, but she pushed through the panic and arrived at a joking tone. She needed Maxwell to be pretending that he'd forgotten. Otherwise, things were much worse than she'd dared to think.

"That's the bouquet *you* sent me, Handsome. It was outside my door Friday evening."

Maxwell's brow furrowed, eyes darkening. That was not the expression that Nora wanted to see. Not even a little bit.

"Gorgeous, I definitely should have, and I absolutely will in the future, but I didn't send you those flowers." His voice was low and quiet and had an edge of both fear and danger to it.

Her fingers were shaking as she reached out for the card. She took it from him, thankful that there was a florist's address on it. She'd take it to the detective, see if they could trace back who'd bought them.

David had never before threatened or even bothered her where she lived. The fact that he even knew her address was cause enough for her to feel like vomiting.

The urgency to get to the police station and change

her address or at the very least her locks hit her with the force of a Mack truck at highway speed.

Maxwell hung around a moment more, holding her as she tempered her panic, then kissed her thoroughly as he stood on the other side of her threshold.

"Message me, please. Let me know what's going on. I'm hoping to be done by the time you're finished at the police station."

"I will."

"Sure you don't want to call Devon or Steph to take you? Go with you at least?"

Her head shook. "I think I'll be okay. If I start to feel worried I'll call them, I promise."

He hesitated but left, regret straining his features.

"Go. Really. Nail down this investor." She made her lips form a reassuring smile as she pushed him out the door.

Maxwell didn't seem to buy her confidence, but nodded and turned to leave, anyway. His indecision was palpable on the air that once again was redolent of vinegar and salt.

Nora stood watching for long seconds after Maxwell's back disappeared from view. She finally closed and locked her door as solidly as she could—the flimsy piece of wood between her and someone who was clearly ready to sabotage her whole life and who also knew where she lived felt pretty useless all told—and immediately dialed her landlord.

Since it was Sunday, she hadn't expected an answer, but she had been hoping for that miracle. The message she left was brief and to the point and she hoped he had his phone on for emergencies. And that he counted what she was dealing with as urgent. Who knew with him, nothing short of the complex flooding or burning down had raised much concern thus far.

The kiss she had shared with a worried Maxwell at her door hadn't been nearly satisfying enough, but it had held a heavy weight that spoke of true concern and attachment. The promise of regular check-ins and assurance of, at the very least, a date at some point in the week left her feeling needy. Having to arrange meetings with security teams, deal with her landlord about changing locks and maybe even moving units and the inevitability of changing her phone number again had her feeling itchy. Nora desperately wanted to go back to Saturday evening in Malibu, but she didn't have a time machine.

Their magic weekend bubble had been effectively, though regrettably, burst.

NORA EXISTED IN a state of suspended reality for the next few weeks. The time passed in a strange vortex of too fast and then too slow as she waited for another message from David or the photos to pop up on TV and the internet.

Everything was a mess and her body was a giant ball of tension. Every time her phone buzzed, she tensed, expecting more threats, more danger, a Google alert that she was trending for what amounted to a sex tape she hadn't explicitly agreed to film—at least not for public consumption—and had paid out tens of thousands of dollars to keep under wraps.

Thanks to Maxwell and Detective Rutherford, her phone was monitored and every unknown number text was traced. They had decided to delay changing her number, hoping to get a hit on David's actual location before they did so.

That didn't make her any less twitchy when her phone buzzed, no matter who was on the other end of the message.

Her mother never did respond, but she saw the money had been accepted the same day it was sent. It irritated her deeply that Athena couldn't be bothered to send so much as a thank you, but maybe total silence was better. Maybe that was the best possible way to confirm total severing of communication.

She'd never be the person her mother wanted her to be, and she'd never move back to Alabama either.

Her landlord hadn't been able to offer much of a solution but did agree to allow her to put on new locks as long as she was the one who paid for and installed them.

Between Maxwell and Devon and a hilarious trip to the hardware store, she ended up with a new handle, deadbolt, and chain that would have been better suited to the house in Malibu than her crappy apartment. Admittedly, she did feel a little safer with the shiny new hardware and that day had been great for her overall mood.

The pair of less than handy men debating between them the possibilities of added features, number of keys, metal strength, and then taking a whole afternoon to install it all had been nothing short of amusing.

Nora had literally made popcorn so she and Stephanie could sit on the couch and watch the show. Hands down the best afternoon entertainment she'd had in quite some time.

Maxwell staying over after the Greene's had departed for the evening also didn't hurt one bit. She much preferred to try out the chaise at the house Malibu, but her sofa had functioned just fine for their needs.

He never once pushed for more information about what was actually going on, nor her past and her guilt gnawed at her for not being open with him.

Nora could feel herself slipping down the *like* slope, and was struggling with that too. Being in a stable, comfortable relationship with Maxwell was equal parts terrifying and delightfully fulfilling. There was something about being near him that spoke to her soul in a way that she felt she couldn't ignore, but until they got the David situation handled, they were having to be secretive and mostly avoid seeing one another and she hated that. It wasn't fair to him.

The gossip shows had gotten word somehow that she was getting threatening texts and that somehow translated to more attention on her from the paparazzi instead of them respecting her privacy. She couldn't go anywhere outside her apartment without a crowd of cameras in her face. She had taken to looking at the photographers closely, and noticed that the same two or three guys were always there. She could pick them out of any lineup if need be, and she mentioned as much to the police.

Even though no physical violence had been threatened, Alan had been called in as her bodyguard, and while she had been completely terrified of him at their first meeting, she quickly learned that he was a large man with a big heart. She felt nothing but safe when he was around, and he readily agreed to a full-time post.

Alan met her every morning at her door, drove her to work in his giant black SUV, lingered in the background on set (where he had no shortage of friends himself, she learned very quickly), and then drove her back home at the end of the day. It was exhausting, and somehow really isolating when it should have been anything but.

Her routine should have helped her sanity, but instead, she wanted to scream every time she got home to her quiet apartment and had to breathe in vinegar while going through her yoga poses. They weren't relaxing, anyway.

She needed Maxwell, but she wasn't brave enough to ask and he was being respectful and giving her space while they both tried to lay low until things were sorted out.

July gave way to August and the heat was nothing less than totally oppressive. She was never so happy as to be working inside a giant concrete box that was generally far too chilly.

Nora was miserable. Things were shifting, and everything felt like it was outside of her control. It was driving her mad.

TO CELEBRATE THE final shoot of the season, there was a wrap party at Avalon. Normally not one to go out to a club, Nora decided to go for a change. She needed a chance to be out, in public, and let off some steam.

Alan drove Nora to Avalon, and she loosely mingled with her co-stars, chatting mostly with Devon and Stephanie near the bar. She was a couple of cocktails in, finally feeling some tension release from muscles even her habitual yoga couldn't manage to loosen when she got a prickly sensation like she was being watched.

Scanning the crowd nervously, she realized that her friends had left her to hit the dance-floor together and it was too loud to signal Alan, though he had her in his line of sight. Oddly, he winked at her just as she felt a warm hand on her hip and mouth at her ear.

"You look stunning tonight Elle. Has anyone told you that yet?"

Nora's muscles loosened as she absorbed Maxwell's warm presence behind her. She turned, wrapping her arms around his neck. He was missing his regular polo, but she could really get behind the black button-up he'd selected. It made him look even more dashing than usual and somehow dangerous. Based on the number of eyes not even trying to be casual checking him out, she wasn't the only one who thought that.

"You'd be the first, actually." She smiled at him and he pulled her tight to his body, fingertips gently brushing the top of her ass. There was no way to suppress the shiver his touch elicited.

"That's a shame." He lowered his head to hers, devouring her mouth with his own. She could swear she heard Alan clearing his throat at the other end of the bar. "You invested here? Or could I convince you to run away with me?"

Devon chose just that moment to pop up like an annoying big brother.

"Hey, guys. Enjoying the party?"

Nora hissed at him. "Go away."

He threw his head back in a broad laugh, and she could see Stephanie shaking her head behind him. Stephanie winked, and Nora wasn't sure if it was meant to encourage her or Maxwell, but it didn't really matter.

The music was too loud for much conversation, but Maxwell molded his body to hers and took her onto the dance-floor. Everything but them disappeared when they were this close in proximity. She danced, allowing the music to flow through her, feeling every shift of his muscles around her as she swayed to the heavy, throbbing beat of the music. Her pulse matched it, and by the time Maxwell pulled her into the dark hallway that led to the bathrooms she was sweaty and desperate for his touch.

He seemed to be struggling similarly, both of them breathing heavily as they made out in the corridor like horny, love-starved teenagers. Maxwell's hands were everywhere at once and yet nowhere she needed them most. Trying to remember that they were in a public place with plenty of onlookers was becoming increasingly difficult. Maxwell shifted them so that she had her back to the wall and he was caging her in, mostly blocking anyone from seeing who she was. Her blonde hair might give her away, but she was beginning not to care.

That seemed to be a dangerous side effect of being near Maxwell.

His knee pressed between her thighs and she moaned into his mouth, putting everything she had into their kiss as she ground herself into his leg, needing some kind of relief from the intense sensations rioting through her body.

"I want it," he grumbled, nipping down the column of her neck, hands guiding her hips through rocking motions and pressing down slightly on her body so it got more pressure, more contact with his muscular thigh. "Give it to me, Elle."

The dirty talk coming out of Maxwell's mouth was the last spark she needed. As the two of them moved together in the hallway all thought disappeared. Her body was pure sensation, thrumming to the beat of bass in the club. She could feel herself climbing, and he must have as well because he plastered his mouth to hers, thrusting with his tongue in a pattern she knew his body could match.

That was all it took. Climax took her as he made love through his kiss and he groaned into her mouth at the same time she offered her moan to his.

"Can I take you home, Elle?"

"Yes," she whispered, realizing that they were still in the club hallway, foot traffic for the bathrooms passing them at regular intervals.

After some quick discussion with Alan and seeing Devon wink at her with that damned smirk in place, Maxwell hustled her out the back door of the club and into his car. She thought they were mostly unnoticed, but there would likely be a couple of photos popping up over the next few days. Flashbulbs were inevitable anytime you snuck out the back door of a club known to be a locale for celebrity parties.

"Hey. Don't worry," Maxwell said, noticing her tension.

"I'm not worried." She smiled at him, trying to make herself believe it.

Instead of her place, Maxwell took her to his condo.

It was very luxurious—a lot like Devon and Stephanie's place actually—but somehow also very bare and without personality. For someone like Maxwell, who oozed large, enthusiastic personality it was a surprise. She didn't have a chance to comment on the lack of energy in his home, however, because the second the door was closed Maxwell had her pinned against it and was rapidly shedding clothing.

Seeing his need for her spiked the lust in her own body, and she gave wordless permission for him to take what he needed from her as she lifted her mini-dress above her hips.

Maxwell all but growled, pushing her panties off her body and sheathing himself inside her in what seemed like one motion. Nora cried out, and her body clamped down on the intrusion, making him groan as he began to move. She wrapped her legs tightly around his waist, and just rode the wave as he took his pleasure of her against the door.

"You with me Elle?" he asked as she felt the peak of her arousal within reach.

"Yes. Don't stop."

Maxwell increased his speed and she saw white light behind her lids as her orgasm consumed her.

Before she could come down even a bit, he marched them into his bedroom and started the whole climb again, licking and sucking and teasing her flesh into nothing more than a trembling pile of nerves and need.

Nora fell asleep sometime later, boneless in her satisfaction, and worried about nothing for the first time in weeks.

SHE SHOULD HAVE been prepared for the fall after the high, but she was too wrapped up in how good she felt, how happy she was and how quiet things had been to even consider that there was anything else that could fall apart.

The universe took the first opportunity to slap her it could get, and that came in three parts.

First, TMZ somehow had footage—not just photos, but *video*—both of Nora and Maxwell in the hallway of the club and then leaving from the back door and of them departing from Maxwell's condo together the following morning.

Nora's rage and shame knew no limits as she scrolled through her news-feed Sunday morning.

Images of her grinding on his leg in a dark hallway, them kissing, them hand-in-hand leaving the club, and then his condo were everywhere. Speculation ran wild and there was nowhere she could go online where they were not on the front page.

Secondly, she got a barrage of texts from the Private number she now knew belonged to David, the content ranging from anger to threats. She was disgusted with her reaction to what was happening and propelled violently down a shame spiral as she scanned the messages.

> ***Private****: You're nothing but a stupid slut. Everyone will know just how much soon since you clearly can't seem to behave in public.*
>
> ***Private****: Who will want to hire a common whore dressed as the pure and clean Nora Chase? Nobody. Your bullshit wholesome, perfect image won't survive this.*
>
> ***Private****: Why would he want you after he sees how well used you are? When he finds out the trash you come from? When any time you're together his picture might end up splashed all over? Think he wants every time you get naked together to be public knowledge? You're disgusting.*
>
> ***Private****: Does he like screwing my sloppy seconds?*

Private: *I'm the only one who will want you after this and I've already had you.*

That's what it came down to, she realized, heat infusing even the tips of her ears in rage and embarrassment. He wanted her to feel isolated and unwanted. He wanted her attention, and this was the best possible way to get it.

Her blood ran cold when he sent her a photo of Maxwell's front door. Hers. Devon's. He even had a picture from that weekend in Malibu of them sitting outside the seafood shack. And one of them on the patio. She was obviously naked, and Maxwell's ass was on full display.

Nobody she cared about here was safe. It was all her fault too; she knew the danger of being seen in public with Maxwell. She knew that was David's hot button and still, she had prioritized her lust over Maxwell's safety. Over the safety of everyone she cared about.

She could feel the mental breakdown encroaching as she screen-shot the messages and sent them all on to the detective.

Thirdly, her mother decided to chime in, calling her all the same names she'd slung at Phae, plus a few new, interesting ones. Naturally, the messages concluded with an allusion to the fact that if she'd never left home and had just settled into a life that matched Athena's, everything would be peachy.

All of this put together and Nora's brain completely imploded. Fight or flight instinct took over and she'd been fighting so long, the only thing left to do was fly.

Before she could think twice about it, she had booked a ticket that would get her to Auburn and packed a bag. The only way to keep everyone safe here was to not be here. There was no job to go to, no reason for her to hang around right now. The idea of leaving without telling Maxwell made her want to vomit, but it was the only way to keep him safe. Right? He'd find out from Devon eventually, anyway.

But leaving him with no word at all didn't feel right. Not at all. They were closer than that. Weren't they? She felt like they were. Her stomach threatening to revolt at the thought definitely made her think twice. Her anxiety was not being overly rational about anything and thankfully she was with it enough to recognize that; telling herself she'd find a reasonable, logical solution before she left.

Nora located a box of temporary hair color under the bathroom sink and applied it, taking the time it needed to set to pack her suitcase and stash everything she most valued in a backpack. She decided to get a new phone once she got to Alabama. This one could be kept safe in Detective Rutherford's hands in the meantime. After she had emailed herself all of her important contacts and photos and scribbled out a note for Devon, it was time to rinse out the color.

The brunette version of her that appeared in the mirror following her shower was like looking at a photograph of her mother. She was not the biggest fan of that, but beggars looking for a disguise to get the hell out of town couldn't be choosers.

Once she was dressed in layers that could easily be removed and felt like she had everything he needed, Nora texted Alan and asked if he could pick her up.

Blind copying in Detective Rutherford so that there was a record and a better chance at a trace, she carefully scripted a text message to the Private number David was hiding behind.

> **N**: *You went too far. I'm your target, not them. This has to stop, now.*

To her surprise, he responded almost immediately.

> **Private**: *You know how to make it stop.*
> **N**: *I don't have that kind of money, and you know it.*
> **Private**: *How or where you get my million dollars isn't relevant to me. The scraps you've been sending so far are pitiful. A million, or I send everything to the media. And what then? What will pristine Nora Chase do once she falls from grace?*

Rage and bile rose and Nora's fingers shook as she sent what would be her final message to her extortionist. She realized at that moment that no matter the consequences for her image, her career, her relationships, she couldn't continue like this.

> **N:** *Do what you think is necessary. I don't have any more money. I'm done.*

After hitting send, she sat on the edge of the bed for what felt like the longest minutes of her life. Heart pounding in her chest, breath loud in her ears, head spinning. She'd done it. Whether or not it was the right choice or just poking the bear would be revealed over the next few days she guessed.

Before she could lose her adrenaline rush, she pressed on, preparing a message for Maxwell. She used a handy app she knew he'd appreciate to schedule the message to deliver after her flight had taken off. She tried to keep it simple without giving anything away.

> **N:** *I have to get out of town for a bit. I'm okay. I'll be safe where I'm going. I'll find a way to get in touch when I get there. I'm sorry.*

It wasn't goodbye, but it was something like it, or at least it felt that way. She could only hope that Maxwell and her friends would understand. She was doing this for them as much as herself.

While she waited for Alan, she cared for her plants, offhandedly swiping at the tears that wouldn't stop slowly tracking down her cheeks. Making sure her babies were well watered and ready for her to be gone a was a good distraction from the extreme mess her whole life had become.

She couldn't protect her good-girl image any longer perhaps, but she could protect her friends from the invasive mess that was her stalker ex.

Twenty minutes later, Alan knocked on the door. He raised an eyebrow at her appearance but said nothing as she stuffed her hair into a baseball cap and put on the largest sunglasses she could find. He carried her bags to the SUV and she climbed into the back seat, slipping out of the outer layer of clothing and stuffing them in her bag once they were out of view of the photogs that liked to linger in her apartment parking lot.

She tucked the cap into the large purse she'd brought and let out a sigh.

"You alright?" Alan asked, meeting her eyes in the rear-view.

She shook her head. "No. I'm so sorry to put this on you, Alan. Can you take me to LAX? I'm going to skip town for a while. Things are…bad."

He only broke eye contact long enough to keep them on the road safely but he nodded.

"Want to talk about it?"

She shook her head, not trusting that her voice wouldn't crack if she tried to get it out.

"Could you please take this backpack to Devon? My keys are in the front pocket. I can't take this stuff with me but I don't want to leave it in my apartment."

"I will. But I feel quite compelled to try and convince you to let me come with you."

Nora couldn't help but smile softly at his words.

"Sorry, but no. I understand why you feel that way, but it has to be this way." She pleaded with her eyes, and he let out a heavy breath but didn't argue with her. "I'm not in physical danger."

"I know you think it has to be this way, but I'm betting it doesn't. Not really." He turned the full, heavy weight of his gaze on her. "You know this is going to completely freak out your friends, right? What about lover-boy? Give me something to make me feel better about putting you on a plane by yourself. Anything."

Nora sighed, looking at the phone in her hands. She zipped it into the front pocket of the backpack where her house keys and the note to Devon were waiting.

"I'm removing myself to keep them safe."

Alan grunted.

"You know that's not really how it works right? You disappear, things may escalate."

"I'm trusting *you* then, to make sure they're all safe and taken care of. Call in your friends, your co-workers—

whatever that means. Get everyone covered if you think it will help. I'm leaving my phone in here—" she tossed the pack into the passenger seat. "—with instructions for Devon to get it to the police. They can monitor my messages. Maybe that will help them find him faster."

Alan attempted a few more arguments and finally agreed to tell him where she was headed and that she'd message them all from her new number as soon as she could.

"I'll hit the first phone store I can that isn't in the airport," she swore. "Tell them I'm sorry, okay? I promise to let them know I'm alright when I can."

Alan pulled the SUV up at the passenger drop off area for her airline. Tension made his features extremely angular. "I'll do what you ask, but I'm still going to worry about you little one."

Gratitude flowed through her warmly. "I appreciate that Alan. You've been so kind to me."

He took a moment to scan the area for paparazzi before opening the back and retrieving her bag. He leaned down and gave her a tight hug.

"Be safe."

"I'll do my best."

After a short nod, he folded his arms over his chest, watching the area as she scurried into the airport, praying she wouldn't be noticed. He didn't leave until she waved from the other side of the glass, and even then he took his time about it. The worry on his face started to seep into her veins but she turned away and headed deeper into the airport as quickly as she could manage to avoid allowing regret or doubt to take root. There was plenty of time for that once her plane was thirty thousand feet above the ground with no way for her to change her mind or escape.

CHAPTER
Fifteen

THE HUMIDITY SLAPPED Nora in the face the moment she exited the plane and stepped into the jet-way. The climate control of the plane itself and the airport could keep the oppressive blanket that was the wet, hot air at bay, but the thin paneling of the movable hallway was no match for it.

Her half-hearted disguise of temporarily colored hair frizzed and curled instantly with the moisture. Thankfully, the brunette hair and large sunglasses had already worked way better than anticipated. There had been very few paparazzi hanging around the airport in Los Angeles, none of them looking for a brunette Nora Chase. She had sprung for business class which maybe had been a less than wise move, but nobody seemed to be looking for Eleanora Chatzi in Atlanta.

From Atlanta, she'd switch to a smaller plane and fly to Columbus, and from there she'd be able to rent a car to get to Auburn.

It wasn't until she was wheels down and had the keys to a non-descript black Nissan Altima in her hand that she allowed herself to breathe easily.

The relief she felt when she finally let go was immense. The guilt was as well.

She had about an hour on the road to get to Auburn and decided that it was best if she went ahead and bought a phone. She needed GPS to locate Phae's house at the very least, and getting one now meant she could message Alan and let him know she was safe. Not far from the airport there was a shopping strip boasting a phone store, salon, and a variety of restaurants, so Nora steered her rental into the parking lot and braced herself for the harrowing experience that was buying a new phone.

The sales guy who was on deck for her seemed nice enough and was way more interested in flirting with her than paying any attention to the information he was putting in for her account. Instead of linking to her old one, Nora started brand new so that people like David and her mother and even well-meaning fans couldn't find her new number. Everything went in under Eleanora Chatzi, and she decided she'd put the billing down as Phae's address to further complicate the trail. She'd maybe get a post office box near Phae and change it to that just in case. Her new number would be an Alabama one, with a different area code than her mom had. It felt like the best idea she'd had in a while.

When she was all paid for and had her new tech in hand, she hit the salon. The bored stylist was no Janice—and she'd have one hell of a lot of explaining to do when she got home—but she gave Nora a cute bob without once pausing in her monologue about how expensive everything was getting and how she'd have started saving when she was younger if she'd known then what she knew now.

After paying her and leaving a reasonable tip, Nora took a chance on the small deli a few doors down.

Body fueled, haircut, and phone activated, she directed her rental car toward her sister's address.

The sedan ate up the miles, and she desperately hoped she wasn't wrong in assuming she could show up unannounced.

It took about three tries and a number of curse words at her GPS, but she finally found the large two-story house near campus. It was spectacular as far as a rental went, looking like every suburban fantasy come true in red brick with black shutters flanking all the windows.

Nora parked on the street in front of the house, exiting the car with a deep breath of heavy, wet air.

It was Sunday afternoon, and the house seemed really quiet for being somewhere that boasted six full-time residents. She knocked on the door and waited. After a few minutes, she rang the bell. A few minutes more and she was beginning to feel nervous and foolish.

She stood on the porch and sent a text to her sister, praying that she was at the very least nearby or could meet her somewhere.

N: *You home rn?*

She hesitated, then realized Phae wouldn't have this number and that was a totally creepy question from a number you didn't recognize.

N: *This is your sister, btw.*

The dots just sat there for a moment and then thankfully began to dance.

P: *Prove it. What's your middle name?*
N: *Really? Anyone with Google can find that information.*
P: *Fine. What was Yiayia Lou's favorite flower?*
N: *Still too easy, Phae. Orchids.*
P: *Who else would know that? Nobody's asking Wikipedia about our grandmother to text me, Nora.*

Nora felt herself smiling and reveled in that sensation. She had missed her sister something fierce.

N: *Fine, whatever. Are you home?*

P: *I'm just leaving work. What's up?*
N: *If I said 'surprise' would you be mad?*
P: *!!!*

The dots bounced for a moment and Nora couldn't help but smile wider.

P: *I'll be home in ten.*

Nora took a seat on the dusty and slightly worn wicker rocking chair that sat to one side of the front door. Phae had said ten minutes, but Nora would have put down good money that she pulled into the driveway in less than eight.

Phae was both beaming and had tears streaming down her cheeks as she all but leaped from the car and ran across the yard.

"What did you do to your hair?" she sobbed, throwing herself into Nora's arms.

"Trying to keep myself on the down-low." She realized that she was crying too as she held her sister and they swayed on the porch. "You dirty little liar. You told me all this time you were okay and you are clearly *not* okay."

Phae laughed wetly. "I am. I am okay. I'm not great, but I'm okay. You're *here*!"

"I'm here!" Nora agreed, and they finally broke apart, laughing through their tears as they looked at one another.

"Come on, let's go in before the neighbors think I've totally lost it."

Phaedra unlocked the front door and Nora followed her into the house. It was cleaner than she expected, and very well kept up for something that was probably closing in on thirty years old.

"This is nice, Phae. Where are all your roommates?" Nora followed her sister up the stairs and into her bedroom.

"Most everyone works weekends because of school." She looked at her phone. "Usually everybody is home by seven or eight though." Phae stared at Nora for a moment and blinked. "You're here," she sighed the words again, a smile lighting up her face.

"I'm here," Nora repeated, sitting on the bed with her sister.

"Wait. You're *here*. Are *you* okay?" Phae's face transformed from joy to concern. She and Nora looked enough alike that it was a little bit like looking into a mirror of the past to see her features in person after they had been separated for so long. Phae's hair was darker than Nora's normal blonde, but with the brunette dye, they could still pass for siblings.

Nora thought her sister was gorgeous but didn't dare tell her so. She wasn't great with compliments, thanks mostly to their mother's constant nitpicking and criticism.

"Things are a hot mess," Nora admitted.

"Mom?" Phae guessed with a snort.

"Among other things. And honestly, Mom is the lesser evil at this point."

Phae's eyes grew wide. "Oh wow. This calls for pizza and daiquiris." Her fingers flew over the screen of her phone.

Nora laughed, and her whole chest loosened up with the effort.

"Can I crash with you for a couple of days?"

"Of course you can! Pizza can be here in 45 minutes."

"Are you ordering for just us? Or for everyone?"

Phae's face wrinkled up a bit. "You realize there are four grown men here? I can't afford that much pizza."

Nora laughed again and gestured toward the phone. "Log back in. Order whatever you think everyone will eat. I got dinner."

Money was a concern for everyone, but Nora's cushion was much more generous than most.

Phae looked a bit constipated as they added and adjusted and added some more to the order. After finally hitting send—which Phae seemed hesitant to do—the pizza place called to confirm the order was accurate and that they weren't getting pranked. The time was extended also, which wasn't really a surprise.

"So? Tell me," Phae said quietly, reaching up to touch Nora's bottle-brown hair. "This is so weird on you. You look like Mom." Her nose wrinkled with distaste.

"I know." Nora took a deep breath and tried to decide where to start. She gave a brief overview of what was going on with David, trying not to stress Phae out.

"Holy shit, Nor. That's a big deal. Why didn't you tell me before? How in the world have you kept that from Devon?"

Nora nodded, then shook her head. "I don't know. It felt like such a dirty secret. I felt so ashamed and *stupid*. It just spiraled out of control." For a moment, she hid her face in her hands. "Oh god Phae, I totally freaked out. The only place I could think to come was here."

Phae pulled her in for a side hug. "I'm really glad you did. But what about your bodyguard? Devon? That guy you've been seeing?"

The smile came at just the thought of Maxwell, then faded.

"What do you know about a guy?"

Her sister bumped her shoulder with her arm. "I have a news-feed too, you know. And maybe a Google alert set up for my famous sister."

"Do your roommates know about me?"

Phae shook her head. "No. They don't really know a lot about me, either though."

"What? You've been here a whole semester and then some. What does that mean?"

Phae shrugged. "I just kind of do my own thing. They're more interested in their sports and partying."

Nora filed that information away.

They both looked at Phaedra's phone as it began to ding repeatedly.

"Whoa." Her sister was holding the device at arms' length as though it might bite her. Finally, the chimes stopped and Phaedra started laughing. "Holy crap, you've got Devon's panties in an *epic* twist." She showed Nora the screen.

D: *Phae—is she with you?*

D: *Have you heard from her?*

D: *She disappeared and all I got was a backpack and a note.*

D: *A fucking NOTE, Phae. Like handwritten on paper. About her PLANTS.*

D: *Plus, she left her phone. Obviously, or I'd be messaging her.*

D: *Tell me she's there.*

D: *Is she safe?*

D: *I know she didn't go to your mom's house.*

D: *She doesn't keep secrets from me but she kept a big one and it's bad enough she freaked the hell out, so I'm freaking the hell out.*

D: *Phaedra Helena, don't make me call Daniel to come over there and check on you. You know I'll do it.*

Nora found herself tearing up a bit. The rush of emotion was unexpected and she blinked against the liquid pooling in her eyes again. She loved that crazy guy.

"Text him back, tell him I'm here and safe." She lifted an eyebrow. "But what's this about Daniel coming to check on you?" She was just teasing, but the deep and sudden blush in Phaedra's cheeks told her everything she needed to know. "Wait. You and Daniel? Seriously?" The crimson in her cheeks only deepened, and that was reasonable confirmation. "We *are* going to talk about that."

Instead of texting, Phae hit the video call button.

"No, Phae—" Nora started to protest, but Devon answered on the first ring.

"Tell me she's there." Devon sounded beyond stressed. Phae, the traitor, just grinned and turned the phone so Devon could see Nora. "Thank God." Nora expected that proclamation to be followed by some kind of lecture, but it wasn't. "Your hair," was all he said.

Nora chortled a small laugh. "Funny, that's what Phae said too. Is it terrible?"

"I don't give a shit about your hair, Nora. I was just worried about you. Alan showed up with your pack and basically ding-dong-ditched after grunting some deep philosophical crap at me about friendship. I open it up and there's your keys, your phone, your jewelry. I didn't know what to think."

"I left you a note."

"About watering your goddamn *plants*."

"My babies need to be cared for."

Devon sighed, and it was long-suffering.

"*Nora.* Why did you vanish?"

"Clearly I didn't. You found me easily enough. I was going to text you in a few minutes, anyway. I swear."

"Nora." His azure gaze bore straight into her soul and she couldn't take it.

She sighed and gave the quick and dirty version—she didn't want to be responsible for anyone she cared for getting hurt because David had photographic ammo against them too. She couldn't be photographed with Maxwell if she wasn't with Maxwell. If Detective Rutherford had her phone, maybe they could find the whacko who couldn't seem to leave her alone. He'd been slippery so far and avoided getting caught despite his regular check-ins and demands for money.

"I don't want anyone hurt because of me. He's not afraid to trash everyone else's reputation just to get to me. Everyone else has already been completely exposed because of me. He had pictures of me and Maxwell at his parents' house. He had pictures of everyone's front door, Devon. Front. Doors. I don't want any of you hurt because of me."

"Nor." His tone was sympathetic.

Phaedra was watching Nora with concern heavy in her eyes. She hadn't so much as lowered the phone.

"I'm just taking a break, Dev. Everything is too much. Everything's going to blow up bad in the next day or two. I couldn't be there."

"Okay. I kind of get it. I mean, I don't, and I wish you'd told me way before now, but I see kind of what got you here. But check in with me okay?" He paused. "Should I tell Maxwell anything? I mean other than what your dumb ass decided to do instead of just talking to your friends—who could have been helping you this whole time I might add—what was going on."

She sighed. "Tell him I'm safe with Phae and that I'm sorry. I'll reach out soon. I just don't know what to say right now. I'm embarrassed and…" she shrugged.

"Nor—"

"I'm okay. Thank you, Devon."

He recognized her discomfort and nodded tightly, kissing his first two fingers in a gesture of love before saying goodbye.

Nora pressed the disconnect button on the call, tears building again.

"What are you doing, sister?" Phaedra asked quietly.

Guilt and the feeling that she'd made the absolute wrong choice again and again crushed down on her. If only she'd listened to that voice in her head telling her the camera was on and David was lying. If only she'd asked him to prove it. If only she'd never started paying him off. If only, if only, if only. The regrets stacked up deep.

She didn't want to admit that out loud, so she just whispered her admission, hoping that releasing the words on the air would soften the ache in her chest, but knowing that it wouldn't.

Everything felt wrong.

"I don't know."

JUST ABOUT THE time roommates started trickling in downstairs in a chaotic chain of door slams and exclamations, the pizza guy rang the doorbell.

Phaedra and Nora collected all the food and Nora made sure to tip the guy an extra $50 just because he looked like he was braced for the absolute worst. Instead, that tip made his eyes bug out and made his day when she reassured him she hadn't handed over the wrong bill. She thought for a moment she'd given herself away, but he was just really happy for the money.

The celebration around the arrival of pizza was intense, and it took a moment for the crowd of large men and one petite woman to clear enough for them to recognize that there was an extra body and that Phaedra was even there at all.

"Who's this?" one of the guys asked Phae, finally acknowledging the sisters' presence. He gestured with his chin, mumbling the question over a full mouth of pizza. He was tall, broad, pretty, and almost certainly a hazard to the hearts and panties of campus co-eds. Blonde hair and blue eyes sealed the deal on his all-American good looks.

Nora registered that he was handsome, but also that his looks were nothing compared to Maxwell. Her heart tugged painfully.

"This is my sister," Phae said quietly.

"Thanks for dinner, Fade's sister." A second large dude responded. He was dark to the first one's light, all black hair and deep brown eyes but still that broad, muscular football player body type.

The roommate situation was interesting, to say the least. No wonder their mother was having kittens over it.

Nora assessed the room as they went about filling paper plates and plastic cups.

All five roommates descended on the food like locusts. The four men were all large, probably played on the same sports teams, and ran the spectrum of features. Phae advised that the blonde was Jace, tall dark and handsome was West, the quiet one with dimples for days and interesting gold eyes to complement his chocolate hair went by Rusty and the seemingly disinterested guy with additional bulk, fewer words and greenish eyes and light hair was Carson. The other female was a vibrant young woman that reminded Nora of Olivia. She had stunning blue eyes, dark brown hair, and exuded nothing but flirt. Phaedra said her name was Harmony.

None of them seemed very friendly with Phaedra, or even to acknowledge her existence much which was honestly kind of hard to watch for the protective older sister.

The roommates all gathered in the living room, the four boys playful with Harmony; touching, joking, flirtatious. Phae stepped forward with her plate of pizza to join the group on one of the couches, and the weirdest thing happened. Nora wouldn't have believed it if she hadn't seen it happen with her own eyes. Big male bodies shifted in a way that physically blocked her out from entering the living room space. They didn't turn around to look, didn't anything—it was like a strange automatic response. Magnets, but in a bizarre, backward, hurtful way.

It happened once, and Phae gave a weak smile, then tried again, between two different bodies and it was the same thing. All the while, they were chatting and laughing and teasing with Harmony.

Nora watched her sister's face fall, and then she met her eye. Phae shrugged, and instead sat at one of the two stools at the breakfast bar.

"That happen a lot?"

Phae nodded. "It's a little weird, right?"

"Definitely." She considered. "Why do they call you Fade? I mean, it's not an inaccurate shortening of your name but I feel like there's something there."

A grimace took over Phae's pretty features.

"Because I fade into the background. I'm a ghost, a phantom. Even when I'm here, I'm not here."

Nora's heart clenched.

"That sucks, Phae. Have you said anything about it?"

"What would I say? They'd just make fun of me, probably. I'm not like Harmony."

No, she definitely was not. She was kind, and interesting, and smart, and fun. Not that Nora was biased about it or anything.

Phae finished her pizza and tossed her plate in the trash. Nora was still slowly working on hers.

"I'm going to go take a shower. You okay?"

Nora nodded, and her sister vanished back upstairs.

Jace was the first to return to the stack of pizza boxes. He appraised Nora, noticing that she was alone at the kitchen island.

"So, Fade's sister. You got a name?"

"So, *Phae's* roommate. Do you even realize that you're a total dick?"

He jolted and then started laughing.

"Most of the time, yeah." His smile was a panty-melter, but she was immune. It was a dime-store knock-off of Maxwell Caine's. Hell, it was a shadow even to Devon's. There was potential there, though, even she could admit that.

"Nora." She held out a hand.

He shook it. "Nice to meet you. Fade-Phaedra—" he corrected himself. "—hasn't mentioned you."

While that should have hurt, it was actually comforting. As was the fact that he knew her sister's actual name.

"Are you sure she hasn't? Do you ever purposely speak to her?" Nora's head cocked to the side. She knew full well she was busting his balls and had zero regrets about doing it.

His eyebrows drew together and West joined them at the island, foraging for seconds.

"She's not a talker," West confirmed.

Nora nodded. She tried not to react when she heard the opening theme song for her show start on the TV, but her blood pressure spiked and she could feel the blood rush to her cheeks.

Dammit.

"I need to catch up on *Destiny Falls*. I'm starting episode nine!" Harmony declared.

"Can I tell you something I just saw happen?" Nora started in, trying for distraction.

Both men nodded.

"Everyone but us was in the living room to eat. Without knowing or thinking about it, you guys physically blocked her from entering the same space as you. She tried twice, even politely cleared her throat, and you just shifted, keeping her out of the circle." They both frowned. "The four of you are playful and flirty with Harmony. Don't get me wrong, she's cute—I get it. But you don't even look at Phaedra. You all make her feel invisible, and stuck on the outside of your group, so what else could she be?"

She slid off the barstool and caught Carson's eye. He too was frowning at her assessment.

"That's not on purpose," Jace said, looking like he felt a bit ashamed. "She's sweet. Quiet. She's a good roommate."

Nora shrugged, tossing her plate. "Doesn't really matter, does it? The result is the same."

Carson's eyes dropped to the floor, then shifted to the TV. Harmony bounced back into the kitchen.

"What are we talking about?"

"Just thanking Nora for buying the pizza," Jace lied, and wasn't *that* interesting all on its own?

"Oh, yeah. Thanks." Harmony gave a smile that Nora recognized from miles away before bouncing back into the living room. She was exactly like all the Olivia's of the world, what Maxwell saw in her was still confusing to Nora—that woman was *so* transparent. Olivia had assets she used for manipulation and personal gain. Collateral damage was not a concern. Harmony was no doubt quite the same.

"My pleasure," She said. "I surprised Phae with this visit so it's the least I could do."

"Where are you visiting from?" West asked.

"The west coast," Nora said, noticing Carson scrutinizing the Nora on the TV then turning his attention to her. Rusty was doing the same. Her skin started to itch a bit and she knew she was about to get busted. "Just something to keep in mind." She said, looking pointedly at Jace. He nodded and she excused herself, finding Phae clean and quiet in her room.

"You mind if I take one too?" Nora asked from the doorway.

Phae smiled, looking up from her laptop. "Of course not. My towels are the green ones."

Nora made her way to the bathroom that her sister and Harmony shared, trying desperately to wash away the day. It only partially worked, and about a quarter of the brown color leached down the drain along with her tension, but it was a start.

CHAPTER
Sixteen

PHAE HAD MORNING classes and a partial work shift at the garden shop she'd been employed at, but said she would be home around 3. The roommates had an assortment of schedules, but it looked like at least one of them would be home with Nora all day long. She had no plans to go much of anywhere, and to her delight, there was a huge expanse of back-yard with plants of all kinds she could sink her hands and energy into. Her sister had confessed to being behind on her regular upkeep because of her class load and finals coming up so quickly, and that was all the motivation Nora needed.

Well, there was that, and the fact that as of late the night before, news outlets and gossip sites had picked up the photos and videos. The shit had officially hit the fan.

David had released *everything*. There was no avoiding her naked body, though partially censored, on any form of media.

She had known that this was the most likely result of her last message, and it was awful to have herself so exposed, but she couldn't have continued as she had been. Hundreds of thousands of dollars gone. Years' worth of time. Mountains of stress. She was done.

The result of her rash decision to finally call a halt was that her naked rear end, mid-coitus face, and breasts were plastered all over the TV and internet. And they would be there forever.

Eventually, she'd make her peace with that.

Confusion was overlaid over even her horror though, because at this point, what could he gain from it? If she wasn't paying him hush money and his ammunition against her was gone, what was the point? Sure, her pristine image was going to be tarnished to hell and back and she'd fought long and hard to be that clean, good girl in the eyes of the press, but it just didn't make much sense. David was giving up any and all leverage and for what? What was his plan? Did he think she'd magically come up with the money once the photos were out? Payoffs from the media outlets were almost certainly a thing.

Maybe that was his endgame.

Nora hoped that it was worth it to him. It was to her if it made him disappear from her life forever, regardless of the fallout for her career. She just hoped that her friends, who had been dragged into the middle and a number of the photos floating around could forgive her.

She left her phone plugged in upstairs but muted, and after doing all the nice and very distracting but slightly invasive older sister guest type things like a load of laundry, dishes, fridge science experiment clean out and even a quick sweep of the hard floors needed somewhere else to direct her energy. It was far too tempting to check her phone when she didn't have anything else occupying her hands.

Once she could no longer reasonably wander around inside the house, she went out into the large back-yard and decided to start with simple pruning and shaping, and then she could water. The garage had a little workbench that could only belong to her sister, so Nora helped herself to a pair of gloves, a sun hat, and some pruning shears. There was a wide, flat basket as well as a five-gallon bucket underneath, and she took those too.

Working left to right, she followed the fence-line and methodically worked her way through hibiscus, oleander, knock out roses, and a variety of jasmine she hadn't seen or smelled since leaving Alabama. She allowed the blossoms and thorns to become her only focus … or at least she tried.

Hours passed as she worked, and it was the best therapy she could have asked for, but her mind still wandered.

No matter how immersed in her work she became, Maxwell continued to pop into her thoughts. She wondered not for the first or even fiftieth time what he was doing, what he thought of her now, whether or not he regretted getting involved with a girl that trouble followed around.

A girl from a questionable background with parents who only contact her to ask for money.

She wondered why she hadn't just told him. Or Devon. Or anyone. How she let it get so far away from her control. She'd started, that day on the way back from Malibu, but had not said everything. Not the important parts.

Nora realized now, she had withheld the parts that he probably would have told her straight out could be handled under the law, by him or otherwise.

By two o'clock, Nora was sunburned, dehydrated, exhausted, and every plant in the quarter-acre back-yard had been groomed, loved, watered, and pruned to within an inch of its life. She'd pay for the extra sun and exertion, but her heart held a sense of fulfillment she hadn't had in quite a while.

Nobody had bothered her all day, but she was glad to see Jace crossing the wide expanse of grass toward her, a large glass of ice water in his hand. He extended it toward her like an offering when he got close enough, a small grin on his face.

"Looks like you could use this."

"Thanks." She tried to sip but found herself gulping.

"Would it be a bad time to mention that the landlord sends a landscaping company at least twice a month?"

He crossed his arms over his broad chest, mirth bright in his eyes.

Nora found herself laughing. She shook her head.

"Nah. They clearly aren't doing their job very well if there was that much for me to do. Phae said she usually does it."

Jace nodded. "She does. Says it relaxes her." His expression was perplexed. That was obviously not how he found relaxation. He probably lifted weights or ran or something equally physical for stress relief.

Nora met his eye, smile persisting. So he *had* been paying attention to her sister, at least a little. Her muscles were aching from being used, but she was rather relaxed. "Can attest and relate," she said.

He snorted. "I'm going to go pick up burgers I think. Can I get you anything?"

Nora nodded. "Whatever you'd get Phae is fine." She dug in the pocket of her jeans for some cash, coming up empty. "I've got money in the house." She turned and Jace held out a hand.

"That's alright. We'll square up later. Besides, you got the pizza."

"Thanks."

He nodded and smiled, and even if he wasn't Maxwell, it gave nice warm feelings.

Nora took the opportunity to put away all of the gardening tools, gulp down two more glasses of water and take a shower while Jace was retrieving the burgers, and Phae was finishing up her work shift at the local wholesale nursery and greenhouse. Rounding the bottom step after yet another trip through the shower where she had to put shampoo back in the bottle because she was used to way more hair and therefore way more product, she heard her sister gasp.

"Turn it *off.*" Phae all but growled, attempting to get the remote from Harmony's hands.

They hadn't noticed Nora yet, as she was frozen at the bottom of the steps just inside the kitchen.

"Oh. My. God." Harmony stood, eyes dancing with glee. "I knew you looked familiar but *damn.*" The smile she turned to Phae was almost predatory. She could see pretty much see the dollar signs flashing in her eyes. It reminded Nora of her mother.

"Nora Chase is your *sister*?" Carson breathed it out heavily.

"Whoa." Rusty chuckled, as always, a man of few words.

Jace and West showed up then, the front door banging loudly in their wake, a cluster of bags of burgers with tell-tale grease spots in their massive hands.

"What'd we miss?" Jace asked, seeing the tension in the air the second they walked in the kitchen. They set the bags down and started unloading them. He looked from his roommates to Nora, then back again.

Instead of the TV being turned off, it was paused on a still of Nora from her first dinner date with Maxwell.

"Oh shit," West said and started to laugh. "Damn. We got a movie star in our house, bro."

"I'm not a movie star. Please turn it off." Nora's voice was quiet, and she was fairly certain that the wobble in it was the catalyst for Rusty to snatch the remote out of Harmony's grasp and hit the power button.

Everyone was quiet. Phae gave Harmony a death glare and came to Nora's side.

"I'm sorry," She said, though what for Nora didn't know.

"None of this is your fault."

The group of roommates moved cautiously, Carson all but slapping Harmony's phone out of her hands as she started tapping away, glee in her eyes.

"Hey. *No*," He said, and his tone commanded respect.

"Why? It's not every day you find out your phantom of a roommate is related to someone famous! I wasn't going to take a selfie or anything I just wanted to put some vague post up on my Instagram story." Harmony's tone was entitled and whiny. It made Nora's skin crawl.

"No," Jace added, shaking his head as he handed out burgers. "That would be super shitty Harm. Ever think there's a reason she's here? Maybe that it has something to do with the crap they're posting all over the internet and TV?"

She pouted like a scolded toddler, turning a scowl on Nora before flopping into the sofa, pouting. "*Fine.*"

Nora met Carson's eye, and they were on the same wavelength because he nodded. Someone would be on duty keeping Harmony off of social media for the next little while.

"I'll admit it's an interesting development. Didn't see that coming at all," West mumbled, taking a massive bite of what looked like a fantastically large, greasy, hand-made burger.

Nora slid into the same barstool she'd made friends with the night before and Phae saddled up next to her. She claimed a burger for herself and one for Phae as well as a paper boat of French fries.

"Maybe if any of you ever talked to Phae you'd learn something," Her tone was gentle, but the accusation loud and clear.

Jace met her eye and nodded. Point well taken.

"Do you want to talk about it?" West offered, leaning onto his forearms on the island countertop.

"No, not really."

There was a quiet moment as everyone ate.

"It's not true," Rusty said. It wasn't a question.

Nora met his eye, and then others around the room. Everyone was watching her.

"Some of it is. You can't fake the pictures or the film." She sighed. "A lot of the circumstances around it are greatly exaggerated."

There were some irritated male grunts which honestly, was incredibly reassuring. Nora heard Phae's phone going off every few seconds. A glance her way was confirmed with a nod.

"Dev."

Nora's burger was probably one of the most delicious things she'd ever put in her mouth, but she could barely taste it.

"I'll call him in a bit."

"Dev? Like Devon Greene?" Harmony's eyes flashed and she all but screeched in her excitement.

Lord love a duck. She'd put money down that her middle name was Olivia. Or maybe Athena, like her mother. Both were equal opportunists and it appeared as though Harmony was cut of the same manipulative cloth.

"Yes," Nora said plainly. She turned her attention to her sister. "We need to discuss Daniel, by the way." Phaedra turned a satisfying shade of red.

Jace shifted uncomfortably. Nora tried to keep her smile on the inside.

Everyone ate, but it was a little awkward. She knew they were all waiting for her to set the tone, make a statement—something.

Finally, she pushed the remnants of her meal aside.

"I didn't know the camera was on. He was a low-level aspiring director trying to break into the legit film business from—" she breathed out heavily. "—from *porn*, and there was a camera in the bedroom. I was dumb enough to believe him when he said it wasn't turned on." Her eyes squeezed shut. "I was a stupid girl who thought she was in love with a guy she met basically the minute she moved to Los Angeles. We had been dating a very short time and he convinced me to go back to his place with him and he filmed us having sex. I thought his giving direction the whole time was just his kink." Nora took a breath, the little she'd eaten rocking uncomfortably in her gut. "When I first found out he'd lied about the camera being off, he claimed he made the tape just for himself, just for us … something like that. He almost had me believing that I'd given him permission to film it—I was so upset I really didn't remember straight what all had happened that night. So, I told nobody, not even my best friend or my sister, and I tell them pretty much everything." She smiled at Phae, who gave a weak grin back. "Well, except for my mother. I made the grave error of telling her thinking she'd have some wisdom to share. She didn't."

Phae's face morphed from shock to sadness to rage. Nora felt terrible that she'd confided in her mom and not her sister, but she wouldn't make that mistake again.

"Anyway, we broke up not long after and he's been extorting money out of me since I got the part on *Destiny Falls* and got even a little famous to keep that tape quiet. He's clearly still following me or has someone he's paying to do so." Anger lit up her veins. "I have no idea how those pictures were taken in Malibu. That was just a few weeks ago and the person who was there with me doesn't deserve to be exposed that way."

There was a continued silence and some shifting of bodies.

"For the record, you don't deserve to be exposed that way either," Jace said.

"Thank you."

"You aren't here," West said quietly.

Harmony made a noise that half disgust and half shock. Nora could pretty much hear her protest but she didn't voice it.

Jace shook his head. "Nope. I mean, Phaedra's sister came to visit, but I don't think her name was Nora."

The desire to go by Elle was momentarily overwhelming, but she didn't want to hear that name roll off anyone else's lips. It was sacred to her. That name belonged to Maxwell.

"What's your full name?" Carson asked.

"Eleanora Demetria." Nora couldn't help but grin a bit at the mouthful that was her given name.

"Jesus. What about you, Fade?" West piped in.

"Phaedra Helena," Phae responded, a grin tugging at her lips as well.

"Alright. Well, we can't call you E.D., because there's no way in the world you could fail to make a man stiff."

"Jesus Christ, Jace," Rusty swore. Trying hard not to laugh.

"What? Truth is truth. Where's the lie there? How about Demi? Or Ellen?"

Nora shook her head. "Nora should be fine. My last name is actually Chatzi. I don't have the same dad as

Phae—if they come looking for her sister, they will probably be looking for someone with her same last name."

They considered. "Alright. No posting pictures." All eyes went to Harmony with this declaration from Jace. "No social media at all. I'll turn off the wi-fi if necessary. You're good here until you're ready to go home."

Nora felt the crushing weight that had been sitting on her chest lift a bit.

"Thank you."

Phaedra lit up as well, and Nora had the feeling this was a turning point for her wallflower sister and her roommates.

"Ugh. I'm going to make margaritas," Harmony proclaimed, still scowling as though the display of positive emotions offended her. Carson, Rusty, and West filtered away to the living room to see what else was on TV while Jace cleaned up after the burgers and helped with the drinks.

Phae bumped Nora's shoulder. "You should call Dev before my phone explodes."

She nodded, a pit roiling in her stomach. The onions from her burger were biting back unpleasantly in her throat.

After retrieving her phone from Phae's room and accepting the margarita Jace was offering, she stepped out back, fingers hesitating over the contacts.

Taking a deep breath, she engaged the video call.

"*Finally.* Why is Phae ignoring me?"

"Why are you blowing up my sister's phone? You know you could just message once or twice and quit bugging us."

Devon clucked his tongue. "No, I certainly could *not*." He gave her a gentle smirk. "You look better today."

Nora nodded her head a little and raised her margarita, offering him *cheers* through the phone screen.

"Feel better today. Spent it taking care of all the plants in Phae's yard."

Devon chuckled. "Well, good." He angled the camera so she could see Stephanie's sympathetic face in the background.

"I hope it doesn't piss you off, but we've initiated project clean-up," She said.

Nora felt her face pull in confusion. "What's that?"

Devon smiled at his wife and then turned back to Nora. "You don't get to be friends with Stephanie Von Feldt and never take advantage of the fringe benefits. That footage and the photos are getting the full-on spin treatment. Marty and Samuel are both pulling every string they can. We've even got a private detective working on finding that limp-dick, David."

Tears sprang to Nora's eyes. Her heart tugged at the mention of Samuel's name also. Anything Caine was sure to do so.

"You guys. That's so…"

"Friend-like?" Devon suggested with a thick layer of sarcasm frosting his words.

"I was going to say unnecessary. Unexpected. More than I could ever repay."

Devon *tsk*ed at her again. "It's like you don't know me *at all*. Come on, Nor. We love you. Why didn't you tell me about this sooner?" He looked hurt.

Nora shook her head, taking a drink of her margarita in the hopes that it would chase away her tears.

"I don't know. I was ashamed. I was scared. I didn't know what to do, and I had already been trying to keep it buried for so long I didn't know how to do anything else. He's been taking my money all this time, but it's only ever seemed to be about sabotaging my good-girl image for him. It doesn't really make sense, honestly. I couldn't stay when anyone I was seen with, you guys included, became a target. I don't even know how he's getting some of those pictures."

Stephanie made a furious growling noise in the background. "Well, either way, this stops *now*. You stay with your sister for a few days, try to breathe and get your head on straight. Things will start to blow over in the next 24 hours or my name isn't Alex Felton."

Devon grunted. "Babe, your name is Stephanie Greene."

Nora could see her friend's hand wave in the air dismissively. Her amber eyes were glowing as she looked back at Nora through the phone screen. "It's both. My point is, the next big scandal is always right around the corner. The outrage about how the media's been responding is already reaching a fever pitch. One would think with all the revenge porn laws out there this crap would stop."

She exhaled a deep breath. Nora was immensely grateful for Stephanie's passion. "Anyway. He's sure to take the much-deserved role as the villain. You have all of us behind you, and the law."

"Thank you." Nora managed over a huge lump in her throat. She felt really dumb for not classifying his blackmail in the realm of revenge porn. Things could have been very different if she'd thought that way. The weight of her stupidity crushed down on her chest.

"He's not mad, you know," Stephanie said quietly after a moment, sympathetic expression deepening as she stepped closer to the phone, face displacing Devon's in the viewfinder.

"What? Who?" Nora's heart began to pound. Even if she wanted to play dumb, her heart knew who Stephanie was talking about.

Stephanie clucked her tongue as well, a half-grin on her mouth. "Maxwell. You know who I meant. I mean, he's mad as hell that someone did that to you, that they've been blackmailing you for so long. He's super irritated that someone managed to get pictures in Malibu. He mentioned something about drones being outlawed or something like that. I think Olivia's been making him crazy popping up at odd moments too, come to think of it. He's worried about you. I'm sure he'd love to hear from you, though we're happy to pass messages if you like. But you need to know that he's not angry with you. He's angry *for* you."

Nora's chest compressed fiercely. She'd address the Olivia popping up issue later; there was no room in her mental compartments for that on top of everything else.

"How could he not be mad? He's getting smeared in the media because of me. I didn't warn him. I just disappeared with a vague 'gotta go' text like a total coward. Someone took a photo of us *naked* and sold it—his literal naked ass is all over the internet. The Bar Association—"

"He's. Not. Mad." Stephanie repeated the words slowly and with emphasis. "He won't get disbarred. He might consider it a blessing if he's no longer wanted or expected to practice law. And he's actually been pretty unbearable lately with all the positive press about his abs and bare ass."

Nora suddenly laughed, and it came with a flood of tears.

"But I just *left*. I didn't say anything. We were … we were *something*, and I didn't trust him with the whole truth."

Devon sighed. "You're still something with him. And you didn't trust *us* either. While we feel bad that you've been dealing with this all by yourself for so long, and while I could absolutely shake you for doing that, we're not pissed at you about it. He's really not mad, Nora. Are you even listening? He's *worried* about you. It's kind of disgusting how stressed out he is. I think he *likes* you or something. Just call him. Text even. Smoke signal. Just reach out, okay?" Devon's attempt at injecting humor was appreciated, but Nora couldn't quite embrace it.

Nora felt her head shaking. "I'm not sure I can yet."

Devon nodded, and Stephanie bowed her head for a moment before turning those amber orbs back to Nora, searing straight through her. "Can I tell him that we talked at least?" she asked. "Tell him that you're okay and that you'll think about reaching out soon? I won't give him this number if you don't want me to."

Her head bobbed gently. "Yeah. That's okay."

Stephanie gave her a smile that felt a lot like a hug.

"Then we have a plan."

Nora's heart lightened. She was conflicted because aside from just Devon himself and of course, Phae, she'd never had a whole team on her side and all of a sudden, she had two.

"Thank you. Really."

"Of course. Call me tomorrow." Devon said, and it didn't even consider being a request.

"Okay." Nora couldn't help but grin back at him and even Stephanie was smiling.

"We got you," he said, and they disconnected a moment later, Nora staring at the blank screen for what was probably way too long. She sat in the quiet of the back yard, trying to come to terms with the riot of emotions ricocheting through her. The desire to call Maxwell was intense, but she needed a little more time.

She decided to buy herself some with a text she agonized over for a ridiculous amount of time.

N: I'm with my sister. I'm safe. I'm so, so sorry. I promise we'll talk soon. If you want.

Phae must have noticed she was done with the call and came out to join her on one of the sun-loungers.

"Okay?" she asked, seeing her tears.

Nora nodded while tipping back her nearly empty margarita glass.

"Yeah."

She gave Phae the short version of the efforts Devon and Stephanie were making on her behalf to make the drama go away.

Nora's phone began to buzz and jitter across the table as texts arrived. Phae smiled.

"I knew he wouldn't be mad. Are you going to call him?"

Nora glanced at the handful of short texts, a smile appearing on her own mouth.

He wasn't mad. He was glad she was safe. He missed her. He was ready to help if she needed it.

"Not yet."

"Why? Nora, come on! Don't be an idiot. He really likes you. If he's not mad, reach out."

"Tomorrow." She agreed. Phae sighed at her but nodded.

"Alright. Tomorrow."

The sisters sat in the deepening twilight, drinking margaritas and critiquing Nora's efforts with the foliage.

"You okay?" Nora asked Phae, who was leaning her head against Nora's shoulder.

Phae smiled. "Yeah, I'm okay. I don't know what you said to my roommates, but Jace has been sure to say something to me or include me in whatever's going on every time I'm around. It's weird."

Nora returned her sister's grin. "Well, that blocking you out shit was *bizarre*. I don't think they meant to do it; I think they mostly thought they were giving you your space. I think they'll all try a little harder, at least for a while."

Phae nodded. "They're all good guys. Harmony…"

Nora made a choking noise in her throat. "Don't worry about her. There are thousands of Harmonies in the world. I know one named Olivia." Something tickled in Nora's brain all of a sudden. Something she'd have to come back to because she couldn't quite latch onto it, but it was niggling there in the recesses. "They are never nearly as interesting or amazing as the Phaedra's of the world."

She was rewarded with a quick squeeze from her sister. "Love you, sister."

"Love you back."

At that moment, that's all that mattered.

CHAPTER
Seventeen

TRUE TO STEPHANIE'S promise, by morning Nora's scandal had been spun to make it look like the person who took and posted the images was the bad guy—rightfully so—and that Nora couldn't possibly be held responsible for something that had been done without her knowledge or consent while being intimate with someone she trusted. The news about him blackmailing her and extorting huge sums of money from her was just the icing on his shit cake.

While she usually lived by the rule about never reading the comments, she allowed herself to do so on a couple of posts and was brought near to tears by the positive and supportive statements she found there.

All that wasted time, effort and money. She couldn't help but wonder what would have happened if she had done things completely different, right from the start. The weight of her stupidity was heavy, but she felt she deserved to wear it, at least for a while.

There was no way to express the obviousness of the logical spin and outpouring of support short of throwing her hands in the air and releasing a frustrated "Thank you!" to the universe.

Phae only had a couple of morning classes and another short shift at work, so Nora was only alone for a few hours. With nothing to occupy her hands, she was only building anxiety so she decided to be a grocery fairy.

Wandering around the local market, she found herself breathing easier than she had in quite a long time. Nobody was paying any attention at all to the girl with short brownish hair who might have a passing resemblance to a lady that was on TV. It was so nice to be able to browse and wander. It was fun to fill her basket and not be rushing through the aisles. It was extra fun to be buying food for college-age dudes that didn't have any interesting dietary restrictions.

A few hundred dollars and a completely stocked fridge and pantry later, Nora found herself in her rental car again, headed in the direction of her sister's job. She wanted to see how this particular nursery and garden center operated. If this is what Phaedra wanted to do, maybe there was something worth taking notes on.

I WET MY PLANTS was a family-run operation with a whimsical sense of decoration, a huge variety of offerings, and a wonderfully comfortable store. It was like stepping into a cedar-lined jungle, and Nora felt her spirits and her smile lift as the humid smell of soil and greenery embraced her.

Phaedra was assembling a large dish garden of various succulents for a customer, so Nora just wandered the aisles, unable to resist touching the delicate blown glass hummingbirds and bamboo wind chimes, breathing in the heavy air laden with the tang of fertilizer over the more earthy scent of the plants.

"Can I help you with something ma'am?" Phaedra teased, finding Nora in the outdoor section admiring the array of vegetable starters and succulents.

"Just browsing, thanks." Nora smiled at her sister. "And ma'am? Ew."

Phae giggled at Nora's horrified reaction, then sighed. "It's pretty great, right?" She turned her head into the sunshine and took a deep breath.

"It is," Nora agreed, walking a bit further down the aisle so she could admire the collection of waist-high concrete cast statues and some made from metal. "It suits you."

Phaedra beamed. "I love it here."

"Would you want to have your own place like this someday?"

Phae considered, gently picking away some dead leaves and debris from some flats of purple and yellow pansies.

Nora could never not see the singing and dancing ones from *Alice in Wonderland* when she saw them. A couple of times, she'd been served them in a fancy salad at a studio dinner.

"Maybe. I'd rather have a custom nursery. You know, high-end specialty stuff. I'd love to get Yiayia Lou's orchids back." She swallowed, and Nora could feel the same lump in her throat.

"She'd love that, I'm sure."

Phae nodded.

"I'm really proud of you," Nora said quietly. Phae's eyes turned to her, half shocked, half embarrassed. "I mean it. You're a fantastic human being, Phaedra."

"Thank you." Her sister wiped at her face, leaving a smear of dirt.

Nora laughed, drawing her sister in for a hug. When they separated, she helped clean off the smudge.

"Mom may not ever come around." Her voice was quieter than she expected it to be like she was telling her sister an obvious secret.

Phae nodded. "I know. I can't help wanting her approval, but I know I may never get it. Having yours means a lot though." The lopsided grin combined with tears in her baby sister's eyes threw Nora over the emotional edge too.

"If it helps, I'll never get her approval either. Not after this … scandal."

They laughed through their tears, hugging again.

"You're going to get me fired." Phaedra mock complained, scrubbing at her face.

"Nah. I saw the owners smiling at us from over there." She gestured toward where the smaller citrus trees were kept. There had been a husband and wife she assumed, smiling beatifically at the sisters as they had their moment.

"That sounds about right. They are pretty nosy." She tossed the word without malice, and with a smile.

"They like you."

Phae nodded. "I like them too."

Nora followed Phae as she made her way back inside.

The female owner approached.

"Phaedra didn't tell us she had family visiting. If she had, we'd have taken her off the schedule."

Phae looked vaguely horrified.

"Oh no, no reason to punish her because I'm here," Nora confirmed. "She loves this job. I can see why. We're both anthophiles and plantsman."

The woman beamed, her bright brown eyes bouncing from Nora to Phae and back again. "We're so lucky to have her. But please, go visit if you like, we're not busy."

Phae looked around. Nora jumped in again.

"If it's alright, I'll just hang around with her here until she's done?"

The woman nodded. "That sounds lovely."

Nora enjoyed the next two hours of wandering, watering, and chattering with her sister.

It fed her soul in ways she hadn't realized she needed to be nourished.

After the shift ended, they went out for lunch at a cute little salad and sandwich place.

"Did you call him yet?" Phae pulled no punches as she took a bite of her bright beet and spinach salad.

Nora rolled her eyes at her sister. "No."

"You need to," Phae admonished.

"I will." She appraised her sister. "Explain what the deal with you and Daniel is."

Phae blushed and shook her head. "There's nothing going on. He's helped me out a few times."

"Helped you out like…"

Phae sighed, her head dropping back, eyes to the sky.

"Like we're friends. We talk sometimes. We have for a long time like since I was in high school, I just never made a big deal about it because it *wasn't* a big deal. We met at your college graduation, remember?"

Nora nodded, vaguely remembering introducing the Greene brothers to her sister after tossing her cap and taking a dozen photos with Devon.

"He helped me move out of my crappy all-girl apartment. He helped when my car stranded me in the middle of nowhere one day and none of the guys I live with could be found. He's just … always available," Phae gave an awkward shrug and Nora couldn't help but laugh at her sister.

Phae didn't usually do embarrassed, but she was right now.

"Uh-huh. Well, I call first dibs if anything develops there. I can tell you like him. No way is Devon going to be the first to hear about it. Can you imagine? He'd never let me live that down."

Her sister's tinkling laugh made her smile.

"Okay. I swear."

"For what it's worth, Daniel's a good guy. I think you could do way worse. He couldn't even hope to do better, either."

Phae smiled. "Thanks, sister."

They fell into their old selves as they sat there nibbling at sandwiches and crunching through salads. It was them against the world, just like old times. They decided that Mom and Charlie could do whatever they wanted and promised to try and let go of any feelings they had about that. They both knew it was much easier said than done, but it was worth trying. There was no amount of money or emotional energy worth the scraps of approval they would get. It didn't matter. Knowing it and applying it were going to be two very different things though, and they recognized that.

After they finished their meals, Phaedra relaxed into her seat.

"It's better today," she said, and Nora nodded, knowing exactly what she meant.

"Devon and Stephanie are pretty incredible."

Phae's face twisted in disgust.

"I hope they find him. He should be arrested."

Nora sighed. "He should. Maybe he will be. What feels likely to happen with my luck is that he'll be fined, and he'll pay that fine with money he got from me. So, I'll be paying to bail his ass out too."

Just then, her phone buzzed in her bag. Good money had even odds on Devon or Maxwell. Both had been sending encouraging texts, and both were trying to coax her into a phone call. Neither had succeeded so far.

Phae grunted. "That's stupid." She stared at her sister a bit longer. "You need to go home."

Nora barked a short, surprised laugh. "You tired of me already? Are you kicking me out?"

"No. Of course not, but nothing gets solved with you here. What if the police need you? And if you're hiding…you look guilty too." Phae sighed heavily, the look of sadness on her face hitting Nora right in the chest.

The truth in her sister's words rang clearly in her head. She knew that was exactly how it looked, and it didn't matter at all that it wasn't out of guilt that she was in Alabama. Or at least not mostly.

Shit.

With a deep breath, Nora nodded.

"How long do you need me to stay? Or how soon do you want me to go?"

Phae shook her head. "It's not about me. You *need* to go. I don't care if it's days or weeks, but I've got class and work and I know you're going stir crazy at the house." Eyes that were similar to her own bore into Nora's soul. "Go home, Nora. Apologize to the cute guy. Go be brave and make the bad guy pay. Go fix your life."

Nora grumbled. "When did you get so wise?"

Phae smiled widely. "I had a good teacher, and I definitely don't mean mom."

Heart soaring at that compliment, Nora beamed back at her sister. They really were quite good at taking on the world, just the two of them.

DINNER THAT NIGHT was a full taco bar thanks to the quick catering availability at a local Mexican restaurant.

"We're going to miss the hell out of you when you're gone," Jace teased. "Great meals, full fridge, and the back-yard has never looked better."

"Hey," Phae protested, smiling. "The yard looks like that when I don't have finals coming up."

Jace winked at her. Nora chuckled. Well then. If Daniel didn't make a move soon, Jace just might. Phae wouldn't know what hit her, and oddly, Nora was here for it.

Harmony was still pouting about being banned from social media posts, but Nora had a plan to make it up to her.

"Thanks for letting me lie low here. Phae's right though—I need to get home. I'm flying out in the morning."

Phae had convinced Nora to let her book a flight and had helped her pack as soon as they got back. Nora was still resisting but allowed her sister to boss her around and take the lead. It was an interesting but not a totally unwelcome role reversal.

"The press seems to be shifting." West nodded, hitting the button on the blender to mix up another batch of margaritas.

"Yep." She turned her attention to Harmony. "You ready for that selfie?"

Harmony nearly choked. "What?"

Nora gestured for her to get her phone. "You and me, having margaritas. You in?"

Harmony made a noise that surely sent the neighborhood dogs into a frenzy. She snapped a few, choosing her favorite, and then the whole household got in the photo for a few.

"Thank you!" Harmony nearly vibrated with excitement.

"I just ask that you don't post them until tomorrow, okay? Let me get on the plane before you hit the button."

The girl nodded enthusiastically. "Okay. I can do that."

Nora prayed that the girl didn't abuse her generosity and get slippery posting fingers.

The doorbell rang as they were cleaning up after dinner, and Nora noticed that Phaedra's eyes slid over to her, an inscrutable expression on her face.

Nora was instantly suspicious of the way her sister looked, but couldn't put her finger on why she should be.

Rusty was the one closest, so he went to answer it.

"Remember that I love you," Phae said cryptically, dashing off to join Rusty.

Nora's blood stopped pumping for at least a handful of breaths when she heard his voice.

"Is Nora here?"

The kitchen island supported her for a moment, the white and blue granite cool under her suddenly sweaty palms.

Jace's eyes slid to meet hers, and she noted the gentle concern but also amusement.

"Oh damn. Fade called the lawyer," he said grinning. "You okay?" Worry overrode the joy for a moment.

Nora gave a tight nod and made her feet move.

Rusty passed her in the doorway between the kitchen and entry hall. "Some pretty boy in a polo here to see you." He winked at her.

Phaedra was shaking Maxwell's hand in the doorway, gesturing for him to come inside. He looked up and her breath was compressed in her lungs as their eyes met.

"Elle."

He breathed it, and she nearly launched herself at him, only barely managing to resist her limbs propelling themselves his direction. Every cell screamed at her to move closer.

His forehead was wrinkled with fatigue and worry and there were dark circles under his eyes.

"Thanks for coming," Phae said to him before spinning to Nora. "*You're welcome,*" Phae intoned breezily, leaving them in the entry hall alone.

She could have killed her sister. Or kissed her. One of those.

"Hi," she said numbly, unsure what to do with her

hands or her body, which had started alternating hot and cold in response to her anxiety level going up.

Maxwell was not so affected.

He took two large steps toward her, gathering her into his arms without hesitation. She could feel the steady beat of his heart under her ear and the way his arms banded her to his body made her release any doubts she might have had about the situation between them.

"I've missed you so much, Elle," he said it heavily into her hair, breathing her in just as much as she was doing to him. His spicy male scent situated itself firmly in her lungs.

"I'm so sorry," she sighed, tears prickling. "I feel so dumb."

"No." He pulled away and lifted her face gently with one large hand cradling her cheek. He made sure she was looking into his eyes. "I'm not sure why you thought leaving and not calling was the best answer, but this is not. Your. Fault. You don't need to apologize to me."

Nora nodded and let him pull her back in for a hug.

"But I do," she said, pulling away a bit so she could see his eyes. "I'm sorry that you got stuck in the middle of my mess. They violated your personal space, Maxwell. They got photos of us on the second-floor patio."

He shook his head. "We can handle all that. I'm just glad you're okay."

Nora gave a short nod. Phae reappeared with Nora's bag and Jace.

"Here's your stuff."

"You're kicking me out?" Nora asked for the second time that day.

Phae sighed and hugged her sister. "Yes. Go work this out. I'll come visit soon, okay?"

Jace looked amused and a little impressed by the significant surprise Phae had pulled off. "If you want to leave your rental car keys, I'll take it back for you in the morning."

"How long have you guys been working on this?" she asked, handing over the key. Her eyes narrowed a bit and Jace barked a laugh, putting up his hands in surrender, then gesturing at Phae. Phae just shrugged, non-plussed, and not at all guilty.

"Not that long. It came together nicely after I started answering Devon's calls." Maxwell admitted.

"Stephanie promised me she wouldn't so much as give you my phone number," Nora said, unable to keep the lift from her lips.

"She didn't. Her scheming husband—your good friend I might add—is the one responsible." Maxwell smiled and took her bag from Phae. "I'm pretty sure he got a sound tongue lashing and maybe even a frying pan to the side of the head this afternoon when she found out. Lucky for him, you'd already texted as well so maybe she went a bit easier on him."

Nora smiled. She wasn't upset. She felt like she should be, but she couldn't muster that energy. Relief weighed too heavy for the anger to rise up.

"Come home with me?" Maxwell asked. She could see the edge of fear in his eyes that she might say no.

"Okay. Let me say goodbye."

Jace called over his shoulder. "Everyone tell Nora bye!"

There was a messy chorus of "nice to meet you" and "see you soon" and Phae was ushering her out the front door.

Maxwell ducked down, kissing Phae on the cheek and hugging her lightly on the walk. "Thanks," he said, smiling. "Nice to meet you, Phaedra. You should absolutely come to California to visit soon."

"Anytime," she confirmed, then drew Nora in for a tight squeeze. "And I will. Swear." Phae turned her attention to Nora, who was half-heartedly glaring. "Sorry not sorry," she said. "You need him, he's been completely miserable and your whole life is back in California. Get the hell out of here, get your apology on, and don't screw this up."

Nora couldn't stop the laugh. "Wow. Who are you? What have you done with my sweet little sister?"

Phae laughed and hugged her one more time.

"I'm your grown-up little sister, and you know I'm right."

Nora nodded and got into the car. "I do." She blew her sister a kiss, waving as Maxwell pulled the car away from the curb.

The silence in the car was terrifying and oppressive. Wordlessly, Maxwell reached out for her hand. He twined his fingers in hers as he watched the road. At a stoplight, he glanced over to find her staring, drawing her palm up to kiss it.

"Stephanie said you weren't mad, and I guess I didn't believe her. Why aren't you mad?"

Maxwell chuckled and shook his head.

"I'm mad as hell, Elle. But not *at* you. *For* you. I was a little frustrated and a lot disappointed that you didn't come to me for help or even to tell me what was going on, but I get it. Now? I'm just so damn happy to see you."

"Why?" Nora said, realizing that she sounded ungrateful. She wasn't, in fact, the gratitude threatened to drown her. She just didn't understand.

"I like you," Maxwell said simply, grinning at her.

"I like you too."

He nodded, and they were quiet as he navigated them out of town and back toward Atlanta. He'd booked them into a hotel right at the airport so all they had to do was get on the plane in the morning.

"I meant it, you know. When I asked what *we* needed to do when you got that message. I wasn't just offering because it was something that sounded nice."

Nora shivered, feeling the blanket of shame descend again.

"I get it. I do. I'm so sorry, Maxwell. I'm used to having to deal with everything on my own. My instinct was to run. I knew that the fallout was going to be messy and I thought disappearing was the best way to protect you. All of you. I never considered that I might have … what I have. Not for this. Not like this." Her eyebrows pulled together.

"Family? Friends?" He turned his attention from the highway for a moment and met her eye.

"Honestly? Yes, all that. My mother…" she just shook her head. Athena was not a good example. She too had plied Nora for money and had done nothing but make her feel guilt for what happened. "I have Phae. And Devon. But this seemed like a *me* problem. Not an anyone else problem. Especially because you were becoming … collateral damage."

He grunted, a frown marring his usually smooth features.

"But I won't make that mistake again. I promise." A small smile tipped her lips up and he matched it with his own.

"You'd better not," he threatened, his voice dark for a short moment. Then, it lightened. "I've been making calls to our network of attorneys. I'm sure you'll get your pick for absolutely stellar representation for the case the state is no doubt building against the disgrace of a man that was blackmailing you. Revenge porn isn't taken lightly either. Devon has been fielding the communication from the detective for you as well. If you start to forget what you've got again, be sure that I'll make sure you only get undercooked bacon and Twizzlers for the rest of your life."

That was a threat she could live with.

CHAPTER
Eighteen

ORA WAS FEELING fairly exhausted by the time they dropped off the car and took the shuttle over to the hotel. Maxwell checked them in while she took in the vast expanse of glass and chrome that was the lobby. Even the furniture was ultra-modern.

She hated everything about it.

Still carrying her bag, he put an arm around her shoulders and guided her to the elevator, not letting go until he had to attempt to use the card-reader door lock.

Once inside, uneasiness set in. The click of the door and the deadbolt being thrown had Nora turning back toward him from the view of the single, king-sized bed.

He set her bag on the little luggage cart and she could feel the full, heavy weight of his attention on her body.

"Elle."

That single word was enough to send blood flowing to parts he alone seemed to control.

"Maxwell," she responded.

He advanced on her slowly, the catlike way he moved making her heart pound.

His hands reached up and held her face gently; thumbs caressing her jawline. Her eyes slipped closed, the sensation of his touch echoing all the way through her body.

She could feel his breath just a moment before his mouth met hers. It was hesitant at first, but when she made a noise in her throat, he deepened it, laying another one of those all-consuming, all parts involved kisses on her. All thought vanished and she fell into his embrace, pulling him closer.

When the kiss broke, Maxwell cradling her to him once again, she apologized once more.

"I'm sorry."

He just pressed his lips to her forehead.

"We'll figure it out, okay? Just like we said we would."

She nodded and shivered as she felt his hands gently tugging at her clothing.

"Yes," she whispered, which was all the permission he needed.

Desperation guided them through the motions of divesting one another of clothing. They wrapped themselves in one another instead, Maxwell rocking himself hotly into her pliant body, their breath a heavy sound in the quiet room as they reconnected, Nora's body greeting his eagerly and with enthusiasm, driving them both to a speedy climax.

"Next time."

Maxwell was mumbling to himself, but she couldn't help but smile as they lay there tangled in the covers and one another. He could have meant they would go slower, indulge exploration more, make use of the convenient chaise by the window. Any number of things. It didn't matter, though. She agreed and would gladly join him— next time.

AS IT HAPPENED, there were three *next times* in that hotel room, and they made perfectly tremendous efforts to cover any guess that Nora might have had about what he'd been referring to.

The chaise was everything she'd hoped it would be, and she just knew that the one in Maxwell's room in Malibu would be a favorite for quite some time based on the trial run in the hotel.

Room service had delivered their overly posh stainless-steel pot of coffee and an assortment of pastries and fruit while she was showering.

He'd tried to make the shower into a *next time* situation, but there wasn't time or room for them to attempt that properly.

Just as they were finishing picking over the tray of food, Maxwell's phone rang.

He frowned at the phone, eyebrows drawn together. "Morning Devon." His frown deepened into a scowl. "Hold on, let me put you on speaker."

"Sorry to drop this on you just before your flight, but someone broke into your place, Nor."

"What?" Nora found herself springing to her feet, heart in her throat.

"It was stellar planning ahead on your part to leave all your valuables with me when you left. I'm so impressed and happy you did that." He cleared his throat. "They uh…they trashed it pretty good."

"Oh my god."

Nora's adrenaline pounded as Devon relayed the story. She felt violated, but also somehow relieved. Like she'd known it was going to happen, and having confirmation that it was over meant she could stop waiting for the other shoe to drop. He'd gone over to care for her plants—which at some point down the road she would definitely be simultaneously teasing and thanking him for doing—and the door had very visibly been jimmied open.

"I've got half a mind to return the hardware we just installed back to the store." He sighed. "Anyway. The police are checking it all out, your landlord is involved, everything is a mess though. You don't want to go there when you get back."

Maxwell looked at her, sympathy painting his features. His raised eyebrow somehow managed to communicate his question without him saying anything at all.

"I can stay with Maxwell. I never loved that apartment, anyway. I will need to get a few things, but I'm not heart-broken about anything they might have destroyed. Well, except my plants maybe. They're okay, right?"

Both men sighed at her. She knew it was ridiculous, but they were her babies. "Yes, the plants are fine."

She nodded, noting that her question had made Maxwell turn away with a grin on his face even as he shook his head.

"You have all of my Yiayia's jewelry and important papers. I'm fine. Clothes and dishes and ... *stuff* can be replaced."

Devon sounded relieved. "Yep, I've got you covered. I'll let you know what the police have to say if you aren't back before then. Safe travels."

Maxwell hung up and Nora let out a breath.

"You okay staying with me?"

Nora smiled, she couldn't help it. He was giving her that grin again.

"I feel like I should be asking you that. Last time I slept over, your bare ass ended up on all the gossip shows."

He chuckled. "Worth it."

They gathered their things, Maxwell left a tip for house-keeping and they exited the steel and glass hotel directly into the noisy, crowded airport terminal.

There was no significant luggage to check, so security was blessedly quick, but while winding their way through the queue Nora couldn't help but feel the eyes on her. She knew the brunette was fading and she was close to getting recognized. Thankfully, nobody called out, nobody asked for a selfie and nobody took her photo. That she noticed anyway.

Hand in hand with Maxwell, he guided them confidently down the travertine hallways lined with shops toward their gate. After a moment's hesitation, he located the closest restaurant that served alcohol and they sat at the bar, quietly sipping their drinks, knees touching.

The television gave a brief blurb at one point regarding Nora and her current ugly situation, but the story was short and moved on from quickly. The bartender had glanced at her a little closely at one point but moved on just as fast.

Slightly more relaxed, once the announcement for their flight came over the speakers the pair boarded business class and headed back to Los Angeles, fingers entwined and something breathing between them that hadn't been there before.

NORA HAD THOUGHT maybe things would relax a bit from then on.

She was wrong.

The hits came hard and fast over the next few days and she often felt like she was trying to swim upstream and couldn't catch her breath.

It was very much like it had been before she ran away, and she was beginning to consider that option again. There had to be an island *somewhere* that was peaceful, right?

Alan had retrieved them from the airport in his huge black SUV. He had thrown Nora a brief 'I can't believe you did that' scowl but then brought her in for a giant hug.

"Don't do that again," he growled.

"Would you mind? I'd appreciate you taking your paws off my girl, Alan." Maxwell sighed.

"I don't mind at all," Alan grumbled, giving her one last squeeze before releasing her.

"Not planning on it," she confirmed, smiling at the large man to make him smile back. She caught Maxwell's eye, and he winked at her, deepening the surge of happy emotions his words had caused.

Once he was sure they were safely tucked into the vehicle, Alan hustled them away from the mess that was traffic near LAX.

NORA TUCKED HERSELF into Maxwell's condo and life like she was meant to be there, and honestly, it felt like she was. If she needed to leave, she was shuttled by either Alan or Maxwell or both.

Over the course of a week, she was shuffled off to a meeting with the police to file a report about the burglary, a meeting with her landlord to discuss how to end her lease and deal with her things, a meeting with Samuel Caine as an introduction to some attorneys from another firm to handle the mounting case against David, who they appeared to be close to catching up to, plus a meeting with both Mel Marty Dennison to get her work affairs straightened out. It was exhausting but necessary and she felt like she'd never work out the cramp in her hand from signing paperwork.

Devon and Stephanie had met them at Maxwell's condo that first evening to talk through what they'd done as far as public relations spin and what she might want to consider doing going forward. They also wanted to 'discuss' with her how she was to *never* disappear again.

"Never. Just no," Devon said fiercely, bringing her in for a hug that left very little room for her to breathe.

"Just reach out." Stephanie had smiled ruefully. "Trust me, I get the inclination. I did the same thing not so long ago." Stephanie and Devon shared a very meaningful look.

"I will. Reach out, I mean. I won't just disappear. Promise."

Nora had returned her friend's smile and hug, thankful to have been inducted into such a wonderful circle of friendship.

The third night back, Nora's phone rang. Recognizing the number as LAPD, she answered.

The officer on the other end of the line had some news and requested that she come down to the precinct in person.

"Of course. We'll get there as soon as we can."

There didn't seem to be adequate words for the shock Nora felt when she entered the station and could hear not only belligerent shouting in David's voice but also *Olivia's*.

Nora met Maxwell's eye, and his expression was that of stunned disbelief. Oddly, it quickly shifted to dispassionate and something bordering on relief.

He'd explained to her over wine the other night that aside from the bizarre coffee date interruption, Olivia had turned up outside his office, outside his condo, and even at his parent's house in Santa Barbara. No matter what he said, she didn't seem to understand that they were more than over and that she needed to stop appearing in places she knew he would be.

Olivia hadn't taken it well, any of those times, which was in line with how she'd taken it when he broke up with her for cheating on him.

Nora couldn't understand what Olivia had been thinking at all. It was perplexing, to say the least, but to have her linked with David? That was a step beyond.

"Sorry. Come with me please?" The police Captain guided them to a private office past a thrashing, swearing Olivia, and David, who was screaming that whatever had happened wasn't his fault. He was yelling something about a drone and the beach and suddenly, where the pictures had come from of her and Maxwell from the second-floor patio made a *whole* lot of sense. What a jerk.

Nora suppressed a barrage of shivers, feeling like she'd been exposed all over again.

Olivia began to shriek about her rights and even pulled out the classic, *"Don't you know who I am?"* line before she was handcuffed and shuffled away.

Captain Ortiz delivered them to a small but quiet private office that smelled like old coffee and musty carpeting. Bookshelves crammed to capacity lined the room and piles of paperwork were stacked haphazardly on the utilitarian desk. He gestured for them to have a seat and closed the door behind himself. It was almost too quiet for a moment, but then he let out a deep sigh as he situated himself behind the desk, fingers steepled together as he appraised them with a patient and kind expression.

After a moment, they were joined by the familiar face of Detective Rutherford. He asked if she could give her version of events, one more time from start to finish, as best as she could recall.

Nora's brain stuttered over a few of the details, but she recounted everything as clinically and as specifically as she could while he took notes, nodding calmly throughout. Maxwell squeezed her hand in support at certain points, and once she finished, she felt completely wrung out.

Nora sat stunned as the kind detective dropped three bombs on them, all in neat succession after verifying that Nora was okay with Maxwell sitting in on the discussion.

Didn't everything come in threes, good or bad? Maxwell held and squeezed her hand as the detective spoke, her brain reeling from the information he was delivering.

David and Olivia had allegedly colluded to break into her apartment. The two had apparently known one another for quite some time as they'd worked together on several adult films before Olivia moved on to more mainstream film parts. That revelation made Maxwell sit up a bit straighter.

As Nora had partially overheard, they had plotted together to take photos by drone but they had also paid off a couple of different photographers to closely watch Nora specifically, but Maxwell as well. David was motivated by his desire to continue extorting money out of Nora, and Olivia was motivated by the same—just as a way to get close to Maxwell.

There was also some information linking David to Athena, Nora's own mother.

Then Captain Ortiz explained that there was signif-icant evidence showing a long history of texts between David and Athena and money transfers that once Nora looked closely, seemed to align with dates that she had changed phone numbers.

Her mother was taking payment to give up her phone number and address to a man who was blackmailing her to keep an unauthorized sex tape quiet.

It was beyond ridiculous.

Nora's rage flamed white-hot. No doubt the money paid to the bad people—her own mother, the paparazzi following them around, Olivia—had originally been *hers.* The fact that her mother was so desperate for money that she didn't earn and that Charlie could just gamble away she'd beg for it, and then use it to pay off people to take photos that could be sold for even more dirty money was just disgusting and disturbing. And hurtful.

She knew her family had its issues but to see her mother go to this extent to not only tarnish her daughter but to further her own wealth broke Nora in places on the inside she had wrongly thought were already shattered.

Nora decided right then and there she'd never again speak to her mother. This was unforgivable. Calling Phae to let her know was at the top of her to-do list.

The information was still being cleared up, but there had also been some contact between David and Athena regarding releasing the videos to the media.

It was ugly and painful and beyond convoluted. Fortunately, the law was on Nora's side, and she didn't have to focus on it any longer. At least after a while, anyway. The detective advised that the state was building a case and there was the possibility of a trial. The other option was a settlement. It seemed likely that past that whole process, they would be punished and she could move on.

Well, mostly. Certainly, it would always be hovering in the background and she might see herself pop up naked online randomly, but based on the positive reaction from supporters when the news broke, she wasn't worried.

She could let go of the anxiety that had been choking her for years.

YEARS.

The money was a lost cause most likely, but that was okay. She'd made many stupid decisions and had paid dearly for them, but it was over now. Maxwell suggested that she may be able to file a civil case to recoup some of that money, and the detective nodded in agreement. Nora decided that she'd look into it, but with low expectations, just in case.

Breath left her in a rush as she started to let go of the fear. She felt as though she'd aged about ten years sitting there listening to the kind policemen.

He gave them a moment to digest all the things he'd told them and leaned back in his chair.

"Your apartment has been cleared. It's no longer the site of a pending investigation—you can go home if you like." He smiled, and it made him seem years younger.

She thanked him—because that's what you're supposed to do, right?

Once everything had been said that needed to be, the officer wrapped up their conversation and led them back through the station toward the exit.

After a manly handshake exchange between Captain Ortiz and Maxwell and a gentle wave to her, all that was left were the formalities—more paperwork, of course—and the promise of an update if anything new came up. There were some signatures made and instructions for the next steps Nora hoped Maxwell could help her remember later.

Nora leaned into Maxwell's warm hand as it rose to her lower back. He left it there all through the station, all down the front steps and all the way to the car where he opened the door and tucked her into his little roadster before climbing in himself.

Her mind spun. That apartment wasn't home. She didn't want to go back there.

She wasn't going to, either—not if Maxwell would let her stay for a while. She was perfectly happy right where she was. There were a few things she might go back to retrieve in addition to her plants—her bed came to mind if it wasn't trashed—but everything else could be tossed or donated and her landlord could do whatever he wanted. She'd pay early termination if she had to, but she had a feeling he'd be glad to see her go along her merry way.

No more crappy apartment. No more Mrs. Gravitz and perpetual vinegar smell. No more of *that* Nora. No more living the way she had been because of outgoing hush money.

Maxwell's grin was broad and his tone jovial when she expressed that she would like to stay if he'd have her. His words stroked pleasantly along the nerve-endings in her spine.

"Are you comfortable where you are then, Elle? Because I'm more than happy to keep you in my bed."

Nora smiled, her heart picking up its tempo as she looked into his eyes.

"My budget is going to change for the better now that I no longer have a significant amount of blackmail money going out."

He grunted. "Hopefully you'll get some of that back. You have the best attorneys in Hollywood at your disposal, after all. It pays to have good connections."

"Don't I know it."

"Have you spoken to your agent yet? I know she's been desperate to get in touch with you. She's been calling the office religiously trying to hunt you down since she doesn't have your new number."

Nora sighed. Guilt pressed on her. She knew better than to avoid her agent. Mel was probably only trying to be helpful, just like the rest of the army of friends and allies she had been dumb enough to run away from. It was not a good place to be as an agent when this kind of thing happened and your client went total radio silence.

"Not really. Just a little bit on a conference call with Marty. Tomorrow. I'll call her tomorrow."

Maxwell nodded, navigating them smoothly through traffic.

"She seems like good people," he assessed.

"She is," Nora confirmed with a nod. "The best, actually."

"Text her then. Don't leave her hanging and stressed out. She sounds like she might already have a bit of an aggressive anxiety problem. Hannah suggested that she might benefit from some cannabis use. Medicinal, of course."

One side of his mouth lifted in a grin and Nora found herself nodding and laughing. So, she'd pegged the unflappable Hannah right after all. The idea made her spirits lift considerably.

"That's an accurate description of Mel, actually. Aggressively anxious."

Heeding his advice, she shot off a quick text letting Mel know that she would be happy to talk or even meet in person sometime in the next week or so.

A barrage of responses arrived shortly, everything from relief that Nora was okay to scolding for falling off the map and not letting her know what was going on. They made an appointment early the following week to discuss everything and as Maxwell pulled into the lot at his condo, exhaustion set in.

"Come on, Elle. Let's get you a bath and some food. Maybe some wine."

"Yes please."

She trudged up the steps, Maxwell's hand at her lower back where she liked it, her feet feeling like lead weights.

As the massive tub in the chrome and marble master bathroom filled up, Nora dialed Phae. To her shock, her sister picked up on the second ring.

"Hey! You okay?"

Nora smiled. "No. Not really. But things will get better from here."

They had to.

"What's going on? There's all kinds of stuff online about your skeevy ex and Maxwell's *skanky* ex and paparazzi?"

Pouring a capful of lilac scented bubbles into the tub, Nora recounted the basics of what she understood to have happened.

"That's not all though, Phae. Mom…" She stopped, a knot of emotion fisting her throat closed.

"What about Mom?" Phae's tone was dark.

"I don't…I don't have all the details, but it looks like she was involved too."

Silence stretched out between them. The water level was good, so Nora turned off the tap and just waited, twisting a soft gray washcloth between her hands, the last drips falling from the faucet echoing off the walls.

Finally, Phae spoke.

"I want to feel surprised, Nor. I do. But…I don't. Is that weird? I'm so damn *angry* with her if it's true."

"Not weird. Same." Tears filled her eyes, and Nora let them. "It seems legit. There's not really a question of if she did it, more like how deeply involved she was. She was the one giving him my new number, my address. He paid her for it."

"I can't…" Phae heaved a sigh. "I'm so sorry."

"Thanks, sister. I love you. I just thought you should know."

They dallied for a moment longer, giving their goodbyes and after they'd hung up, Nora allowed herself the sobs that had been choking her. She sat on the edge of the tub and poured all her conflicted emotions out into her hands, the tears a mix of rage and loss.

Once she could breathe again, she slipped out of her clothes and into the steamy water.

She was trying desperately and failing to soak away her troubles when Maxwell rapped a knuckle on the glossy white door-frame, a glass of rich red wine in hand.

"Thought you could use this." He sat on the edge of the tub as she had, offering the glass.

"Thanks."

"You alright? Phae?"

Serious Maxwell was devastatingly hard on her heart. She was so in love with this man it wasn't even funny.

"I think so. Same wavelength about Mom." Nora hoped that Maxwell could decipher her shorthand as she spoke. Words were not her friend at the moment and thoughts were stilted.

"I'm not surprised." He stroked her cheek with his fingers. "Dinner will be here by the time you get out."

She nodded softly. "Thank you."

He grinned. Damn, she adored that grin.

"Anything for you, Elle."

Maxwell left the bathroom and she resumed her quiet soaking, willing herself to absorb his words and feel worthy of them.

Once she'd had her fill of hot water and bubbles, she pulled the plug and tugged on her favorite spa-quality robe. Maxwell seemed to have nicked a few from his parents' beach house and she wasn't mad about it one bit; they were glorious.

She could hear the front door open and a short conversation in low voices happen. Assuming it was the food, she made her way back through the bedroom to the living room only to be barreled into by an enthusiastic Rufus. His massive paws found her waist and she took a step back to balance, laughing as she did so.

"Whoa! Rufus, easy!" Maxwell was chuckling as he tried to pull the furry bundle of excitement off of her.

"He's okay." Nora found herself laughing, heart light as the dog lapped at her cheeks. She lowered herself to her knees and he buried his head in her chest as she scratched behind his ears, then flopped over onto his back so she could rub his belly.

"Oh wow. I needed that." She sighed once Rufus had gotten his fill and wandered off to find the water and food dishes.

Maxwell was beaming, hand outstretched to help her off of the floor as he watched his dog.

"He's pretty good therapy, I've learned."

"I totally get that."

Maxwell held her hand as he pulled her to the small round dining table where some bags from *Cleo* sat.

"Did your parents…" Nora left off, heart threatening to burst right out of her chest. She didn't deserve this man or his family.

He nodded. "They were on their way back from Malibu and it was on their way. They figured I could use some time with my furry beast so they brought him along too. They like you." His smile was wide.

"They don't really know me," she protested, feeling her brow furrow. "I mean, I met your dad at the office, but what they must think after everything hit the press? I was in a *sex tape*, I was naked—" panic started to rise, her body heating up as her mind to spin out of control.

Maxwell pressed his fingers to her lips and then pulled her into a tight hug, grinning that wolfish easy smile into her hair.

"Elle. Breathe. They don't care about what pictures are in the press. You make me happy. Rufus likes you. You're essentially related to Devon. That's more than enough for them."

Nora didn't have a rebuttal for that and managed a deep breath.

He kissed her forehead and then pulled out a chair for her. It was an unexpected way to end the day, recreating their first dinner date at Maxwell's cozy apartment, but not unwelcome. Rufus underfoot was the best possible addition and not having paparazzi to contend with after the meal ended was spectacular.

They ate, and drank, and laughed.

Emotionally wrung out, she allowed Maxwell to escort her to the master suite after dinner and then a movie on the plush sofa, where he languidly pulled every ounce of pleasure he possibly could from her body before she drifted off to a blessedly dreamless sleep.

CHAPTER
Nineteen

ORA'S DESCENT INTO madness seemed to slow and things thankfully started to rebound as the Summer months gave way to the cooler breeze of early Fall.

TMZ moved on to another scandal much faster than expected, and Nora was grateful. Charges were pending and for as overblown as everything had gotten in her head, they were straightening out with tremendous speed. Credit of course due there to Stephanie, Devon, and Maxwell. Well, plus their connections and money.

She wasn't sure how she'd ever repay them, but as a joke, she would start with jars and jars of pickled goodies courtesy of Mrs. Gravitz. Strangely, the pickle cabinet was spared entirely when Nora's apartment got tossed.

Devon, at least, wouldn't mind. He was a lover of all things pickled. Rumor had it that David was going to settle his case with the state, and even the civil case seemed likely to shake out in Nora's favor which was a pleasant turn of events. The wheels of justice had been greased before being set in motion and they were making an example out of David and Olivia for their part in what amounted to mass release of revenge porn and blackmail. Nora was perpetually thankful.

Athena had not once attempted to call.

Phae had done Nora a solid and called her dad to get the closest thing she could to the truth. Athena was on house-arrest for her part in the illegal activities, which complicated their lives significantly, but neither Phae or Nora really cared. It made them sad, but what Athena had done, likely with Charlie's knowledge if not his blessing, was simply unforgivable.

The show resumed filming on schedule and was extended two more seasons thanks to overwhelming fan support and the network paying attention to viewership instead of just ratings—which honestly were also pretty great. There would be a break in filming for the holidays right around the time Phae was finishing up college and she had a seed of a plan percolating in the back of her mind for luring her sister to the west coast.

Acting of course was her first love, but it seemed with Maxwell considering transitioning away from law and into the security app business, it felt like just about every-thing was changing. Nora was feeling—and not for the first time—that things in her life were about to shift in another big way and she found herself welcoming it instead of fearing it.

That part was new.

The newly established couple had settled into a very comfortable co-habitation routine at Maxwell's condo. Lazy, half-naked weekends with too much coffee, too many buttery pastries, plenty of overgrown puppy cuddles, and lots of companionable quiet were quickly becoming Nora's very favorite thing.

They'd transitioned over everything that she wanted to keep from her old apartment, and it was a shockingly small amount all told. Her plants were honestly the majority of it, and that fact alone made Nora a bit sad. She'd been stuck a long time, and it took having to sort through destroyed things, things that were not of any sentimental or monetary value for her to realize just how bad it had gotten. The backpack she'd given Devon held everything she couldn't replace.

There's been sufficient space in Maxwell's spare room and closets for her things and she had pretty much just moved right in. He didn't seem to mind.

She didn't either.

It was odd, but cozy and like pretty much everything to do with Maxwell, she was learning to just go with it.

"I was thinking I might take a look at the place Stephanie is renovating." Her voice was low and the words had a strangely powerful feeling once they were out in the open. It was an unusual and unplanned declaration. She'd been reviewing the script for her next episode, words all blurring together when the thought took over and decided to show up out loud.

Maxwell glanced over at her from where he was settled on the other end of his dove gray sofa. It was ridiculously plush and as deep as a twin mattress.

There was something pretty spectacular about the Caine family's uncanny ability to pick out amazing furniture.

Maxwell rarely made sudden or sharp movements, but she could tell that this surprised him a bit with how abruptly he turned her way.

His mocha eyes tracked her face for a moment, and then he grinned.

"I think that's a wonderful idea."

"Really?" Nora's breath caught in a strange way. She knew he wasn't trying to get rid of her, but his enthusiasm was a bit surprising.

"Truly. She's very happy there. It seems like a great way to have a life away from the city. If I kept this condo, and you had a place there, perhaps that would be a good balance for both of us all the way around."

Nora smiled. He said it so matter-of-factly. As if there were no question that they were an 'us' and would continue to be. The sweeping wave of warm tingly feeling she got from making plans for a future that involved Maxwell was oddly pleasant in her stomach.

"Plus, it would get Steph off my back about buying it myself. She's about to start decorating in earnest and she's been driving me up the wall about it." The smile he reserved just for his best friend was kind and endearing.

A thought occurred, and Nora's daydreaming crashed a bit.

"It's probably really, really far out of my price range." Nora's face fell.

Maxwell tossed her that devil-may-care grin and patted the seat next to him. He placed the laptop he was working on atop the massive tufted ottoman in front of him and opened his arms for her. She couldn't resist that offer and tucked herself into his warm embrace.

"Shall we invite them for dinner and discuss it? You know Steph can be bought off for just about anything with Mr. Woo's," He made a thoughtful noise, a sound close to a growl really, and it resonated throughout her body. "We can meet them at the restaurant?"

Nora felt the sardonic laugh dance past her lips, loving the caress of Maxwell's breath in her hair, his fingers gently tracing the outline of her shoulder-blade through her shirt.

"No number of egg-rolls could possibly drop the price-tag of a multi-million-dollar condo into my price range. It's a decent idea, though."

Maxwell's chuckle rumbled under her ear. Her stomach let out a similar noise which felt like it maybe should be a bit embarrassing but wasn't.

"You never know. Either way, dinner, yes?"

Nora nodded and Maxwell got out his phone to text Stephanie. There was a near-instantaneous cluster or dings in response and Maxwell laughed broadly, lowering his mouth to Nora's in a luxurious and stirringly thorough kiss before moving to stand.

"I take it that was a yes?" She laughed, sliding out from under Maxwell's arm and preparing to stand.

"You know it. She'd never refuse. I'm certain she's dragging Devon out of the house by the hand and speeding across town as we speak."

Nora laughed at the thought, gathering her purse and jacket before following Maxwell down to his little roadster.

As Maxwell had guessed, Devon and Stephanie were already seated and helping themselves to some green tea and pot-stickers when they arrived at the somehow simultaneously modern, upscale bistro with a classic and almost cliché Chinese restaurant feel. Red paper lanterns and good luck cats mingled with lots of stainless steel and clean dark wood.

There didn't appear to be many photogs hanging around outside the gates of Maxwell's gated condo complex or the set for which Nora was thankful. There were of course always a handful of paps waiting to take a picture when she left the condo or stepped within view on the back-lot, but not nearly as many as before her case broke. She'd been extra careful to point out anyone that seemed pointedly interested in her alone to both Alan and Detective Rutherford. Anybody that seemed to be constantly around for no real reason was also suspect. Two of the three faces she had been recognizing regularly had vanished completely after everything came out because of David.

Apparently, getting harassment charges filed against you didn't really impress employers, even when said employers were tabloids.

"What's shakin'?" Devon grinned, standing enough to shake Maxwell's hand and lean in to give Nora a friendly hug. Stephanie gave Maxwell a similar greeting and then they sat, the waitress bustling over to fill two more teacups.

"Do we need a reason to want a family dinner?" Maxwell pretended offense at the accusation.

Nora loved that they had all started calling it that. It made her feel so loved and special to be part of a family like this.

"No, but you usually do anyway." Stephanie raised her eyebrow at Maxwell over her teacup.

He sighed heavily, feigning frustration and defeat, but his mouth curled up into a grin as he looked at Nora, giving her encouragement to start the condo conversation.

"I already ordered for the table," Devon said reassuringly, that smirk he was known for taunting her.

"Of course you did," Nora muttered, shaking her head. She was smiling though, and he grinned back.

"Is something wrong?" Stephanie's face grew pensive.

"No, not at all." Maxwell shook his head, helping himself to a couple of pot-stickers. "I think these taste better when tossed directly at my face after I've said something hilarious," he ribbed Stephanie. Clearly, there was some kind of inside joke there.

Shrugging, she picked one up and chucked it at him.

Nora would have ducked without meaning to, but Maxwell reached up with one clever, quick hand and snatched it from the air before stuffing it into his mouth.

"Thanks," he mumbled over the mouthful.

"You guys are ridiculous." Devon laughed.

"He started it," Stephanie protested with a giggle.

TMZ would have a field day with pictures of their friendly food fight, Nora thought. For a change, the notion didn't bring dark clouds with it—it was purely amusing.

She cleared her throat and started right in before she could lose her nerve.

"Maxwell mentioned that you're renovating a space across the hall from your place in Santa Barbara."

Stephanie paused mid-sip, but her face brightened.

"Yes. It's basically finished except for decorating and final finishes. He's not taking my unsubtle hints that I'd like him to buy it. Are you interested?"

Nora glanced at Maxwell who just sat appraising his friend with a placid grin. Without moving his warm chocolate gaze from Stephanie to Nora, he placed his warm hand on her thigh, a reassuring weight.

"I am. But I'm afraid it's probably way out of my grasp as far as cost."

Stephanie made a noise in her throat. "I see. Well." Her smile was radiant. "I'm sure we can arrange something if you're interested. We should make plans for you to come out and see it at least."

Nora nodded. She could use a few days at the beach. It would be nothing but welcome to find that lovely bubble of peace and lust that she and Maxwell had inhabited in Malibu.

That weekend seemed like it was lifetimes away but it still shone bright in her memory, tasting like salt and wine.

"Yes. Definitely."

Stephanie beamed and dinner was delivered, breaking the moment.

"It's a good idea, Elle." Maxwell leaned in to whisper into her ear as the meal continued on all around them. Devon was similarly telling Stephanie something up close, making her smile and even blush a little. They were adorable together, the happiest newlyweds she'd ever seen.

It occurred to her then that she and Maxwell probably looked like that to people. She wasn't mad about it either, not even a little bit.

She was happy.

There were no more skeletons tapping at closet doors, no more looming threats, no more than the every-day dramatics that came with being a public figure. With a new phone and one of Maxwell's apps working in the background at all times, even the friendly texts from strang-ers had stopped. Only the people at this table, Phae and Alan were reaching out to her personally—and she liked it that way.

It was strange and lovely and she found herself wanting to freeze that moment and hang on to it, emotional in a good way for the second time in as many days.

Try as she might, there was no way to freeze time, so instead, she leaned over and took a selfie with her friends, posting it to Instagram as a bold middle finger to any paparazzi that might be lingering nearby and the tabloids as a whole.

Her media presence was hers to control, and she was going to be doing just that from now on.

WASTING TIME WAS apparently no longer something Nora chose to do.

That very weekend, the two couples headed out to Santa Barbara so she could take a look at the apartment. Devon and Stephanie needed to check on her place anyway, and they said they could use what Devon called a vacation, and Stephanie called a day off. It was clearly one of their own inside jokes, but it was cute.

They were a ridiculous couple, but Nora admired them.

There was a palpable shift in the air the moment they left the city limits, Nora effected just like she had been when she and Maxwell had taken a weekend in Malibu. The press of all those millions of bodies crammed into a compressed space, the energy of the city as a whole, and all the pressure of being Nora instead of Eleanora—or Elle—lifted. It was glorious and she understood wholly and completely why Stephanie enjoyed being away from Los Angeles.

Santa Barbara, with its mountains, bluffs, and Mediterranean influenced architecture spoke to Nora's soul in a way she hadn't expected. As they followed Devon down cute little side streets with lots of touristy foot-traffic, lots of hole-in-the-wall restaurants and kitschy shops, she found herself leaning forward in her seat and smiling.

"Uh oh," Maxwell teased. "I can only imagine what that look means."

Nora turned his way slightly, closing her eyes and drinking in the sun on her face, thankful the weather was still mild enough for him to put the top down on his little roadster once they'd hit city limits.

"Do you feel it?" she asked.

"I do," he confirmed after a short moment, voice quiet, almost reverent.

"Really?"

He released a warm laugh, and Nora could see that they were filing into an alleyway behind what must be the building where the apartments were.

"Yes, Elle. I feel it. I can't accurately describe it, but yes."

Nora couldn't have described it either really, but it was…light, and clean and tasted like salt and sunshine.

Fingers linked, they followed Stephanie and Devon through a quiet concrete hallway that sat between a clothing store and an Irish pub, then up a set of stairs. To the left was Stephanie's apartment and to the right the one undergoing remodel.

"I won't bother showing you my place first," Stephanie said, warm brandy-hued eyes bright. She unlocked the vacant unit and gestured for them to go in first.

There was nothing that didn't immediately take Nora's breath away. It was one large open space, and it was full of light. The kitchen was missing cabinets and counter-tops, but there was an assortment of samples laid out on a makeshift table made from plywood and saw-horses. And professional stainless appliances standing at the ready.

It was a blank canvas, and Nora's mind was painting it aggressively.

Nobody said a word as she walked through the space, the quiet tap of her shoes echoing off of the bare walls. Well, some bare walls, quite a bit of exposed brick, and some enormous windows.

Stephanie had taken care to blend the history of the old mercantile store the building used to be with clean modern lines and conveniences. Nora adored the old red brick and hardwood flooring no doubt made from re-purposed original lumber. Every texture she could put her fingers on and touch, she did, and it was like the space hummed back at her in greeting.

The skylights and wall of windows were everything her green-thumb heart could ever ask for, and she envisioned islands of plants all over the space; planters hanging from the vast ceiling and on the walls and clusters of pots on tables and the floor and on shelves in front of the windows.

She could very clearly visualize dark wood cabinets with frosted-glass fronts, some kind of quartz or marble counter-tops, a farmhouse-style table made from more planks of the flooring material and even a casual living room area with furniture from the same set as in either Maxwell's condo or his parents' house.

Nora could hear Devon making a thoughtful noise and Stephanie shushing him as she made her way toward the area that would be a bedroom. The bathroom was built out, but still bare. Nora wanted those amazing river rocks in the shower and slate on the floor.

One more trip around the space revealed that there was a balcony outside the glass and a staircase up to the roof. With her friends following her, still quiet, she gasped when she got to the top.

Someone, long ago, had planned a rooftop garden. It was only about half the size of the apartment below her feet, the space she desperately wanted to be hers, and it was perfect. The brick edges of the roof came up nearly to her waist, and there were some really sturdy wooden shelves already lining one side. Old buckets, some full of soil remained, and it looked like the flat area was well-drained and maintained.

Tears sprang to her eyes. There was no avoiding the sudden wave of emotion that surged, telling her in no uncertain terms that she had arrived *home*.

From her place on the roof, she could see the rolling ocean, taste the waves, hear the gulls. There was the not unpleasant smell of a restaurant grill from the place beneath Stephanie's apartment, and her friends were all talking quietly behind her.

"I need this," she finally said, not intending the words to be aloud.

Turning, she met Stephanie's pleased brandy-toned eye. Devon, the cad, was smirking, and Maxwell looked positively angelic.

"See, Alex? I told you that you weren't waiting for me to decide. You were waiting for *her*."

Stephanie gave a *tsk* with her tongue, but conceded.

"I suppose you're right. Come on, Nora. Let's go pick your finishes out." Stephanie reached out a hand toward her.

Nora couldn't help but smile at the thought but shook her head.

"I don't even know how much you're asking. I could barely afford my crappy apartment and ancient car."

Stephanie *tsk*ed again, shaking her head as they all filed back down the stairs and into the empty apartment.

"We can all see clear as day that this place is yours." Stephanie sighed.

"Yes, but I can't afford it. I just know I can't." Nora felt crushed at the very thought of someone else living here.

Maxwell cleared his throat and stepped closer, putting his hand at her back.

"I was going to tell you at dinner, but they've gotten your bonus situation settled. Maybe you could use that as a down payment?"

Nora gaped at him. "Really?"

He smiled. "Dad let me know last night. I wanted to surprise you."

"Tell me what you see," Stephanie requested. "I've been delaying finishing for months—" she turned a glance to Maxwell, who just shrugged, that grin of his firmly in place. "Tell me, Nora—how would you do it?"

Nora cleared her throat and gazed around the room, starting with the kitchen. She noticed Stephanie's smile getting bigger and bigger as she described what she thought would fit—dark wood, glass, chrome. Next up was the bathroom, and Devon started laughing in earnest.

"What's funny?"

"Come next door. You'll see." He was shaking his head, but they all went over, Nora stunned into silence and then giggles when she saw that what she had asked for, minus a few adjustments, was basically what Stephanie had done with her own place.

"Wow," Maxwell said. "That's…"

"Totally creepy," Devon confirmed with a firm nod, brows drawn together, his hands in his pockets.

"Why don't you gentlemen go get us a table downstairs? Nora and I will work out some particulars," Stephanie offered, equal parts enthusiastic and diplomatic.

Maxwell and Devon both sighed, resigned to leaving them for some girl talk. Once they were gone, Stephanie put her arm around Nora's shoulders for a moment before grabbing a notebook and pen. Then, she guided her back into the empty space across the hall.

"Tell me everything. Whatever you like—that's what we'll do. Surely one of us knows a real-estate attorney we can have draw up the paperwork. I don't really care if it takes you a hundred years to pay off the loan Nora, you need this place as much as I want you to have it. We'll make it work."

Nora felt emotion clogging her throat again and swallowed against it. Stephanie brought her into a warm, gentle, friendly hug.

When the two stepped apart, they laughed and grinned at each other.

"I've missed having that," Stephanie said quietly, and Nora agreed. Having a solid, true female friend was a rarity for them both.

"Me too." Nora finally released the reigns she'd been holding on her imagination. "What are your counter-tops made out of?"

Stephanie laughed again, the rich sound filling the space.

Nora spared a quick thought for Maxwell and Devon, hoping they ordered drinks and appetizers and even a main course because this conversation was going to take a while and she was going to love every single moment.

CHAPTER Twenty

"ON'T EVER THINK about doing that to me again." Bulldog Mel was the one who showed up to their lunch meeting at a quiet cafe near her office downtown, all bright red lipstick, ballerina bun, and navy power-suit.

"Sorry, Mel. I've been hearing that a lot. I swear, it wasn't intentional and won't be repeated."

The fierce woman dropped the scowl and her expression softened into something like concern edged with relief.

"Damn right."

There was a brief pause as the waiter took their order, and then Mel wasted zero time launching information at Nora like it was her job. Which, honestly, it was.

"So, Hollywood Law got your bonus situation all settled, which is fantastic." She sipped at her hot water with lemon, hold the tea. "I got a call I really want you to consider, Nora. It's a feature film and they want you to come in and read in a couple of weeks. There are a couple of other readings for less interesting projects I want you to look at, but this one—this is the one I want you to really, seriously think about."

Mel pulled a ream of papers out of her bag and plunked them down on the table in front of Nora.

Shaking off some surprise both of Mel's news and the title adorning the top page in bold black letters, she flipped through the script, fingers trembling as she tried to remain casual.

"This is part of the Borderline franchise." Which was only the biggest, hottest movie franchise since … well, aside from something like Star Wars or Harry Potter, maybe ever.

"Yes." Mel nodded simply signaling to the waiter across the room with a raised mug and her red-lacquered fingernail that she'd like additional lemons. He hustled over a whole bowl full as well as a metal pot full of steaming water before Nora could find her voice.

"Mel."

"Nora?" The brash woman appraised her over the top of her mug, crimson lipstick staining the white ceramic.

"This is a big deal." Breath left her in a rush. "They want *me*? I'm just a TV actress—"

"And a damn good one. And yes, they asked for you specifically. It's just a reading, darling, don't get all in your head about it."

Mel looked right through Nora, who was floundering for words as her adrenaline spiked, making her hot then cold then hot again.

"Hey."

Nora met Mel's eyes, finding them kind and oddly soft. Mel was not soft.

"This could be a fantastic opportunity for you. No lies, for *us.*"

The laugh at Mel's honesty was short and genuine. They paused as the waiter efficiently delivered their meals.

"Just *read*, Nora. That's all you have to do. I know you're committed to the show, but I have a feeling this would be pretty flexible," she stabbed the deep green arugula and cherry tomatoes on her plate like they owed her money.

As she dressed her own green salad with the rich balsamic reduction provided, Nora nodded. Her head spun. Daring to dream wasn't even the half of it. This was above and beyond.

"You're thinking things are too good, aren't you," Mel grunted.

Nora met her eye, embarrassed at being so transparent. "Yes."

"Well, knock that shit off. Things come in cycles babe. Ride the tide to your fame and fortune while you can."

If that wasn't the best possible advice ever, Nora didn't know what was.

NORA AGREED TO go to all the readings that Mel presented. The first was a total bust before it even started, which was a bummer, but the second one had promise. She wasn't going to hold her breath, but it was nice to be putting herself out there at someone else's request instead of clawing for any possible opportunities.

Waiting outside the room for the third project on Mel's list, Nora appraised the cluster of actresses similarly seated in terrible folding chairs both in an oddly empty waiting room and down a long, generic hallway. It was a bit strange because there wasn't a type represented like usual—typically, she'd walk in to find a handful of blonde women, or be the only blonde in a room full of brunettes. All variations were present here, and that by itself was interesting.

The people waiting for the audition were also exclusively women.

The latest auditionee came out of the closed door, looking flushed and near tears. Oh, dear. Not good then.

"Nora Chase?"

She pulled her sympathetic eyes away from the poor woman doing all she could not to outright run down the hall toward the elevator and put on a smile for the man holding open the casting room door for her.

"Hello."

"Nice to meet you Nora, please have a seat."

Prickles of tension rose to the surface of Nora's skin as she sat on the white leather love-seat facing a table behind which, four middle-aged men sat. Nervousness about readings was something she worried she might never get over. The reaction of the last woman wasn't sitting well with her, either.

"Welcome, Nora. Would you like to jump right in then?"

She nodded, trying not to appear as wooden as her movements felt.

"Sure. What part would you like me to read?"

Feeling like something was off, she had palmed her phone before setting her purse off to the side. With the device disguised behind the script, she unlocked the screen and pressed the button to activate the security app Maxwell had designed for Stephanie and had modified for Nora. Even though there were other ways to do it, knowing that pushing that one button had notified him where she was and that she was uncomfortable with her surroundings was a comfort. Alan would also be notified, and Mel, and if nothing else, Alan showing up to retrieve her would send a clear message.

All four men behind the casting table could have come out of the same factory, off the same assembly line. They were all middle-aged with dark hair and dark eyes. They had similar, plain features. One was balding, one had glasses, one had a beard; other than that, there was no way to clearly distinguish them and they weren't introducing themselves, which was strange.

Nora's intuition was telling her something—everything—was very wrong, but she wasn't sure how she could escape at this point in the process.

Having employed Maxwell's app made her feel slightly better about being in this room, but not enough. Not enough by half.

"Would you mind starting with the bedroom scene?" the man on the far left, the one with glasses, asked.

Nora hesitated but only for a moment, nodding as she flipped through the script the man from the far right, the one who had held the door for her, had handed her.

She could feel her brown crumple as she assessed the words on the page for the indicated scene.

"Sorry, but there doesn't seem to be any dialogue for … Chloe, in this scene?"

A ripple of their legs moving under the table gave Nora chills, nausea teasing in her gut.

"That's correct." Man with a Beard said, and his tone felt slimy, the words somehow hanging in the air between them.

Nora swallowed and forced some steel into her spine, thankful that the app included automatic voice recording.

"Would you please elaborate on what you'd like me to read from a scene with no dialogue?"

Man with Glasses cleared his throat, Nora wanting to slap the salacious expression on his face clean off.

"We were under the impression, I mean, based on previous acting credits—" Balding Man started in, turning a tablet her direction. "—that you were open to this kind of part."

Nora watched in horror as the video of her and David played on the tablet. Her throat clenched tight as she watched her breasts bounce and heard his groan. It would appear that these men had managed to download and save the whole thing too, not just the snippets that some outlets had snagged.

She realized quite clearly through the haze of her distress that she couldn't let this happen to any of the women in the waiting area. Her tape was out there and would be forever, no matter how thoroughly they were trying to scrub it. The internet was forever, and that's just how it was. But she had a chance, here and now, to make a stand about it.

"I just want to make sure I'm not misunderstanding your expectations." She tried to infuse her voice with sultry confidence, hoping it disguised the tremor the adrenaline rush was putting in there.

Everything smelled bitter as she took a breath, waiting to see what exactly these jerks would ask for.

"We could start with your top, honey. Take it off and we'll see what we're working with."

Heart pounding in her ears, Nora stood, placing the script face-down on top of her phone so it remained hidden. How long had it been since she came into the room? Was that enough recorded to get these jerks in any kind of trouble?

Grateful that she'd worn a button-down blouse instead of the pullover she'd originally considered, her mouth played at a sexy smirk and she cocked a hip, slowly undoing the top two buttons with trembling fingers.

"I'm not … I'm not sure I'm comfortable with nudity," she said. "And I'm not sure what good me taking off my shirt will do when I'm here for an acting audition."

She chose her words carefully, making sure there was no misunderstanding for anyone who might only hear the audio. She could guarantee that if Alan and Maxwell were listening, they were absolutely fuming.

There was a brief moment of silence, and then all four men started to laugh. Heat surged into Nora's face, shame and embarrassment warring with rage.

"You're here for your assets, sweetie, not your acting."

Nora's anger took over control at that moment.

"I'm afraid I'm not who you're looking for then."

There was a chorus of protests and even threats, but Nora just calmly gathered her bag and phone, tossing the script back on the table. She could feel the layer of grime it left behind like a stain on her skin. With a few quick motions, she took a photo of the men sitting behind the table.

This did not please them. Not one bit.

As she opened the door, the men grew quiet, as though waiting to see what she would do next. To Nora's immense relief, Alan was just coming off the elevator at the end of the hall as she looked up.

Relief seemed an odd thing to be feeling considering the absolutely thunderous expression on his face.

"Don't bother, ladies. Best if you go home right now. These assholes don't have any interest in your acting—they just want to see your tits," she snarled.

There was a boom of protest behind her, more threats—she would be blacklisted, she was nothing but a whore—it was all there. She realized suddenly that she didn't care what they thought of her, and nothing mattered except getting out of there and taking as many of the other women as possible with her.

Nora met the eye of any of the ladies brave enough to look up as she passed them and walked toward Alan. He was right on it and held up his phone, replaying part of the audio from the casting room at full volume while smirking. His bulk alone gave the four men pause but the audio was irrefutable and totally damning. They'd clearly told her what they were after.

A number of the actresses gasped as they heard the words replayed. Most got immediately to their feet, throwing glares at the copy/paste casting men as they stormed down the hall in Alan's direction.

"You'll be hearing from my agent and my attorney," Nora said, finding strength in the women gathered around her and the mountain that was Alan.

"Damn right," he said, gesturing for a number of the other actresses to go ahead and catch the first elevator down.

"Please get in touch with Samuel Caine at Hollywood Law if you choose to pursue reporting this," Nora said. Many of the ladies' heads bobbed up and down, a frustrated chorus of hair. Red, Brown, Blonde, curly, straight, short—all accounted for, all beautiful and all royally pissed off.

Once every last one of the women had made it out of the hallway and into the elevator, Alan and Nora tucked themselves into the metal box and stared back at the raging men as the doors slipped closed.

Nora lifted one middle finger in a wave as they fell out of sight. Alan laughed, and she felt more powerful than she ever had before.

ALAN HAD A good habit of being in the right place at the right time. It turned out he had been just down the street getting a coffee with one of his trainers when she had pushed the button on Maxwell's amazing app.

Nora tried and failed to adequately express her gratitude. The smile on his face told her all she needed to know—that he was thankful to have been able to be of service not only for her but for the other women who had been lured there to 'audition'. It sounded like most of them had already checked in at Hollywood Law too, Maxwell was texting back and forth with her from the car to Mel's office after a quick call to confirm she was okay.

His voice was just as soothing as Alan's presence had been.

Mel was beside herself, but also in full attack-mode after she too had tapped into the audio coming through in real-time.

"I'm so fucking proud of you," Mel told her, even bringing her in for a tight squeeze as they debriefed in her office the next morning. "And I'm so goddamn sorry I sent you there." Mel was all fire and brimstone as she paced the floor.

"It's not your fault, Mel. And we caught them. With actual evidence. It's one big step in the right direction."

Mel acquiesced and asked for Maxwell's information—she wanted to get his app for all her clients as soon it was through beta testing.

He'd be beside himself with joy at that news, and she couldn't wait to tell him.

In-between some fantastically boring domesticity with Maxwell, as well as some unforgettable nocturnal acrobatics, Nora began to prepare herself for what she was beginning to think of as the BIG audition, all in caps, even in her mind.

The date approached swiftly, and then just as soon, it was over. She showed up, she acted her ass off, she got some neutral expressions from the eight people behind the table, then she was excused. She had no idea how to feel about it, but she was proud of her performance and it would be what it was supposed to be.

Maxwell met her at the door the day of her audition, giant bouquet of stargazer lilies in hand, and a bright smile.

"How'd it go?"

She couldn't help but smile as she accepted the flowers and a hearty kiss.

"I don't know. They had the most incredible poker face the whole time. But I felt like I nailed it." Pride filled her and she smiled broader.

Rufus came to greet her, and she stroked the fur of his head as he leaned into her legs, Maxwell's arms around her middle as he pressed another kiss to her mouth, this one deeper and much more interesting than the first.

"I'm proud of you. No matter how it turns out."

"Thank you."

He walked them into the living room, pulling Nora down on top of him in a straddle as he sat down on the couch.

"Oh?" She giggled at him, his face burrowing into her breasts.

"Mmmm," he said. His mocha eyes met hers and he looked unusually discomfited.

"What's wrong?" she asked gently, cupping his cheek with her hand.

"I did a thing today."

His hands wound into her hair, arms a solid brace against her back. His length was thick against her center, but he was not distracted by it nearly as much as she was.

"Something good?"

Maxwell cleared his throat, looking away from her. Nora shook her head, using her hand to bring his focus back to her face.

"Nope. Don't do that. What is it? Just tell me."

His lazy grin appeared, but it had an edge of apprehension.

"I turned in my notice at the firm."

Nora stared. She could feel the moment her face broke out in a smile. Enthusiastic and rampant excitement for Maxwell filled her.

"You did? How did your dad take it?"

She slid off his lap, holding one of his hands when he offered it.

"Honestly? He was amazing about it. Told me he'd had a feeling I wasn't happy, and he'd love to have me back if I ever changed my mind, but he understood."

"That's so wonderful, Babe." It was the first time she'd called him that nickname, and it brought a massive smile to his face.

"It is, isn't it?"

Nora nodded, pulling him in for a thorough kiss, his body on top of hers on the couch cushions. Not for the first time, she was extra pleased with the mattress-depth cushions. He wrapped his fist in her hair again, stealing her breath with an extra kiss or two, or ten before they broke for breath.

"Does that mean the investor money came through?"

"Yes." He smiled against her throat, peppering soft nips down the column of her neck and across her collarbone.

"Oh good. Mel wants to buy your app for all her clients." Maxwell lifted his head.

"Yeah?"

Nora nodded, a giant smile on her face. "I forgot to tell you. She said that the day of that terrible audition."

"Damn." He grinned bigger than she'd ever seen. "I'd better get to selling the rights to Google or Apple or someone with big money then, hadn't I?" Then he pounced, warm hands running themselves under her loose top, pulling and twisting and pushing until she was naked and he was devouring her like a starving man.

"Maxwell," she breathed his name heavily as he tangled his tongue around her clit, sliding his long fingers into her core.

There were no pauses, no time to protest, or even think as his lush, warm mouth drove her to the edge quicker than she believed possible. He didn't stop either, pushing her past that first climax and into the beginning of another before suddenly scooping her up and carting her off to the bedroom.

She laughed as he dropped her onto their bed, Rufus snorting in disgust as he left the room, his nap having been disturbed.

"Poor guy."

"Poor nothing. He's spoiled rotten."

Maxwell settled himself between her thighs and engaged her mouth in a kiss so fierce she could scarcely breathe, taking the opportunity to slide himself into her body gently but completely.

A long sigh escaped her at the sensation of fullness, and she moaned as he plucked her nipples first with his deft fingers and then suckled them with his mouth.

"You know what I want, Elle," he crooned into her ear, holding her body tight in his arms as he rocked into her.

"Mmm."

Coherent thought was long gone, and he destroyed what little function might have been remaining by pressing a thumb against the tight nub of nerves at her apex between them.

"Maxwell…" her breath was heavy and she felt the muscles all tense as she climaxed, Maxwell's rhythm thrown off the smallest amount as he increased his tempo so he could catch up and fall with her.

Afterward, they lay there for a long while, all loose long limbs, easy breaths, and gentle caresses.

"I love you, Elle. Would you consider hitching your cart to this temporarily unemployed horse at some point in the near-ish future?"

His voice was low, uncharacteristically serious, but there was a levity that was classic Maxwell there as well.

Nora felt her face break into a slow grin.

"This cart could only be so lucky," she said, turning her head toward him.

He glowed in the waning sunlight coming through the window, and she knew at that moment that she was looking directly at her future.

And it was beautiful.

CHAPTER
Twenty-One

NORA'S FEET DRAGGED as she followed Alan to the set from the big black SUV he had resumed hauling her around in.

She was nearly four weeks into two-a-day shoots, and she was worn the hell out. Performing 18-hour days was no joke, but she wasn't complaining. She was the luckiest girl she knew, and so excited to be on both projects she could hardly stand herself most of the time. But she was tired.

Bone-deep, soul level tired.

As a concession for taking the contract for the Borderline film, she'd negotiated with the TV studio that she could film in half the time so she was finished with all her episodes before the movie set required her presence. It would take some creative editing, and many of her parts were trimmed, but it would work.

It was amazing, honestly. Life was so good. Just exhausting.

The end was in sight though—after one more day, she was on a full week break for Thanksgiving and she already had extensive plans to eat, sleep, and maybe drag herself off to Santa Barbara. Stephanie had gone above and beyond getting her contractors and tradesmen in to finish it up, and the apartment was now ready for habitation.

Maxwell had been making some trips back and forth when he had the time, carting some of her plants and things she'd wanted to decorate with.

"Only one more day, then you can breathe a little, Kid," Alan had tried to reassure her as she half dozed in the back seat.

They were getting to set well before the sun even considered rising and leaving well after it had set. Her blood-type was very likely cappuccino because of the amount of coffee she'd been consuming.

"I know. I'll make it. I just need to learn the fine art of power naps."

Alan snorted. "You and me both."

She pretty much slept through makeup and wardrobe and managed to snap herself into character once Devon arrived on set and the second enormous Starbucks cup was empty.

Thoughts of the beach, her new apartment, her boyfriend, and basically anything but work kept her going. Devon poked at her when she started to drift off and couldn't stop himself from laughing at her.

When the director finally called cut for the last time, she sagged with relief.

"Come on. Let's get you out of here." Devon slung his arm over her shoulder and shuffled her to wardrobe to change, then to make up to scrub away the day.

They rode together with Alan, Nora pillowing her head on Devon's shoulder as they traversed the parking-lot that the freeway was.

"You alright?" Devon put his arm around her shoulders.

"Yeah. Just fried."

"I bet." His face was drawn into an unusually serious expression of concern.

"Do you know if Steph heard back about that property? I haven't had a chance to talk to her all week."

Devon smirked.

"Project lure Phae to California is a-go," he confirmed.

Nora's face broke into a broad smile. She could barely open her eyes, but the smile lit up her features.

"Awesome. Tell your wife I owe her at least a dozen egg-rolls."

"You got it."

Alan stopped the SUV and Maxwell was there, opening the door to let Nora out.

There was a very masculine nod exchange between Devon and Maxwell, and then between Alan and Maxwell, and if Nora could have raised the energy to roll her eyes, she would have.

With what seemed like no effort at all, Maxwell scooped her up and carried her up into the condo, not bothering with any conversation as he undressed her and tucked her into bed.

"Take a nap, Elle."

"But we should talk about your day," she protested groggily, feeling the bed dip with his weight.

"Not now. Sleep."

She did.

Like a brick, for at least 12 hours.

Her heart was racing in the best possible way when she stirred into wakefulness, sunlight gently streaming in through the windows, a warm mouth tantalizing the back of her shoulder and neck.

Maxwell pressed himself into her back, and she made a noise in her throat that translated in bedroom language to agreement.

"Don't worry, I'll do all the heavy lifting," he promised, and the giggle that tried to escape her throat stalled into a moan as he lifted her leg and pressed himself into her body slowly, fully and deeply.

He wrapped his arms tightly around her middle, teasing her breasts with one of his hands and her clit with the other. She reached behind her, grabbing onto a healthy handful of his toned backside as he drove into her, their breathing heavy in the sun-soaked air. They were nothing more than one soul, one breath, and total ecstasy.

They lay there for moments after, just being, and it was Nora's favorite place. Nothing could compare.

Eventually, Maxwell rolled away and returned with both a cloth for her and a cup of coffee.

"I already think you're the best, but you just keep topping yourself," she teased.

"We going to see the new place today?" he asked.

Nora couldn't contain a smile.

"Yes please."

He turned that devastating, easy grin back at her, blonde hair flopping into his face in a way that should have felt messy but mostly felt sexy. He'd been putting off getting a trim since leaving the firm, and she was definitely a fan of the more rugged, surfer style he had adopted.

After the caffeine hit her system enough that she could motivate her limbs, she took a shower and they gathered a few more things to take to the new apartment.

Rufus was coming this trip, his large furry body crammed into the tiny back seat of the roadster, hot panting breath brushing Nora's ear.

"I really do need a new car," she muttered, patting the poor dog's head.

"We can look at that whenever you want," Maxwell said.

His easy demeanor was something she might not ever get used to, but would always appreciate.

The drive seemed shorter every time they made it, just because of the regularity it was becoming. Saturday morning traffic was scarce, and they made it in time to get the brunch offering at O'Malley's, eating with Rufus underfoot on the patio before heading up to the apartment.

Nora embraced the amazing sensation that she was home every time she opened the door and crossed the threshold.

Stephanie had heard and come through in a major way with every vision Nora had shared for the space. It was open, light, and everything she had ever wanted in a living space.

Over the last few weeks, things like furniture and dishes had all been delivered and arranged. They could actually *live* here now, and Nora couldn't wait until the bulk of their time could be spent here instead of in the city.

Guilt was naturally on the heels of that thought—she was so lucky to be acting regularly, and on big-name projects, but there was something else on her horizon and she was looking forward to it in a big way.

Maxwell, ever watchful, could sense her mood change.

"Alright, Elle?" He wrapped an arm around her waist, looking out the bank of windows with her.

"Fine. Just thinking. The next couple of years…"

"Are going to be very interesting," he finished for her, that grin melting away any apprehension she had allowed to creep in. "Let's go see it."

She nodded, and they leashed Rufus so he could walk with them.

A few blocks down the street from the apartments was a small storefront attached to an elaborate courtyard. The courtyard was completely enclosed by the high white brick walls of the hotel next to it, ivy having claimed about half the available bricks and moss coming through the very Greco-style detailed pavers. It had felt like stepping into the secret garden minus most of the garden when Nora first put her feet out the sliding glass door that connected it to the glass-walled storefront.

The property was a unique and lucky find that had come up for sale when a hotel decided they no longer needed that space. For Nora's purposes, it was perfect.

Without hesitating, she dialed Phae on video call, muttering to herself that the brat had better answer. Her words made Maxwell chuckle as he watched her, eyes warm.

"Hey. You okay?" Phae greeted her, skin flushed and damp with sweat in the picture.

"Should I be asking *you* that?" Nora laughed, half-worried that she was interrupting something private. "Am I interrupting something?"

Phae rolled her eyes.

"I'm taking care of the *yard*. It's a million percent humidity here still, though at least it's a little bit cooler."

Nora laughed. "Okay then. Thank God. We're fine. I just had some questions I wanted to ask you."

The screen jiggled as Phae settled into one of the loungers, taking a drink from a huge metal water bottle.

"Okay. What's up?"

The smile was enormous as Nora flipped the camera around and started walking around the courtyard.

"Hi, Maxwell." Phae laughed.

"Hello, little sister." Maxwell chuckled, waving.

"Focus Phae," Nora teased, pulling her sister's attention back. "What do you think?"

Phae squinted. "Of what? Is that moss? I'm not sure what you're asking."

Nora gestured to the far wall.

"I'm thinking some dwarf trees, but we could put about three rows of benches here. Maybe four."

"Nora, what the hell are you talking about? Where are you?"

"I'm not sure what to call it yet. But I'm hoping you can help me figure that out."

Nora panned the camera around the courtyard and then stepped back into the store part of the property. She ran a hand lovingly along the wooden counter-top, modeling it like she was a game-show hostess.

"Nora." Phae sounded pissed, but Nora recognized it for what it was—shock. "What did you do?"

"Ta-da!" Nora gestured grandly. She had managed to get in touch with the man who had taken over Yiayia Lou's orchids, and a dozen or so of the plants were already proudly seated atop a glass table. Getting them imported into California was no joke and it was going to be a time consuming and expensive venture to get them all brought in, but she was dedicated to getting as many as she could. "I'm going to need your help Phae. Will you consider coming to California when you graduate?"

"Are those … are those Yiayia Lou's orchids?" Phae had tears in her eyes.

"Yes. Will you come?"

Phae started to laugh and cry at the same time.

"You are *such an asshole*. Of course, I will. I was planning on asking you if I could."

"You were?" Nora was tearing up now too, and Rufus rubbed against her legs as though he could tell there was a disturbance in her emotional state.

"Yes. Did Devon tell you?"

"No. Why, did you tell *him*? Why would you tell him *first*?" Nora could hear the irritation in her voice, but couldn't tamp it down.

Phae snorted. "No, but I told Daniel. I thought maybe he ratted me out."

Nora gasped, then laughed.

"I see how it is. Jace didn't make his move then?"

Phae shook her head. "Nuh-uh. We're not talking about that."

Nora met Maxwell's eye; his grin as broad as hers.

"I love you sister. We can totally do this, right?"

Phae shrugged. "Well, I have absolutely no idea about the business end, but I can grow the plants."

"Awesome. I'll figure out the rest, I guess. Love you Phae."

"Love you too, crazy woman."

Nora ended the call, heart soaring.

She was home, and the future held orchids.

NORA WAS SOAKING up some vitamin D in the bright sunlight coming through the wall of windows in the Santa Barbara apartment a couple of days later when Rufus loped over, something in his mouth.

"You got something, boy? Hopefully, it's a toy."

He dropped the small box into her hands, bored with the whole thing, and flopping onto the floor for a nap once he had done his part and gotten his ear scratches in payment.

Nora chuckled.

"Thanks?"

She looked up to find Maxwell casually leaning against the kitchen island, sinfully sexy in his plain t-shirt and shorts.

"Open it, Elle."

Her heart leaped into her throat. The box was palm-sized and smooth, not velvety, but she just *knew* there was jewelry inside.

"Maxw—"

"Just *open* it." His long legs ate up the distance between them in a few short strides, and he lowered himself to the floor next to her.

Meeting his cocoa gaze, she cracked open the box to find a ring. A ring she suddenly realized she wanted to wear more than anything in the world.

"Eleanora Demetria, my lovely Elle; would you marry me someday soon? Here, I think, or maybe at my parents' house if you like. I just don't want to be anywhere you're not and I'd like to have the honor of calling you my wife."

Nora felt the tears building but found herself laughing.

"Yes. All the yes. Of course, I will Maxwell. I don't want to be anywhere without you either."

Maxwell's devastating grin turned bright as he plucked the simple but elegant pink diamond from where it was nestled in the box.

He pushed the platinum band onto her finger and she admired it, the sunlight picking up and magnifying every sharp facet of the round, rose-hued stone.

"It's so beautiful," she breathed.

"Thank you, Elle," Maxwell said quietly, pulling her into the warm circle of his embrace.

"For what?"

"Everything. You changed everything. In the best way."

"I could say the same about you." Nora smiled.

They sat there, in the sunlight, for what could have

been minutes or hours. It was all they needed, and it was perfect.

"QUIT FUSSING." STEPHANIE scolded Devon, slapping his hand away from the plate of egg-rolls that was situated in the center of the table.

Nora and Maxwell wasted no time at all and had rented out the banquet room at Mr. Woo's for their public engagement party. It was shaping up to be a hilarious gathering that included the Caines, Stephanie's parents, Alan, Mel and some co-stars to round out the numbers. Phae hadn't been able to get away as she was in the middle of finals, but she'd be there soon enough. Graduation was just around the corner and if she hustled, she'd be moved Christmas, the New Year at the latest.

Nora smiled at her friend.

"It's not every day your best friends get engaged," he grumbled, winking at her.

"No, but quit trying to sneak an egg-roll. If anyone deserves it, it's *me*." Stephanie probably didn't realize she was caressing her belly, but Nora noticed the brief, casual gesture right away.

She was pretty sure another kind of announcement and party would be forthcoming very soon. The gentle grin on her lips broadened at the idea.

Devon clinked his glass to get everyone's attention.

"Friends! Family. Thanks so much for coming," he paused to allow some general happy responses. "It's not every day that you get to see your best friends fall in love. We couldn't be happier that Nora and Maxwell were compatible—holidays are going to be *so much* easier for us since they like each other," He joked, Stephanie elbowing him. "But seriously, we love these two, and they love each other. What better reason to celebrate? Let's eat!"

Nora laughed at her friend's unorthodox but still somehow touching speech. It was pure Devon, and she adored him.

The staff bustled into action around them, bringing in entree after entree.

"What's it going to be Nor, beach wedding? I can say with authority that's a decent way to go."

Nora nodded, piling her favorites onto her plate, Maxwell quietly grinning to her left.

"Yes, I think so. We're considering duplicating your wedding pretty much if you don't mind."

"Returning to the scene of the crime?" Devon raised an eyebrow playfully. "Marlowe and my mom did an incredible job. I'm sure they'd take the helm again if needed."

Nora nodded, face falling just a bit. She had yet to decide if she was going to invite Athena.

Thanks to the lovely ankle bracelet she had been provided to keep track of her comings and goings, it was unlikely that she could even attend, anyway.

"Maxwell's mom seems quite thrilled by the prospect." She forced a grin, deciding not to dwell. Stephanie caught her eye and gave a sympathetic look.

"Plenty of time, either way," Maxwell added, kissing her gently on the cheek.

The party wore on around them, to the point where Nora didn't realize they'd lost everyone except the four of them until she realized the staff was doing end of shift side work in a very low-key manner as a suggestion they wrap it up and head on home. Nora noted that she'd need to ask Maxwell to increase the gratuity before signing the bill.

"This was lovely." Stephanie sighed, relaxing into her chair and leaning on Devon.

"It was." Maxwell agreed.

The four friends smiled at one another. Nobody bothered to say it, but they were all thinking it was going to be wonderful every time it happened, hopefully for a very, very long time.

AS TENDS TO happen, things turned around and the positives began to balance all the negative that had happened.

Nora's upcoming Borderline movie was on pace to be an all-out blockbuster, and it was still in pre-production. She had been called in for at least one sequel already, and filming probably wouldn't begin until she was finished with the show, for which she gave thanks.

In the interest of expediency, David had both settled with the state and pled out of his civil case. He would be serving some jail time for his efforts and was ordered to return what amounted to about 80 percent of the money he'd gotten out of Nora over the years which amounted to hundreds of thousands of dollars. Olivia would be fined, put on probation, and sent to a specialty rehab facility for her part in the scheme. As Nora knew, her mother would be wearing an ankle monitor for the foreseeable future. All of them had been punished, and Nora felt satisfied with the judgments.

Devon would hear nothing of missing Phae's graduation, so they all four flew to Alabama to see her walk across the stage and toss her mortarboard in mid-December. Charlie was spotted lingering near the back of the bleachers, and Phae did manage to locate him long enough to get a hug, but not much past that.

Daniel was also in attendance. Devon and Nora exchanged several glances about the interesting chemistry between their mutual siblings but said nothing, interested to see how it played out on its own.

Phae moved as quickly as she could to Santa Barbara so she could help Nora run the shop, which was operating under the name Lou's Exotics. Nora wasn't overly thrilled with the name—she thought it sounded like a car dealership—but it would do for the time being.

Interestingly enough, when the move had happened, Daniel had accompanied Phae across the country, but he hadn't lingered in California past a couple of days to catch up with Devon.

Phae was tight-lipped about what was going on but Nora knew she'd get her sister to crack sooner or later.

There were rumblings that the foundation that the Greene brothers ran that encompassed everything from animal charities to online sales of vegan grocery items was looking into a California expansion. Devon was a clever little matchmaker, but Nora worried that if he made things a little too convenient or pushed too hard, they'd blow up in his face.

Time would tell.

Every now and then, a video or some photos would pop up online again and make another round. Nora would grit her teeth, ignore the comments, and call her team to scrub the source when it happened.

It hadn't ruined her, or her image after all. She had mountains of regret that she'd so fiercely tried to protect an image that she didn't even need all things considered. It was an ugly piece of her history, but it had brought her the most beautiful future, and as strange as it seemed, she was starting to become thankful for it.

Nora watched her sister caring for the plants and customers alike from a distance, Phae wholly in her element. As though she could feel someone watching, Phae's eyes turned her way and Nora just smiled and waved.

Phae shook her head and went about her business.

"Elle," Maxwell's croon came from behind her.

She turned, unable to resist the timbre of his voice or that grin. Never the grin. It was too powerful.

"Yes?"

"Come on. Let's go home."

Nora blushed, recognizing his tone and the unspoken request. Her fingers immediately moved to untie her dirt-smudged white apron. Phae glanced over and winked at her sister, waving her off.

Warmth suffused Nora's chest and she took Maxwell's hand, the sun beginning to set over the water just across the street from the shop.

"Yes, please. Home."

WANT TO KNOW WHAT'S NEXT FOR

Phae

AND THE OTHER SIBLINGS OF
YOUR FAVORITE CELEBRITIES?

Winter
BLOOM

HOLLYWOOD CONNECTIONS BOOK ONE
NOW AVAILABLE
HTTPS://GENI.US/BLOOMHC1

TURN THE PAGE FOR A SNEAK PEEK

CHAPTER ONE

Phae

"CAN ONE OF you get that, please? It's probably my moving truck!"

There was no escape route through the cardboard jungle my bedroom had become to run down and answer the doorbell. Yelling the request at my roommates wasn't the optimal answer either, but beggars couldn't be choosers.

"I got it, Phae!" Jace, one of my five roommates, yelled back.

Harmony, the only other female of the group, had moved out about a week ago and nearly all of the drama had left with her. We were a pretty compatible group, all things considered, but without her, it had been pretty quiet. Considering there were four large, male college athletes in the house, I was impressed.

I finally managed to untangle myself from the maze of boxes and exit my room. It was a good thing I did because there was some testosterone flowing heavily on the air by the time I got to the entryway.

I felt him before I saw him. It was like my cells were attuned to his frequency, and they all stood up and took notice when he was near.

It was dangerous.

It was fantastic.

I hoped we never lost it.

I loved how I could always find him in a large crowd if we got separated. How my body was aware of his, just like magnets. The way everything brightened with life when he was close.

I worried it went a step beyond what we were as friends, but I couldn't help that.

Also, he wasn't supposed to be there.

My eyes fell to the half-open door where football-player Jace was all clenched jaw and tight words, his chest puffed out. He had my friend Daniel - no less fit or imposing, to be honest, though he was less bulky as he was not a college athlete - blocked in the doorway. I couldn't help but roll my eyes and Daniel was smirking calmly like he found Jace's posture amusing.

"Problem, guys?" I asked smoothly, trying to diffuse the tension, but my heart thumped around excitedly in my chest. I was thrilled to see my best friend. I hadn't been expecting to see him so soon. He had just attended my graduation and lived a couple of hours away. We'd said what I thought was our 'goodbye for now' with hugs and promises to talk frequently before he'd left for home. "Hey, you. What are you doing here?"

"You know him?" Jace asked me shortly, gesturing with his chin.

I couldn't suppress the exasperated sigh. Jace had been doing this odd peacocking around me since my sister Nora had come to visit a few months before. It was weird and kind of sweet, but I was pretty sure his motivations were a little... misplaced.

I had been Fade, the quiet, mostly invisible roommate before my sister had come to visit. After she'd left, Jace had started acting strange, perhaps... interested? Friendly at the very least. It was nice, but super strange. He was the total package as far as guys went and a wonderful friend, but he just wasn't for me.

He hadn't figured it out yet, but I had a feeling he was about to.

"Yes. Thank you for answering the door, Jace. This is my good friend, Daniel." He continued to pin Daniel with his glare and refused to meet my eye. Undeterred, I continued, "Whom you met at graduation. *Remember*?"

Jace clenched his jaw one final time before abandoning the doorway. He only stepped back a few paces though, arms crossed over his chest and stance wide, like a bouncer at a club.

"If you say so," he groused.

"We're fine, Jace." I laughed at him, which I knew could backfire depending on how worked up he was but I couldn't help it. Stress levels were high and I laughed whenever I was nervous. And really, he was being ridiculous if he was jealous. Those blue eyes flared at me, but he didn't move a muscle. Well, except the one he kept popping in his jaw that had me worried about his next dental visit. "Daniel is Devon's brother. My sister's best friend. Well, one of them, anyway. One of the *brothers* I mean. Not best friends. That's just Devon and maybe me." I took a deep breath to steady myself. It wasn't often I tripped all over my words, but something about two large dudes facing off over my honor or whatever nonsense this was, on top of a restless night clearly, messed with my head. "We've known each other for a very long time. You've met. Be nice."

"Hi, Pea." Daniel graced me with a smile before turning to my roommate. "Nice to see you again, Jace." He put a hand out, with a smirk that reminded me so much of his older brother still in place. Between the smirk and the sky-blue eyes, it was hard not to see the resemblance. But Daniel was taller, broader and his voice did things to my body that Devon's never had or would. Thank God for that.

I appreciated the fact he wasn't either baiting or cowering to Jace. Honestly, it was a pretty typical Greene boy tactic—smooth and placating ran in the gene pool the same as devilish good looks did. Daniel was just one of four brothers and they all had similar traits in spades.

Surely feeling obligated because of the manly challenge thrown down by performing a simple handshake, Jace took Daniel's outstretched hand and pumped it slowly up and down. I couldn't stop my eyes from rolling again, because I knew they were both squeezing as hard as they dared. I had gone from being completely invisible to causing a full-on pissing match.

Boys are so weird.

Jace stepped back but didn't leave. He was clearly playing bodyguard. I resisted the urge to sigh at him.

"I was expecting my moving truck. This is a pleasant surprise. But what in the hell are you doing here?"

Daniel chuckled at me.

"You didn't think you were going to drive cross country all by yourself, did you?"

My defenses tingled and sprung up, a bit prickly at his tone. I was a strong, independent woman. Of course I could drive by myself.

"Actually, I did. I'm certainly more than capable of taking care of myself in the car for a few days."

He reached out a hand, gently setting it on my shoulder. I could see Jace stiffen. I reflexively relaxed under my friend's touch.

"I have the utmost confidence in your independence and capabilities," He soothed me. "But Phae—you're supposed to go on an epic post-graduation road trip with *friends*. Or at least *a* friend. I volunteered as tribute." He appraised the glare on my face and probably the raised eyebrow as well. "It'll be great. Way better than you going alone."

Jace snorted, and I turned a glare at him. I wasn't quite sure how to take that, but it seemed like he was mostly offering me kindness, not an insult so I accepted it.

"Well. Thanks, I guess."

He quirked his mouth again, and the rest of the defensiveness inside my body melted away. This was a complication I wasn't expecting and definitely hadn't planned for, but it could work out. There seemed to be two options: this would either be a great way to strengthen our friendship bond or horribly destructive.

One of those scared the hell out of me.

Read the full novel today!
https://geni.us/BloomHC1

Everyone does it, right? It's something you do to like... find yourself
ARE YOU LOST, PEA?
I don't know. Maybe.
WELL... THEN LET'S GO FIND YOU.
Winter
BLOOM
HOLLYWOOD CONNECTIONS BOOK ONE
LILY ALEXANDER

Did you accidentally skip Stephanie and Devon's story?
Find out what you missed in

IMAGE
Adjuster

RULE #1: Don't fall for a client.
Catching real feelings in a fake
relationship is a recipe for disaster.

IT'S LITERALLY STEPHANIE'S job as the Celebrity
Image Adjuster to play the perfect A-list girlfriend
to the bad boys in the business. A former actress,
her Hollywood royalty last name and squeaky-clean reputation are great for helping actors move get onto the A-list.
It's all a paid transaction- they follow a script and go their
separate ways when the contract is up. No risk, no feelings—just acting.

Devon's star is rising thanks to a hit prime-time show.
He's got a smoldering smirk and massive…ego to match.
He also has a heart of gold and just needs a little PR push

to put him and his show over the top. A real girlfriend is out of the question—he's never had much luck in love and what you see is never what you get in Los Angeles.

Their chemistry is off the charts—and off the script. Why do their dates feel like more than acting? What happens when the contract ends and the feelings don't?

Image Adjuster is a standalone contemporary Hollywood romance. Perfect for you if you like intense friends-to-lovers chemistry, a guaranteed Happily Ever After!

Image Adjuster is available at Amazon
and other major book retailers!

"ONE OF THE first steps into true recovery is making amends with those you have hurt or wronged."

The perky, well-spoken therapist was the embodiment of everything Olivia hated about rehab.

She didn't even belong there for starters. There was nothing wrong with her—she wasn't addicted to drugs or alcohol. There were no anger management issues. Sure, she'd made some bad decisions when it came to men, but she wasn't a damn junkie.

If it weren't a condition of her probation for the unfortunate sex-tape debacle she couldn't quite bring herself to regret, she wouldn't even be there. Not for a second.

Her eyes met the aqua ones of a man she recognized across the circle of chairs.

Unable to stop herself, she winked at him.

Ollie Parkinson.

Now there was someone who *should* be in rehab. Olivia had heard all the terrible stories about him floating around; everyone had.

"Olivia? Is there something you'd perhaps like to share today?" The pretty enough therapist smiled at her, and Olivia felt the urge to claw her eyes out of her skull rise suddenly. Intentionally folding her hands in her lap, she appraised the doctor. She was brunette but reminded her enough of that bitch Nora that Maxwell was still seeing that it made her blood rush.

"No, thanks."

The therapist's face dropped a bit, but she recovered quickly.

"That's alright. Sharing is never mandatory, but it can really help the process. Maybe next session."

Olivia felt her face form a pretend smile that she hoped came across the same as if she'd flipped Dr. Feelgood the bird.

After the painfully long feelings-sharing session finally ended, Ollie boldly approached her before she could slip out of the meeting space and return to her tiny cell of a room.

"Hey, Olivia, right?"

"Yeah," she snapped, not trying one bit to mask her impatience.

"Look, I know we don't know one another, but I think we have some … acquaintances in common. I've been here for a few weeks, and I can tell you that it gets easier." He seemed genuine, and for some reason that was worse than him propositioning her like she'd thought he might.

"Okay. Thanks."

He ran a hand through his sandy hair. There was no denying he was handsome, but Olivia wasn't interested. See? Who needed rehab for sex addiction? Not her. She was fine. There was nothing wrong with her at all.

"You want to grab something to eat?" Ollie deployed what should have been a very charming lopsided grin.

"Pass," Olivia said, pushing her way past him and out into the hallway.

"If you need anything..." he trailed off behind her.

"Sure," she said, glancing over her shoulder as her feet carried her quickly down the hall toward her room.

As if.

She was here to do her time and get the hell out, not make friends with the likes of Ollie Parkinson.

Image Destroyer, third and final book in the Image series will provide redemption for these villains in 2021!

A NOTE FROM
The Author

THIS BOOK WAS so much fun to discover! When Nora and Maxwell started off as side characters in *Image Adjuster* I never dreamed they'd take on such big, beautiful lives for themselves. I hope you loved their story as much as I do!

As always, hugs and cookies are owed to my faithful team of betas, editors and incredible supporters. You are few but you are mighty! THANK YOU.

Special thanks to the other parts of my writer brain—Shain & Dannie, you're the cat's pajamas and I'm so happy we found one another! Figuring out this writing thing is much more fun and way less stressful with more people in the crazy boat with me! XOXO

And of course to you the reader! Thanks for taking a shot on me!